DEADLIER THAN DEATH

BY

CAROLYN CHAMBERS CLARK, EdD, RN, ARNP, FAAN

Vista
publishing, Inc.

Edited by Jerena Burdge-Rezvan

Cover Design by Noelle Auriemma
Creative Assistance by Thomas Taylor of Thomcatt Graphics

Vista Publishing, Inc.
473 Broadway
Long Branch, N.J. 07740
(908) 229-6500

This publication is designed for the reading pleasure of the general public. All characters, places and situations are fictional and are in no way intended to depict actual people, places or situations.

Printed and bound in the United States of America on acid-free paper.

ISBN: 1-880254-06-9
Library of Congress Catalogue Card Number: 93-060315

U.S.A. Price $9.95
Canada Price $15.95

DEDICATION

For Janice Manaser Geller who helped me learn to write.

For Charlotte Andersen who helped me fine tune my writing skills.

For Alice Avery who loves to read whatever I write.

ACKNOWLEDGMENTS

The author wishes to acknowledge the invaluable assistance of the following people: Noelle Auriemma; Tony Auriemma; Tim Moran, Investigator, Pinellas County Medical Examiner's Office; Wendell Creager, and Alice Morrow, St. Petersburg Police Department; and Kate Richards, Private Investigator.

ABOUT THE AUTHOR

Carolyn Chambers Clark earned a B.S. in Nursing from the University of Wisconsin-Madison, a Masters Degree in Psychiatric/Mental Health Nursing from Rutgers, the State University, New Jersey, and a doctorate in Nursing Education from Teachers College, Columbia University, New York. She is an Advanced Registered Nurse Practitioner (ARNP) in Psychiatric/Mental Health Nursing and a Fellow of the American Academy of Nursing. She is Editor of <u>Alternative Health Practitioner: The Journal of Complementary and Natural Care</u> and is listed in <u>Who's Who of American Women</u>.

Carolyn's work experiences are extensive and varied. She has twenty years of experience as a clinician, educator, consultant and psychotherapist. She has taught thousands of nurses at the baccalaureate, graduate and continuing education level. She has published nine text books and numerous book chapters, learning systems and articles.

In 1980, Carolyn established THE WELLNESS INSTITUTE, offering wellness workshops, consultation and a health promotion newsletter. Since 1980, she has been the editor/publisher of THE WELLNESS NEWSLETTER, which she developed to fill the void of self-care information.

Currently she provides continuing education self-study courses and workshops for nurses in Florida; maintains a private practice in individual, couple and family psychotherapy and therapeutic touch; teaches self-esteem, stress management and self-awareness courses for the community; and provides therapeutic touch workshops for nurses and others interested in learning the skill.

Carolyn has lived in Florida with her husband, Tony, since 1984. One of his daughters, Noelle, created the parrot drawings for the book cover. Carolyn enjoys early morning walks on the beach, tap dancing and puttering with her plants. Although she may have endowed Megan Baldwin with some of her real-life characteristics, Carolyn firmly insists she does not own a parrot named Bucky.

CHAPTER I

I opened the door of my ten year old white Toyota and there she was. Black sunglasses covered the upper portion of her face. They were the kind worn after cataract surgery. I knew this because before I became an avid reader of mystery novels and editor of my own health promotion money-losing newsletter, I was a hospital nurse. I also surmised her condition because a large percentage of the population of St. Petersburg is over sixty-five and wear those glasses. You can't fool a nurse. We're a very perceptive lot.

The woman sitting in the passenger seat of my car smiled at me without opening her lips. The sun dappled across her face, making the red splotches on her nose and cheeks even more pronounced. "Excuse me," I said, "but do I know you?"

A shiver ran through me then and that almost convinced me she was a spy or somebody who was about to become very important to me. But I held my tongue for a minute, mainly because I do have an over-active imagination and a wise-cracking manner that has gotten me into several nasty encounters with physicians and supervisors. So instead of saying anything else, I took another look at the passenger side of my car, thinking that maybe I did know the woman.

A small green parrot sat on her hunched-over shoulder. The bird gave me a glance that said, *We were here first.* The woman's smile broadened and her white-hair polyester wig of curls shook. "Am I in the wrong car?" she asked in a voice that can only be described as drugged.

"I think so." I slid into my seat. The smell of lavender was unmistakable. Trying not to appear rude, I took a closer look at her. A black straw hat with a big red rose dangling off the front roosted on her head. Just a tad too much Naples red lipstick covered her lips as well as a generous portion above and below them. Her face caked into crevices around an over-abundance of white powder.

She was skinny, with a little bump on her back and short legs that barely grazed the floor. The frock she wore was memorable for the white orchids patterning the yellow and pale green of the fabric, and her hands for their covering of immaculate, hand-crocheted, white gloves. A strange-looking woman, but I liked her immediately.

I looked back at her face. "Whose car were you looking for?"

She didn't answer. Her lips curled into a loud snore and her head bobbed on her neck like a frail flower in the wind. I must have sat there for quite a while trying to figure out what to do. Every now and then I poked or shook her, but she only mumbled and went back to sleep.

I gazed around the parking lot of the St. Petersburg Beach Library. A few more cars had pulled into spaces, but their occupants had already gone inside. I got out of the car and went around to the passenger side. Tucking her Jell-O arms in the seatbelt, I buckled her up, then locked both doors carefully, before heading back into the library. Mildewed, cool air came at me. "Anyone missing a lady with a parrot?" I asked, trying to sound nonchalant.

The librarian smiled at me as if she was used to strange requests (which she probably was) and said, "Not that I know of."

I turned toward the man standing at the card catalogue. "What about you? Do you know a lady with a parrot?"

His whole body shook with the slight tremor of Parkinson's disease. He turned and looked down his trifocals at me. "Birds aren't allowed in the library, miss."

A man in plaid shorts and black socks who had been watching, grunted and went back to his world atlas. A woman in a pink smock and sneakers stared at me while her companion just clicked her gum or her teeth, I wasn't sure which.

By that time I was convinced either they knew her and weren't saying or I had made up an imaginary parrot woman. The librarian suggested I leave my name, address and phone number at the desk in case anyone turned up missing such a person. I shot her a grateful look, gave her the information and returned to my car.

The parrot lady was still there, snoozing. A bit of spittle had gathered in the corner of her mouth and her body had slid down a couple of inches in the seat. Nothing seemed to have changed, but then I saw the matchbook resting on her lap. It hadn't been there when I left, but it was there now. Had someone put it there or had she reached into her purse and left it there as a clue for me?

The words on the matchbook glimmered back up at me in the morning sun, *Single Hearts Club*. What was an elderly woman doing with a matchbook from there? She was obviously not about to answer, so I decide to drive her around a while until she woke up.

Keeping an eye on her so she didn't slide farther, I maneuvered out of the lot at a snail's pace. I had only traveled half a block when I looked in my rear view mirror and saw a heavyset man and woman in a blue Ford Festiva behind me. While the parrot lady snored, I pulled over to the side, thinking her family had come to claim her at last.

The man swerved in behind me. After twenty years of living in New York, I didn't trust anyone being behind me that I couldn't see, so I glanced in the rear view mirror again. The two in the car were arguing and the woman wore a particularly ugly look on her face. When she raised her arm, I saw a glint in the windshield and wasn't sure, but it looked like it might be shining off the nose of a revolver.

I didn't wait to find out. My foot hit the accelerator. The parrot lady fell against her door, but I grabbed her by the arm and held her in place. Ruffling its feathers and getting a better grip for the ride, the parrot squawked, then gave me an *are you crazy?* look, but I ignored it.

Taking the back streets, I drove with one hand, skidding and squealing toward my house. The Ford Festiva shrieked behind me on the first turn, but I lost him somewhere between the library and Sixty-Fourth Avenue. To be sure, I went past my house and circled around and back. The street was empty.

I used my garage door opener and gunned my Toyota into the tomb-like darkness of my one-car space. The parrot lady moaned and seemed to be waking up. "Where are we? Are we home?" she mumbled.

"Yes, home." I pushed the garage door opener once more before I grabbed for her arm and hustled her to her feet. She stumbled out of the car with my help and shuffled into the back door of my house.

The garage door clanked down with finality.

CHAPTER 2

In all the excitement, I'd forgotten about Samantha and how birds and cats don't mix. I poked my head in the back door of my house and looked left and right, expecting pandemonium to strike any second. The bird must have caught a whiff of the cat because he started to rock back and forth on the parrot lady's shoulder and punctuate the air with loud squawks. The woman seemed barely to notice, but I knew if Samantha were anywhere nearby, there'd be one dead parrot.

No sign of the cat. I pulled the door closed again, propped the woman inside my huge broom closet as a temporary measure and corseted her in with strips of cloth.

The parrot stuck his head toward me, opened and closed his eyes wildly, rattled his mandibles and said between squawks, "That's a good bird, no foolishness now." They were the first words the bird had spoken and I waited for more, but he went back to mutters and a shriek or two, no doubt sensing what was in the house. I left the parrot and the woman in the garage with the door firmly shut behind me.

I found Samantha stalking in from the living room, getting a little suspicious about what I had dragged in. "Out! Scoot!" I said, waving my arms and shoving her toward the front door. She went, but at her own pace, stopping to give me a *drop dead* look and a hiss or two.

When I got back to the garage, the parrot lady was already sliding out of her make-do corset and had caught her hat in the broom holder. The bird held steadfastly to the woman's shoulder. I pulled the parrot lady out carefully and helped her inside. She walked like a drunk, staggering and stumbling and taking half-snores between breaths. It wasn't very far across the terrazzo floor of my living room, but it felt like miles. At the rattan couch, she bent her knees and slumped down onto the seat. I flipped on the seashell lamp beside her, grabbed for her wrist and counted her pulse and breathing rate. They seemed stable, which was strange, judging from her walk and sleepiness.

I re-adjusted her straw hat so it didn't dangle off her left ear and propped her up with pillows, making sure she was securely on the couch. "How about some tea? Then you can tell me what this is all about."

She waved to me merrily and I went toward the stove. While I heated the water and put some tea bags in cups, I made a few checks on her to make sure she was all right. She had found a *Greenpeace* magazine on the side table and was looking through it as if it were the most interesting thing she'd ever seen. Even the parrot peered down at the pages with curiosity, like a driver rubbernecking on the highway.

When I came back into the living room, she still seemed a little dazed, but that might have been her normal condition. At least I considered it a possibility until I saw how she scarfed down two bran muffins and three cups of tea.

"Feed the birdie, feed Buck," said the parrot. I laughed and nodded to the woman, pushing the muffin dish toward her. The woman broke off a piece of the sweet dark cake and handed it to the bird. He chewed happily, dropping a few crumbs on her shoulder, then bending down to retrieve them.

After I took the last sip of my peppermint tea, I decide it was time to find out more. She gave me a most angelic look when I said, "Perhaps you can tell me what that was all about at the library."

"You mean my getting in your car, dear?" A drop of honey glistened on her chin.

"That and those people chasing us in the blue car."

"I don't know about anyone chasing us, but you should learn to drive a bit more safely, dear." She waved a finger at me as if I had been naughty and she was setting me straight.

"What about the blue car?"

She stared at me. "I've never seen that car in my life."

"Then you don't think anybody is after you?"

"I don't think so. Who would be after someone like me?" She looked around her. "You haven't seen my purse, have you, dear? It's beige and it contains all my important things. I always keep it with me."

"I haven't seen it. Maybe it's in my car. Will you be all right while I go check?" I stood up, but her words held me in place.

She rattled her magazine. "Of course not, dear, I was just reading about the Clean Air Act. It says here President Bush pays money to the oil companies to keep gas prices low and spends no money for things like solar power" She shook her head and glanced back at *Greenpeace*.

I gazed at her dumbfounded. Was the parrot lady wiser and more clear-headed than I thought or was she just repeating back to me what she had read. Either way, I decided not to discount her intelligence anymore.

"I wish I'd known that when I voted for him." She clicked her tongue against her teeth a few times and I got the feeling that if the president were there right then she'd have given him a good scolding.

"I'll just go look for your purse," I said and made for the garage. The beige purse was in the car, squished between the seat and the door. I yanked it out and pushed it back into its original shape, then I did something a snoopy person like me tends to do---I checked the contents. A lacy handkerchief wreaking with lavender cologne lay clean and folded on top of a wallet with a five and ten ones in it. She had no driver's license and no credit cards. Beneath the wallet were two pair of glasses, each tucked in a needlepointed holder. Three plastic bottles of medication rattled around in the bottom, one of Elavil, another of Entex and third of aspirin. The two prescription drugs were prescribed for V. May on October of that year by Stephen Oakes, MD. What was she doing with an anti-depressant? The parrot lady didn't look depressed to me, but she was a bit drowsy. Maybe that was how her depression showed up.

I continued my search. A gold-plated compact and silver tube of Sexy Siren Red lipstick by Forever Yours glimmered up at me in the dim light. I chuckled over that, wondering what romantic fantasies (or real life episodes) the parrot lady had. Reaching the bottom, I stuffed everything back in the purse, trying to keep some sense of order.

When I got back to the living room she said, "Rock 'n' roll is going to save the world, my dear."

"It is?" I mumbled, wondering where she got that idea.

"Of course it is. Says so right here." Her bony finger pointed at *Greenpeace.* Her face congealed into rapture. "Did you know the Thompson Twins have just returned from their triumphant trip to Moscow?"

"No, I sure didn't." She was a bottomless pit of useful information.

"Yes, they were there, speaking about the environment. Good kids, the Thompsons."

All this was very interesting, especially since I hadn't had a change to read my copy of *Greenpeace* yet, but it wasn't helping one bit with my understanding of the parrot lady's plight. "Here's your purse," I said, handing it to her. "Maybe you can tell me who you are now and where I can bring you."

"My dear, haven't I introduced myself?" Her fingers rummaged through the beige bag. "Now I know what happened." She pulled out three plastic bottles. "I think I took three of these instead of the one I was supposed to take." Her fingers pulled out two pairs of glasses and she pushed the sunglasses up on her forehead. Trying on the others in turn, amid much squinting and grimacing, she finally said, "What does this bottle say?"

"Take the pills, mother. Take the pills," said Buck in a nasty tone.

The parrot lady jerked her head and looked at the bird. "Where did you learn such nasty talk, Buck? Shame on you." The bird ducked its head.

I bent down and took the pill container from the woman. "It says, *one tablet three times a day.*"

6

"Isn't that just what I told you? I've taken too many at once and that's why I got into your car. I tell you dearie, the older you get, the more your forget things."

I looked at her, but her explanation just didn't ring true. Still, she seemed to be okay now, so perhaps it was none of my business. The only thing that still bothered me was the blue Ford Festiva. I could tell by the way the man was driving and the look on the woman's face that they weren't fooling.

CHAPTER 3

The parrot lady and Buck finished off the last of my muffins before the woman said, "My name's Veronica May, just like the movie star." Her violet eyes caught fire brilliantly as if she were remembering something spectacular.

My mind tore back to the old-time films I had seen, but I couldn't remember a single name, especially not Veronica May. "She was a star?"

Veronica rubbed her eyes, then put her black sun glasses back on and returned the other pair to her purse. "Not really a star, she was more like my friend, Selma Wyberg, destined to be one. That was before Selma met Luke Pesco and ran off."

"Where did she run too?" Although I was usually able to keep on track when I was extracting information, something about Veronica May made me want to hear more about her. I guess I really liked her, maybe because she was the grandmother I never had. Buck liked her too. He nuzzled against her neck and mumbled to himself, one minute sounding like kids yelling to one another on the playground, the next like any angry man's voice and then switching to an apologetic woman. All the words were unintelligible, but the intonation was clear.

Veronica scratched Buck's head and he bobbed on her shoulder in ecstasy. "I never did find out where Luke and Selma went. They were never heard from again. She and I were best friends in grammar school. We used to practice acting out stories up in her room. What a beauty she was even then, with long red, wavy hair and eyes as blue as cornflowers."

Before I got her entire history, no matter how interesting, I needed to know more about the past few hours. The nosiness in me came out and asked, "If you've never seen the blue car and don't know anybody who might be after you, what do you suppose those two people were doing chasing us?"

Veronica tapped her chin with a gloved hand. "You know, dear, I've been giving that some thought. Maybe they thought I was somebody else. Maybe somebody who'd done them some wrong."

For some reason, I heard Mae West singing, "He Was Her Man, But She Done Him Wrong." It floated in my head, like perfect background music for Veronica. She looked nothing like Mae West, but she did have a seductive quality about her and with Buck on her shoulder, she was one unique lady. I thought I'd try another tack. "Do you live alone?"

"No, I live with my daughter and her husband. I guess I should say they live with me. It's my house.

"Could it have been your daughter and son-in-law following us?"

"You took off so fast, I really didn't get a good look, but I don't think so. Dennis and Mary have an old station wagon. I think it's an awful green color."

"Could they have gotten a new car?"

"I suppose it's possible, but don't you think they'd have mentioned it to me?"

"I don't know, how close are you?"

"Mary's always been a little tight-lipped, she's like her father that way. Edward didn't talk much, but you knew what he was thinking, especially when he got angry. Then his brown eyes would narrow and his thick brows would sink down and you'd know what the preacher meant when he talked about hellfire and damnation."

"Your husband was a violent man?"

"I wouldn't say exactly violent, but he did beat little Mary a few times when I didn't think she deserved it. As a result she turned to food, I know that's why she's always been a chubby child."

"The woman behind us in the blue car was---chubby." She was actually fat, but I didn't want to offend Veronica.

"She was? I really didn't get a good look. Besides, what would they be doing chasing us? That's not a very polite way of doing things."

"I thought maybe you'd know why they acted that way."

"Mary's been a little strange lately, but not that strange. But she'd never do anything like that. And Dennis drives so slow. He's a real poke, if you know what I mean."

"I know what you mean." A lot of drivers in St. Petersburg liked to get in the fast lane and go slow. I guess Dennis must have been one of those. "Must not have been your daughter and son-in-law then. Maybe you should call and let them know you're all right."

"Oh, could I? I would feel much better knowing they're not worrying about me." She opened her purse and rummaged in it. Buck jumped down onto her lap and stuck his beak into the blue bag. "Oh darn, have I forgotten that address book again." She waved him away. "Get out of there Buck, that's no place for a gentleman."

The bird squawked, whistled, then said, "No place for a gentleman --- w-w-a-o-o-ck!"

Veronica giggled at me. "He learns very quickly you know. Have to be careful what you say around him or he'll pick it up."

9

"I see that. Does he fly?"

"Sometimes. My daughter wanted me to clip his wings, but I just couldn't bring myself to do it. It seems so heartless, like taking away a cat's defenses by declawing it." I nodded. Sometimes I'd wished I'd declawed Samantha, especially after one of her *climb the curtains* episodes.

"How do you get him to fly?"

"Generally he just does it, but I did teach him a trick or two. Sometimes when I tap my shoulder, he flies up there."

"Would he fly onto my shoulder?"

"I think so. He seems to like you. He *is* a ladies' man." She giggled.

"How can you tell he likes me?" I set down my teacup on the side table.

"He never talks if he's mad or doesn't like a person. It's like he's punishing you. He stopped talking for a whole week the one time I left him and went to visit my sister in Nebraska. I guess he thought I deserved it. He doesn't talk to my daughter or son-in-law, either. For him, they don't exist. He likes to give them the silent treatment." She looked at the bird. "Don't you, Buck? You sly thing."

The parrot nodded and blinked his eyes a few times before he said, "Buck is a sly thing. A ladies' man."

We both laughed at that, then I tapped my shoulder. Buck looked at it, cocked his head from side to side, then flew over and perched on me. "See, I told you he likes you," said Veronica with a smile.

"Must be the muffins." With Buck doing a balancing act, I stood up and walked over to the table. His feet felt like cold little knobs on my shoulder. Grasping knobs. "Let's see if we have any nuts around here." I opened a drawer in the wicker book shelf and took out a jar of peanuts. "Can he have these?"

"Certainly. He adores them. But I only give them to him for a treat. Too much fat isn't good for them." I took off the jar cap, put a few nuts in my hand and held them up for him to eat. He pulverized them with a couple of clicks of his mandibles, letting me see what he could do to my arm or face with that powerful beak if he wanted to.

I gave him a respectful look, returned to my rattan chair and looked over at Veronica. "Do you remember your phone number?"

Buck squawked, then flew back to Veronica's shoulder. She gave me a blank look. "You know, I don't." She looked down at the bird. "Good bird. Nice Buck," she said, scratching his head.

"Maybe the number is listed in the phone book." I got up, riffled though the place mats and candles until I found the well-creased book in the bottom of the broom closet. It wasn't a book I consulted too often. The numbers I usually called were in the roladex on my desk. I took the phone book back into the living room.

"I see you're a health and wellness writer," she said.

"Does it show?"

"No, but I saw your business cards on the desk. Megan Baldwin, Health and Wellness Editor."

"That's me and that's what I do." I went over and took a few cards and handed them to her. "Here, in case you run into anyone who might be interested in my newsletter."

I went back and sat down. "What's your son-in-law's last name?"

"Dwyer, Dennis Dwyer."

My finger slid down the page. "Here it is. I'll dial it for you." I waited for twenty rings, but no one answered. "Maybe I could drive you there."

"Certainly, dear." She rose and straightened her dress. Buck picked up a clawed foot, then set it down on her shoulder gently. "You've been very kind to let me rest here for so long."

Veronica gave me a fragile look and I almost recanted, but enough was enough. I had done my good deed for the day. She took my arm and we strolled out to the garage and my waiting car. It was a fifteen-minute drive to Veronica's house in the Old NorthEast. Buck stared straight ahead out the windshield, while Veronica dozed off. We pulled up in front of a white, two-story frame house that looked like a transplant from the north with its big porch swing, green shutters and brick chimneys. It nestled between two Mediterranean stuccos, and like the other houses in the neighborhood, had a distinctive look, in this case, a white cupola roof over the front porch. The house had all the trappings of a very respectable home, but something told me it wasn't.

A mixture of flowering and non-flowering trees nearly filled the lawn. Jacarunda threatened to show their purple blooms and flowerettes had already burst into color on the golden rain and orchid trees. Two giant palms swayed sedately in the afternoon breeze on either side of the walk. I thought I spied a royal poinciana in the side yard where grapefruit and orange trees carried their fruit proudly like so many Christmas ornaments.

I didn't see the blue Ford Festiva parked in front, but then in the Old NorthEast, everyone had a garage on the alley, not like in the rest of St. Petersburg where you either parked in the drive or pulled into a house-attached garage. Veronica jolted awake when I turned off the engine. "Are we here?" She looked around her.

"We have arrived." I walked her to the front door, up the brick steps, holding onto the wrought iron railing. There were no signs of life in the house. I rang the bell, but no one answered. Then I picked up a heavy gold knocker and let it fall on the wooden door a few times. Still no response.

Veronica shrugged, giggled, then bent down and extracted a key from under the straw mat at the front door. "For emergencies," she said, opening the door.

"You going to be all right?"

"I guess I'll be fine now," she said, unconvincingly.

"Do you want me to come in with you?"

"No, we'll be fine. Buck and I will be just fine."

I turned to go. "Okay, then. Call me if you need me."

"I will and thanks for everything." I was already regretting my decision and almost went back to the door, but I forced myself to get in the car. I'd check on her later. Besides, there might be a message on my answering machine inquiring about bulk rate subscriptions for thousands of newsletters. I could use something like that, the cat food was beginning to run out.

CHAPTER 4

I didn't have a chance to make the call to Veronica May because when I got back home, my phone was ringing. It was Paula Saunders, the Realtor who had helped me sell the house when Ned and I divorced. It had been a bad time for me. A time of great sadness and depression. I kicked myself around for a few months about being a failure in the marriage until Paula sold the house and brought me a tuna fish casserole to help celebrate the closing. We clicked our grape juice glasses, toasting the start of my new life and it seemed to have taken. That was the night I firmly decided to end my hospital nursing career and start my own business. She had been a friend to me then and I still considered her one.

Her foghorn voice had been worsened by a few hours of crying. "It's Cassie."

"What's wrong with her?" Cassie was Paula's wayward daughter who had been in trouble with the law or otherwise since kindergarten. First there had been stealing in grade school, then drugs and an abortion in high school, and more petty thievery and prostitution after that.

I felt sorry for Paula. She was the kind of woman who I wouldn't have minded having for a mother and I guess she felt the same way about me being her daughter. God knows fate hadn't dealt her any kind blows with four miscarriages (the last one ending in a hysterectomy) and an alcoholic husband who died young. Then there was Cassie, whose police record was anything but something to be proud of and who came home to live with her mother until she could find some more trouble.

"Cassie's been living with me again you know and she hasn't been home for three nights."

"Is that unusual?"

"Sure it is. A night at the most, But---"

"Maybe I'll just come over and you can tell me all about it."

"Would you?" Her voice was a mix of gratefulness and depression.

It was short drive to the Palms, a four-story condominium complex to the west. A few residents, like Paula, still worked, but most were retirees or snowbirds who came down from the north for six months in the winter.

Spotlights highlighted the swaying palms and newly-blacktopped parking lot. Built in the 60's when materials and labor came more cheaply, The Palms was a substantial grouping of beige stucco buildings and red tile roofs clustered around a pool, fountain, and fishing pier. I pulled into a visitor's spot in the section of the lot that wasn't cordoned off. The air smelled of tar, salt air and barbecuing meat.

Paula's unit was on the second floor, facing out over the pool. She met me at the screened door with a haggard look on her face and purple shadows under her eyes. The light over her door glinted off her silvery hair and drew deep cervices alongside her mouth. I put out my arms and she grabbed me like a swimmer going down for the third time. We must have hugged for five minutes before she released me and pulled me into the kitchen.

It was one of those comfortable places with chintz curtains over the sink and glass jars full of noodles and cookies and other good things lining the counter. *Bless this House* hotpads hung above the stove and a matching hand towel dangled from a nearby hook.

I sat down on one of the heavy maple kitchen chairs and waited for Paula to put some steaming coffee and brownies in front of me. No matter how busy she was with work and her daughter, she always baked. From the smell of the kitchen, she was baking then. It smelled like oatmeal cookies to me. Paula said baking was her therapy. The way she looked told me she needed a lot more hours before she was cured.

Her face was puffy from crying and she'd lost weight. Her ample flesh hung sadly on her body as if it preferred to be anywhere but on this planet. She wore a purple striped apron with flour fingerprints on the bib over her plaid Bermuda shorts and matching blouse.

She lugged over two steaming cups and a piled-high plate of chocolate goodness. While she talked, I managed to put away two of the chewy delights. "Cassie promised me she wouldn't stay out without calling." She gave me a sheepish look. "No, really, she's gone straight. No more men for pay. She even joined the Single Hearts Club and planned to meet a nice guy."

I knew the club. It was one in St. Petersburg I had thought of joining myself. It had a good reputation as a place where you could meet halfway decent dates who were well-screened. Given the AIDS fear and my track record with men (two divorces and no long-term relationship in sight), that was a definite plus.

Then it hit me. The parrot lady had a matchbook to that club, too. What did a prostitute and an elderly woman have in common?

Paula took a sip of her coffee. "Until Tuesday, Cassie hadn't broken her word. That's why I think something has happened to her.

"You could be right." Imagining the crowd Cassie ran with, anything was possible. "Do you have the names or addresses of any of her friends?" I was being polite so I didn't say johns or tricks.

"I may have." She reached for the side counter and picked up a small red address book. "Cassie kept their names in this book." She browsed through it while I wondered how her daughter could be so brazen as to leave such evidence in front of

14

her mother. I was the rebellious type too, but tended to keep my sexual life pretty much to myself.

Paula's chubby finger traced down the pages. "These are all from the old times. I don't know if they'll help now."

Do you want me to call for you?"

Paula nodded and sniffed. "I remember her mentioning this guy, Rick Stetson. He may be someone who knows something."

Have you tried to contact him?"

Her face turned an embarrassed pink. "I didn't think that --- I didn't want to ---"

I understood. I wasn't exactly experienced in the world of sex for money, but for some reason I felt I had to make her think I was. Just a slight insecurity I was nursing along until it gave up and left me alone.

She put an arm around me and kissed my cheek. Her lips were warm and wet and sad. I almost started to cry myself. Sometimes I get a distinct feeling when something irreversible has happened. This was one of those times. I hugged her and we sat silently for quite a while.

"More coffee?" she said, standing up and moving to the stove.

"Sure, why not? I don't like to sleep anyway." That nearly brought a smile to her face and I felt good about that.

She poured us each a cup, then set the pot on a straw pad. "I want you to find out what happened to Cassie."

"I'm not an investigator."

"No, but you told me you used to help the police find missing patients."

"But I'm not an investigator."

"No, but I can't call the police. I just can't."

I smiled at her and kissed her on the cheek. Sometimes I can be conned into anything. This time it took three brownies and two cups of coffee. With Cassie's red address book tucked in the pocket of my off-white pants and another brownie (carefully wrapped in aluminum foil to prevent soiling) buried deep in the pocket of my cotton shirt, I was ready for a couple of more hours of work.

When I got home, I gave Samantha a can of her favorite cat food, then tried to ignore the silent treatment she gave me. I took time out for a cup of tea. I needed something to soothe my bubbly stomach. The paper wasn't much help. An article on page six was particularly distressing.

15

SUN PARTICLES BOMBARD THE EARTH

UNPRECEDENTED LEVELS OF SOLAR ACTIVITY PREDICTED

"Oh, God," I think I said, throwing down the copy of *The Times*. "That's all I need." First there was red tide, then acid rain, global warming, Tammy Faye, Ollie North, the parrot lady, Cassie Saunders---and now, particle bombardment.

I took a sip of peppermint tea and considered. What was this particle bombardment about? Did it mean we were all under some kind of horrific force, like when there's a full moon and gravitational pulls make some of us act a little crazier than usual? Although the thought scared me. at least it might explain the parrot lady's appearance and Cassie's disappearance.

I snapped up the newspaper, my eyes furiously scanning the wrinkled mess, hoping to find out more. Of course there wasn't any more. It was one of those short articles written by some sadistic reporter who hopes to scare the heck out of you with too little information and terrifying headlines and was probably at that very moment glowering with glee over the havoc he was causing me that morning.

I kept my eyes off Samantha, who I knew was eyeing me with her most penetrating glance, making me feel I was taking the whole thing too seriously. Samantha is the cat who lives with me. Correction: the cat I live with. Notice I didn't call her "my cat", because she is nothing if not a free spirit who deigns to reside in my house when she doesn't have better things to do.

From her perch on the windowsill of the Florida room, the feline let out a soft hiss and I just knew *she knew* I was thinking about her. At various times I've been convinced that cat is either the reincarnation of some mystical, pagan goddess or the ghost of my dead, ex-mother-in-law who swore she'd come back and make my life miserable.

I snorted, just to show I wasn't going to let Samantha have the last word, and headed for the kitchen with my cup. She hated being booted out of the house (as she was for Veronica's parrot, Buck) and always paid me back in one way or another. That night she refused to eat and wouldn't even come to me when I called.

I picked up her dish and dumped the food in a plastic container. Two could play this game. I had read in a book somewhere that if the cat doesn't eat after twenty minutes, take up the food and put it away. Samantha gave me a disapproving look, her brilliant copper eyes glistening back at me, then she flicked her tail and went into the living room. Good thing my family had made me nearly immune to the silent treatment.

I sat down at my kitchen table with the telephone and Cassie's address book. Rick Stetson was an attorney with a downtown office and an uptown home address. I tried the office first, hoping I might catch him working late. Whoever answered let the phone clatter against some annoying surface like a desk, then picked it up and mumbled, "Hello."

"Mr. Stetson?"

"Yes. Who's this?"

"Megan Baldwin. I'm looking into the disappearance of Cassie Saunders."

He banged the phone down and I heard muffled voices in the background. When he picked up the receiver again he said, "I don't know anyone by that name and please don't call here again." Before I could answer, he hung up.

I gave the phone a Bronx cheer before I picked it up again and dialed his home number. A woman with a nasal voice said, "Is this my husband's slut? I told you not to call here anymore!"

Now we were getting somewhere. Mrs. Stetson knew about Cassie and had probably heard from her recently. "Don't hang up. I'm Megan Baldwin and I'm investigating ---"

"Did my husband hire you to spy on me?"

"Not at all. I don't even know him. I'm looking into the disappearance of Cassie Saunders."

"That's her! She's the one! You just tell my husband he'd better stop running around with tramps or I'll divorce him and take him for all he's worth ---"

I interrupted her threat and said, "I don't know your husband. I'm trying to find Cassie Saunders.

After a long pause, her nasal voice said, "Is she blonde with emerald green eyes and about six feet tall?"

"More like five ten."

"I know who she is. She had the gall to come here and try to blackmail me."

"Then you've seen her?'

"Two days ago."

"What did she say?"

"She said to give her five thousand dollars or she'd go public."

"Did you?"

"Of course not. I hope everyone finds out about him. Let him see how it feels to be a laughing stock."

"Maybe I could come over there and you could give me the details on Cassie ---"

"Don't you dare come over here and don't call again!" For the second time that night the phone slammed down in my ear. It must run in the family.

I copied down Attorney Rick Stetson's office and home address and headed for my car. His office was in a white stone building on First Avenue North near Maas Brothers department store. I parked down the block and walked in the shadows until I found the front door. On the other side of the street in front of a newsstand, a bearded man swayed back and forth as if he was either on drugs or drunk. I moved a little faster and tried to look like I belonged there and was on a mission. Which I was.

The only light on in the building flickered under his attorney-at-law sign. Two cars were parked on the street nearby, but neither one looked like something an up-and-coming attorney would drive. I walked to the corner and went around the alley. No car there either. That entrance was locked.

I walked back to the street, hearing my sneakered feet make squeaky noises on the cement. The man across First Avenue North stumbled onto the cement bench and sat staring at me. Not wanting a confrontation, I pretended not to see him, put my head down, got into my car and drove off as quickly as possible.

It was only a mile or so to the Stetson's house. They lived in the Old NorthEast too, but in a more expensive section with magnificent water views. I parked on the corner and walked up the sidewalk as if I lived there.

The Stetson residence was a two-story stone house with turquoise and white awnings. A stone lion lantern stood on the lawn, lighting my way up the brick steps. Arguing voices came through the open windows. They sounded like Rick and his wife.

I ducked behind a thirty-foot oak and watched and listened. "I told you this would come back and haunt us," shouted Mrs. Stetson. She wore a flimsy satin robe and her small breasts stood out against the material like aerial weapons ready to be launched. Her red hair was the bottle variety, but had been done at some fancy salon where they knew what they were doing. Her skin was china-doll perfect, even without makeup. She had the kind of look I used to wish I'd grow up to have before I learned to like my attractive, but nothing-sensational-look. She pushed back a clump of curls from her forehead with her carmine-tipped fingers, using a dramatic motion as if she might faint at any moment.

"Don't get hysterical on me, Janice. I've heard all this crap before." Rick Stetson towered over her, at least six-four to her five-five. His face wasn't handsome or even attractive, especially since he held it in an angry bear look. His high forehead ran back into tufts of woolly black hair and his body was skinny and probably out of shape beneath his Brooks Brothers tailoring. He moved like a man who needed to be noticed and his hands waved continually within inches of his wife's livid face.

"I'm not getting hysterical. I told you she called and knew all about Cassie."

"What she didn't know you probably told her, right?"

"I didn't say anything she didn't already know."

They moved away from the windows and their voices turned into incomprehensible noise. I crept back to my car and drove home. At least I knew they were hiding something. I didn't know what it was yet, but it had to do with Cassie Saunders.

CHAPTER 5

On the drive back to the beach, my stomach told me I hadn't had dinner. Not wanting to go home and face eating by myself, I pulled into B.J.'s, a cafe overlooking the Gulf of Mexico, where you can get a decent piece of fish and endless salad bar. The Blue awnings and the red geraniums in the window boxes looked very inviting at that moment. B.J.'s is a place I sometimes go for a little talk, a cool drink, and a glimpse of a magnificent sunset. I don't usually stay to eat, but it seemed like the time to splurge. Maybe the idea of investigating a disappearance made me giddy or just plain unwilling to recognize I couldn't afford to eat out.

B.J., the owner, moved here when construction came to a standstill in Texas. He had planned to build condos, but when he saw the cafe on the beach, he fell in love and used his money to buy it. B.J. (short for Billy Joe) was usually behind the bar, if he wasn't in the kitchen sampling or cooking. Sometimes he even waited tables.

I pulled my jacket out of the back seat and scooted through the wooden saloon half-door leading into the cafe. B.J.'s lanky body leaned over the pine-carved bar, his mustachioed mouth twisting in a low tones of an intimate conversation with a long-legged blonde wearing a white skirt and a halter about two sizes too small for her breasts. He waved when I came in, then disentangled himself from the girl and came sauntering over, stopping at the hefty wood tables in the center of the room to slap a back or throw hello to a customer. He never missed a chance to talk to me, so I had a hunch he would have made a move if I'd given him the slightest encouragement.

I leaned into the high-backed wooden booth and watched him. He wasn't a bad-looking guy if you liked the rugged, western look. Maybe it was the dim, cigarette-smoky light that made him look attractive. Or maybe it was the sad love song on the juke box. Or maybe it was just that I hadn't been with a man for a long time. Whatever it was, I started to have fantasies of what his body might look like under his western shirt, faded jeans, scuffed boots and ten gallon hat.

"You look like hell," he said in a western twang, destroying any fantasies I may have thought of pursuing.

I gave him a weak smile. "Thanks. You look pretty good. Must be that young thing you were talking to." I looked toward the bar.

"Ramona?" He grimaced. "She's the daughter of my cook. Trying to hit me up for money again. I swear she's snorting something."

"Probably." I glanced at the daily specials hanging above the bar. "How's the sea trout?"

"I wouldn't recommend it. Stick to the grouper."

B.J.'s honesty was one reason I came to his cafe. He never steered me wrong. "Give me that and put me down for the salad bar."

He nodded. "Beer?"

"Perrier."

"You New York types always screw up a perfectly good meal."

"I know. It's what I come here for."

He winked and clumped off to the kitchen while I got up and filled my plate from the track-lit salad bar at the back of the cafe. Broccoli and cauliflower hearts sat in artful arrangement in huge wooden bowls, next to shredded carrots, olives, creamy coleslaw, cheese squares, mounds of escarole and romaine, three-bean salad, cottage cheese and bacon bits. I grabbed one of the warm plates from the stack and started to fill it up.

I was basically a vegetarian who ate fish once in a while. That had started when I was a child and my father gave me the T-bone out of his steak. "The nearer the bone, the sweeter the meat," he'd say, winking at my mother. (Then I resented having to chew the bone while he ate the meat.) Later I found out I felt better eating potatoes, squash and salad and chewing on an occasional bone, so I became a vegetarian.

Returning to my table with vegetables heaped high on my plate, I turned to the sound of a familiar voice. I hadn't seen Lou Rasnick in weeks but that hadn't made me forget what a handsome creature he was. His well-muscled body leaned casually against the bar. A blue-and-white striped shirt emphasized the width and firmness of his chest. Smooth-fitting, beige deck pants showed off his narrow waist and long legs. He and B.J. were having a bull session about something, probably football or fishing.

Watching them, it occurred to me why I like B.J.'s so much. Lou and I came here a lot when we had been a couple and had watched more than a few sunsets on B.J.'s deck overlooking the Gulf. We had also lived together in my house eons ago (or two years depending on which time frame you used) when he was on the St. Petersburg police force and I was working nights at Bay General. I was also taking courses at the local junior college to learn writing. When I started working weirder hours than he did, the whole thing between us fell apart, but the chemistry remained.

Sensing my glance, he turned and gave me the famous Lou Rasnick, dimpled smile. "Megan. I was just thinking about you," he mouthed and started toward my booth.

Same here, partner. "Really? Where's Susan?" Unable to work out our relationship, he had finally quit the force, became a private detective himself and married Susan, a (you guessed it) nurse. As much as I hated to admit it, I liked the woman. Right then, she came between us like an invisible screen, keeping our primal urges in check.

"She's working the evening shift," he said in that rich, deep voice of his that reminded me of something sinfully good, but forbidden, like chocolate. "Thought I'd catch a bite to eat. My cooking's dreadful."

"Mine, too."

Track lights shone down on his glossy black hair and across the angular planes of his face, making his brown eyes glow. "As I recall, you were a pretty good cook."

"I've gotten rusty. Want to join me?"

"Actually, I was thinking of eating out on the porch. It's going to be a great sunset. Want to join me?" We both knew the sun had set hours ago, but maintained the game.

"Sure. Tell B.J. to bring my fish there." Lou turned and walked away, long legs loping across the floor, leaving me with a bittersweet feeling that we weren't together anymore. He came back a minute later with two drinks and we went onto the open porch. We picked a round wooden table away from the bustle. I arranged my jacket around the back of the captain's chair and sat down. The sky blazed with glittering stars, but I was imagining the bright pinks and blues of a Gulf sunset and the red disk of a sun hovering on the horizon as if it didn't want to leave.

We sat and sipped and pretended to watch the orb slide out of sight. Every sunset in St. Petersburg was a unique experience, one of the few things in my life that could still bring back in me that childlike sense of awe at the majesty of the universe. With Lou's strong presence and the beauty before me, I didn't once think of being bombarded with particles.

"So what you working on?" He asked a few minutes later, taking a sip of his Chablis.

"It's not what I'm working on that really bothers me." I pulled my jacket over my shoulders and told him about the parrot lady, Veronica May.

"She does sound like a character. But what are you really working on?"

"A missing persons case for a friend."

He raised an eyebrow. "What? That's the craziest thing I ever heard of. You don't know anything about investigating."

I knew what he meant and I probably shouldn't have said yes to Paula but she was one of my few friends. "I know, damned if you do and damned if you don't, but Paula Saunders needed help and I doubt she'd go to someone she didn't know."

"Saunders. The Realtor?"

"She's the one."

"Isn't it her daughter who's always on the report sheets?"

I nodded. "Cassie. She's the one and she's also the one who's missing."

Another raised eyebrow. "She's the type to go underground for days at a time, so what's the big deal?"

"I just want to reassure Paula. She helped me out when I needed it and ---"

His hand touched my arm with a pressure of warmth and excitement and I turned to look where he was pointing, paying more attention to the havoc inside me his fingers were creating than to the splendor before us. "Look at those colors."

Lou was one of the few men I knew who wasn't ashamed to admit an emotional response to natural beauty. I suppose that wasn't strange because one of his hobbies was oil painting, yet most men, at least in my business, maintained a veneer of toughness and inattention to such *feminine* things. It was one of the many traits that endeared him to me.

By that time, the sky would have been a palette of lavenders, blues and oranges if the sun was really setting. For a few minutes, we sat silently and pretended to watch the show. The air turned chillier and I pulled up the collar of my jacket. He looked at me. "Cold?"

"I'm fine." I said it automatically, holding back the wish for him to put his arm around me like he used to.

Later, over our fish, I asked about his work. He was following up on an insurance case for Brian Taub, a local lawyer. "The guy is obsessed with a case that goes back a year or so. He says he doesn't have time to follow all the leads, so he hired me."

"Obsessed?"

"There's this woman, another friend of the family." He glared at me as if to show only bad can come to those who get involved professionally with friends. He cleared his throat. "Anyway, this Nancy Rodgers has been trying to collect on the life insurance for her daughter's accidental death and she's having quite a time doing it."

"Isn't she the beneficiary?"

"That's just it, the insurance company is giving her the run-around about that."

"And that's where you come in."

"You got it. Should be a pretty simple thing to check and that's what I'm going to do as soon as the insurance office opens tomorrow."

A blotchy-faced waiter with a white towel tied around his jeans took our food plates and plunked down two mugs of coffee. We sat sipping from them for a long time, talking around the subject of us. I had almost forgotten the intensity of his blue eyes and the lazy way he smiled at me when he was enjoying my company. I didn't want the evening to end, but I knew it had to. He had a wife to go home to and I had to find the parrot lady. It took all the moral courage I had to get up, go to my car and drive home, when all I wanted to do was just curl up in Lou's arms and forget particle bombardment, Veronica May and Cassie Saunders.

CHAPTER 6

Samantha waited at the door for me and twisted her silky body against my legs. All was forgiven or she was hungry and conning me again. Whatever, I reached down and scratched behind her ears, bringing out purrs of pleasure.

I threw my jacket over a chair in the kitchen and took out the teapot. If it was one thing I needed after a few hours of hormonal arousal it was something calming, like chamomile tea. The teabag had barely hit the bottom of the cup when the phone rang.

I poured the water in the cup with one hand and retrieved the kitchen phone with the other. It was Lou Rasnick. Before he could say more than "hello," my mind crowded with visions of him saying he couldn't live without me anymore, that he was leaving his wife and was coming right over to see me.

Instead, he said, "They found Cassie Saunders."

I gulped down some tea and burned the inside of my mouth something fierce. "Who? Where?"

"Joe Ferguson called. A couple of his sergeants dragged her out of the water off Gandy Bridge."

"Dead?"

"Totally. She washed ashore and some fisherman found her in his net."

"She was in the water awhile?"

"Not long. About a day they think, but the medical examiner will know more soon."

"How'd they I.D. her?"

"She was wearing a bracelet with information about her health status. Guess she was a diabetic."

I remembered then that Paula had told me Cassie had been diagnosed with diabetes at age ten. Maybe without that bracelet the police would never have known who she was. And if she'd been in the salt water longer than a day, she's have blown up like a balloon. Water does strange things after a while. I remember reading that in a mystery someplace. It wasn't a picture I wanted to contemplate, so I asked, "Does Paula know yet?"

"Somebody's on the way over there now."

"Thanks for letting me know, Lou. I think I'll go over too. She'll be needing some comfort real soon."

I hung up, slumped into a chair, and took another sip of the tea before I realized my mouth was scalded. Setting down the cup, I stared at the blue and yellow walrus hotpads hanging by my stove. All I could think about was how Paula was going to feel when she found out.

I pulled a sweater over my shirt and put my jacket back on. The wind had picked up and it was going to be a cold evening by Florida standards. Samantha gave me a Can-I-Go-Out-Again look, but I snubbed her. I wasn't in any mood to play games.

I backed my Toyota out of the drive like one of those car chases in "Smoky and the Bandit" and gunned it to Paula's. I left the windows rolled up and still could feel the cool air through them. A few snowbirds in shorts and short sleeves walked the streets. I honked at two of them, having no patience that night with people walking in the middle of the road.

A police car stood in front of the Palms, alerting the neighborhood to trouble. Lights blazing from Paula's condo pointed to its source. Except for the car and lights, everything looked quiet and ordinary. Like the calm before a storm. I ran up the flight of stairs and across the walkway to Paula's condo.

A slender woman in a red plaid robe and pink pajamas was stationed at the front door with a look on her face that reminded me of a bouncer I had seen once. "Yes?" she said through clenched teeth. Her eyes were steel gray, hard and unmoving. Her hair was braided in a tight line down the back of her head, pulling the skin of her face tight. I wondered if it had been painful to achieve.

My mother used to braid my hair when I was little and I remembered the agony of each before-school session as she twisted and pulled, making sure it hung in two perfect shiny streams down my back, while ignoring my tears and pleadings to stop. One day I put a stop to the daily pain. I took out her shears, made two swift cuts across the braids, about ear-high, and threw the plaited demons under my bed. That was the end of braids for me.

I took a step forward, closer to Paula's door. "I'm Megan Baldwin, a friend of Paula's."

The woman's face changed in an instant to warmth and approval. "Come in, come in. I'm Stella Dodson. Paula's been talking about you."

Stella held the door open and I stumbled in. Paula was in the kitchen with a look on her face like I'd never seen before, something between shock and utter despair. A sergeant in uniform sat in the chair next to hers, talking in earnest tones like a doctor telling a patient these were her last days. He was young, maybe twenty-five, and looked like he didn't even shave yet, but then the older I get, the younger everyone else looks.

A plate of cookies and cups of coffee cluttered the otherwise neat table. Nothing stopped Paula from being hospitable.

The policeman looked up. A name tag on his shirt identified him as Sergeant Hennessey. Freckles spread out across his nose and cheeks and a knot of reddish hair stood up in a cowlick at the back of his head. A kid, they've sent a kid, I thought, but his voice was deep and authoritative. "No visitors, please. Mrs. Saunders has had a bad experience." His partner was at the stove, pouring more coffee. "Show her out, will you Sergeant Dubrowski?"

The plump sergeant in police uniform at the stove turned around and stared at me. Frizzy brown hair stood out in clumps around her head. Her eyes were blueberry blue and friendly in a pasty face that looked like it had too many pies and cakes lately. She nodded to the man at the table, then came toward me with a confused look on her face and a coffee pot in her hand. She looked as if she didn't know whether to pour me a cup or shoo me out.

Paula leaned forward in her chair. "No! Let her stay." Her face was so angry and her tone so commanding that Sergeant Dubrowski nodded, turned and went back to the stove.

Paula looked at me and the tears tracking down her face glistened in the kitchen light. I moved to the table and put my arms around her. A million reassuring phrases ran through my head like, "It's all right," and "I'm so sorry," but it wasn't all right and being sorry wasn't going to help. There was really nothing to say, so we just hugged.

She clung to me like a small child who had been lost and just found its mother. Reversing the roles like that kind of threw me, but I stood there and tried to pretend I knew how to handle it. Finally she began to make sounds, first half wheezes, gasps and sobs, then words. "Dead?...How could this happen?...My, God...I knew something was wrong...I never guessed this...Is this punishment?...Cassie was never an angel ... I just never thought ..."

I held her for a few more minutes while the sergeants exchanged uncomfortable looks. Finally Paula's arms began to relax from around my body. She looked up at me and said, "Do you want some coffee?"

I sniffed a few tears back. "Don't worry about me now. I'm fine." I drew a tissue out of my jacket pocket and handed it to her.

Paula honked into it a few times and wiped her eyes. "What now?" She looked at the sergeants.

Sergeant Hennessey slapped his notebook closed. "We have the information we need." He stood up and motioned to me. I followed him into the living room. His green eyes blurred with indecision before he said, "We need you to come down and identify the body."

I'd seen quite a few dead bodies, but that didn't stop me from feeling squeamish about it. "Isn't the bracelet enough?"

"Could be somebody else's bracelet on her. We need personal confirmation, ma'am. Now if you'll come with me ---"

I stood next to him, placing my face a little too close for both our comforts. He stood about five-four to my five-five. "Can't that wait until morning. This poor woman has just been through the wringer. She needs someone with her and right now, I'm it."

Sergeant Hennessey looked at his partner who stared at the flower print wallpaper. "I --- I guess that will be all right. You do promise to come down ---"

I whipped out my nursing license and shoved it in front of his face. "I promise."

He nodded. "Okay, okay." He motioned to his partner and they clunked out, closing the door behind them. I was left with a dull ache in my chest for Paula and no idea of what to do next.

I went back in the kitchen and found Paula fingering a linen napkin. We sat at the table and drank the rest of the coffee. By then I didn't think either of us would sleep that night and it was going to be a long couple of hours until daylight.

"How about trying to rest, Paula," I finally said.

"No," she stood up unsteadily. "I think I'll bake that bread I was planning to make yesterday."

I thought about trying to stop her, but she wasn't going to rest then anyway, so she might as well bake. I nodded to her. "Okay, will you be all right for a while?'

"Sure. I could make bread in my sleep." She opened a cabinet door and took down flour and measuring cups, then turned and gave me a frightened look. "You aren't leaving, are you?"

"Me? Nah. I'd like to go look in Cassie's room if it's okay with you." My snoopy, investigator side just would not stay put even though I knew the police wouldn't want me messing up their case.

Paula turned and set her chin. "That's good. The police looked already, but they weren't in there long enough to find anything. I want you to find out who did this to my poor Cassie."

"The police will do that."

Paula's eyes snapped like tiny little firecrackers. "No, they won't. They sent two kids here to tell me. Do you think they'll put anyone better on it to find out what happened to my Cassie?" Her voice quavered and her lips trembled with anger.

"Okay, I'll look into it, you just bake your bread."

She nodded and reached for the yeast. "Don't be surprised at what you find. I don't clean in there. Strict orders from Cassie."

I'd lived in a college dorm and had roommates in an apartment so I knew not everyone was as tidy as Paula and I were. If I remembered correctly from my few sojourns to the bathroom while visiting Paula, Cassie's bedroom was down the hall from her mother's.

The door to her room was closed and resisted being opened until I put my weight against it, then it jolted open with a loud creak, releasing odors of soiled clothes, cheap perfume and cigarette smoke. My hand fumbled around on the wall for the light switch, finding nothing. Almost giving up the search, my finger touched the switch at last, clicking it on.

The walls were painted a hideous mauve that seemed out of place in Paula's condo. In the center of the room, a single bed lay unmade. Black satin sheets jumbled together with a mauve bedspread as if a battle had been raged there. *True Confession* magazines covered the floor on one side of the bed, keeping company with the dust balled terrazzo floor, while a pair of high-heeled satin slippers hung on the edge of a white fuzzy rug on the other side.

Tightly closed lavender drapes hung unevenly at the windows, despite metal weights in their corners. One of them had a circular tear in it as if Cassie had made a peephole for herself. I looked out the slot and wondered who or what she had been watching.

Tangles of dresses, stockings and soiled underwear nearly covered the lavender-flowered chaise lounge in the corner and spilled onto the floor. A black bra hung suggestively from the desk lamp, next to an ashtray piled high with red-lipsticked cigarette butts. I sat down at the mahogany desk and opened the top drawer. I found a carton of unopened Pall Mall cigarettes, a half-empty package of emery boards, three bottles of nail polish in various degrees of drying out, and a half-chewed stick of gum sitting in its wrapper.

The first few side drawers didn't bring me much better: a pearl-handled mail opener, broken pencils and leaky pens, a monogrammed pink notepad and paperbacks describing woman's sexual fantasies. I hit the jackpot on the bottom drawer. There, nestled between a plastic Teddy bear filled with chocolates and a book entitled, *How to Increase Your Vocabulary in Seven Days,* was a matchbook from the Single Hearts Club.

My mind spun back to Paula telling me Cassie was member of the club. I hadn't given it much thought then, but now I did. What did a prostitute need a Single Hearts Club for? Was she picking up paying customers there? Unlikely. People who went there weren't in the market for paid sex.

This was my first clue and I wanted to chase it down. Then I remembered Paula in the other room and that I still had to visit the medical examiner.

I yawned and stretched, feeling sleep coming over me like a dark blanket. I stumbled over to the unmade bed and fell on it. The next thing I knew sunlight was streaming in through the hole in the drape like a laser beam. I jolted to my feet and staggered out of the room, wondering what had become of Paula.

I needn't have worried. Wandering down the hall, I smelled fresh bread, cinnamon and cookies. Paula was still going strong in the kitchen, her pot holder-covered hand just extracting a sheet of chocolate chip cookies from the oven. She turned, raising her dark eyebrows. "Did you get some rest?'

I yawned and stretched. "A little. Did you sleep?"

"Not a wink, but I did bake three loaves of bread, two cakes and these cookies."

"It smells great in here." I checked my watch: 8:30. I didn't want to leave Paula alone, but I had things to do, places to go. The front doorbell rang then and I opened it on a chubby woman with a look on her face that said she was unforgiving of weakness in herself and others. Her mud brown eyes scrutinized me. "I'm Rachel Windom, Paula's sister. And who might you be?" A shapeless black suit hung on her heavy body and a brittle black straw hat clung securely in place on top of her graying hair, probably held there by a very sharp pin or a dagger.

"I'm Megan Baldwin, Paula's friend." I extended my hand but she ignored it.

Instead she shook her head and mumbled, "It's a terrible thing when your own children don't outlive you." She pushed inside, setting her blue suitcase down by the door and removing her jacket coat.

I led her to the kitchen. The sisters hugged and then Rachel pulled on an apron by the stove. "I'll have breakfast ready in a jiffy. You have to keep up your strength." She nodded to me. "You may stay too, young lady."

I didn't quite trust Rachel with Paula yet, so I stayed until I had a chance to try the cake and fresh coffee. Besides, Cassie wasn't going anywhere, she'd wait for me.

CHAPTER 7

After we polished off a good quarter of the cake, I left Paula's house. By then Rachel had taken over, directing Paula to bed and starting to clean up the clutter of cookie sheets and baking bowls.

At my house, I found Samantha in the Florida room, cleaning her feet and acting as if she couldn't be bothered with me. I knew she was angry for being left home alone the whole night, but she had a double standard. It was perfectly all right for her to stay out all hours, but if I did, she let me know about it.

I pretended I didn't notice and went into the bathroom and took a cold shower to wake myself up. In keeping with the solemnity of the day, I pulled on a gray cotton skirt and sweater and topped it off with a black-and-gray jacket.

I left the house as soon as I was dressed, wanting to just complete my visit to the medical examiner's and get on to other things. It was balmy, a spring-like day of clear skies and dazzling sun. I drove up Gulf Boulevard to the Tom Stuart Causeway and turned left on Seminole Boulevard. Traffic was brisk, with the usual number of young people whizzing in and out between cars, fooling themselves they were saving time, and the same number of retirees rubbernecking at the malls from the fast lane.

I turned left on Ulmerton Road at the Shell Station and pulled into the road by the blue sign that read: County Medical Examiner. On my left, palms rustled in front of a sizable beige stucco building with chocolate trim. On my right, a matching, but smaller building's marquee announced: John J. Shinner Forensic Center, Office of Pinellas County Medical Examiner.

I hadn't been there before, but I had spoken with a woman named Edna a couple of times, and she had been very cordial, even inviting me up for a tour of the place. I pulled in front of the building, then moved my car when I read the reserved parking sign. I found the last spot on the grass by the road, pulling under a cluster of tall maples that dangled their Spanish moss like skinny green fingers. Some of the other cars carried the Sheriff's insignia, but most had regular Pinellas County license plates like my car. It was a busy place.

When I walked in the front door, I immediately had a feeling of peace and calm, making me wonder if my perception had been put on tilt by the events of the last two days. The reception area had an aura of newness, with clean walls painted a pleasant off-white and a floor covered in an absolutely clean octagonal brick red tile. It almost made me afraid to step on it, but I took a deep breath and headed across the eight feet to the reception window. It was a huge mass of sliding glass (then tightly closed) that went from halfway up the wall to the ceiling.

Behind it four secretaries sat at their computers. The woman closest to the window, a skinny blonde with bright red lipstick and a high-collared blouse, looked at me through straw-colored eyes. I mouthed through the closed glass, "I'm Megan Baldwin. Came to identify Cassie Saunders."

She gave me a brief smile, opened the glass a crack and said in a soft, professional tone, "I'll need you to answer some questions."

"Sure."

"I need your name, address and home phone." I passed my business card through to her. She read it over quickly then attached it to a clipboard in front of her. "Are you related to Ms. Saunders?"

"No, I know her mother. I've met Cassie. I know who she is."

"Fine, then please have a seat, someone will be with your shortly." She pointed to the corner opposite her.

"Is there a bathroom I can use?" Either the amount of coffee I had consumed or my nervousness about being there made a rest stop necessary.

"Right over there." She pointed to a wooden door in the corner.

I walked to it and went inside. More off-white walls, eggshell tile and floor. It was a big room, but contained only one toilet and sink. I used all the facilities, then turned to the mirror.

I don't usually wear much make-up, but that morning my face had a gray pallor. You'd think someone in my family had died. Good thing I carry emergency supplies. A little blush on my cheeks and a dab of pink lipstick and I looked almost normal.

I wash my hair in the shower and let it dry in the breeze. Consequently, it does what it wants to. That morning it stood up a little higher on the right side than on the left so I flattened it down with a handful of water. That's about the extent of my hair dressing. When the bangs get too long I cut them myself and when the back grows past my shoulder blades I grab it up in a hunk and make one cut across it. I call it my *au natural* look.

I grabbed my bag and went back out to the reception area. Arranged on an island of imitation Persian rug, two comfortable chairs and a mahogany table sat beneath an oil painting of pastel flowers. A lamp with a corrugated shade and a healthy-looking ivy plant in a rattan holder stood on the table.

I plunked down on the chair to the right of the table and waited. On my left next to the bathroom was a corridor leading to a door carrying the sign, Restricted Area, Authorized Personnel Only. That door had a heavy lock on it. The kind that can only be opened by the flip of a switch controlled from the other side.

A man in slacks and long-sleeved white shirt came in and looked at me as if he knew me, raising his thick eyebrows quizzically. "Hello," I said and he smiled and returned a warm greeting, then turned and sauntered up to the reception glass. The secretary opened the window a crack so they could converse. "Here is the report for that baby back there." He slid a few pieces of papers through to her, then turned and left by the front door.

The locked door clicked open and a woman in a plum-colored blouse and cranberry suit skirt scooted out. She wore high heels and walked as if she wasn't quite used to them yet. She had a deeply-lined, sensitive face and a long thin nose. Her lavender eyes were well-shielded behind thick bifocals, but her smile was friendly. "I'm Dr. Owens, one of the medical examiners. I understand you're here to make an identification."

"That's right."

"Come with me. The viewing room is this way." Someone turned the switch and the heavy door clicked open. I followed her down the corridor, past the secretaries. Huge detail maps of Pinellas and Pasco Counties hung on the left walls. On the right a small room held shelves of manila folders. The hallway jogged to the right and we walked into a small room carpeted with light green industrial grade rug. On my left stood a copier and a table with shelves holding various pathology forms. Straight ahead loomed a glass window about four feet by five feet.

Dr. Owens signaled through the window and a pinkish light came on over a cart. A blonde woman lay on it, her head to the window. A clean white sheet covered everything but her face. The skin was wrinkly and pale even under the cosmetic lighting and a bit of flesh had been removed from her right cheek. The medical examiner turned to me. "Do you recognize her?"

"Yes, it's Cassie Saunders all right. What happened to her cheek?"

"Could be a fish bite." She glossed over the next sentence, perhaps trying to spare me. "Sometimes when the body has been in the water a while, the fish get interested. Do you know anything about her medical history?"

"I know she was diabetic."

"Yes, we found the bracelet." She made a note on the clipboard she carried.

A man in his early thirties came into the room. "This is Ira Wickstein, the investigator working with me on the case."

Ira gave me a shy smile. He was a tall man with a thin, eager face and kinky, coppery red hair. He put out his hand and I shook it, looking at the small lines of pride and sensitivity around his thoughtful brown eyes. He gave me a warm, firm handshake, then stepped back.

"Ira will answer any other questions you might have and take any other information you have to give." Dr. Owens smiled, nodded and left the room. The pink lights went out and someone on the other side closed the blinds.

I turned to the investigator. "I thought you were going to yank open a drawer somewhere, pull back the sheet and I'd see Cassie."

He laughed, a deep, warm laugh. "Things aren't like you see them on television. I especially hate the stories where the doctor doing the autopsy is eating a sandwich or something ghoulish like that. We try to be professional here and make it as easy as possible for the family and friends. Of course we're not a funeral home, but we use the pink lights so the face doesn't look so pale and we cover the body except for the face. Makes for the least amount of shock."

"I thought you wanted a family member to identify the body."

"No. We're against it. They're already traumatized by the death. We always ask for a friend of the family."

"You weren't by any chance on duty when Cassie was brought in, were you?"

"Yes, I've been on call for the past two days."

"Busy, huh?"

"Not this stretch. One time I had fourteen homicides during my on-call days. I was really tired that time." He gave me another of his shy smiles and his pale skin turned a rosy pink.

"I'll bet. Do you by any chance remember how she was dressed when she was found?"

"I didn't go to the crime scene, but I can find out for you."

"Sometimes you go to the crime scene?"

"Sure, if foul play is suspected. The police will ask for an investigator to come and videotape the area, take photos of the body, the scene, that kind of thing. But there isn't much of a crime scene by the water."

"I guess not. So in this case foul play isn't suspected."

"No. They were pretty sure it was either an accident or a suicide. If it were an open case, I wouldn't be able to answer your questions now."

"How do you rule whether it is suicide or accidental?" I remembered some of this from books I had read, but it was a little fuzzy in my mind. Besides, I wanted him to tell me as much as possible and I had discovered long ago that playing dumb often got me what I needed to know a lot quicker than looking it up.

34

"We rule it suicide or accidental according to the autopsy, information we get from the family and the medical history. If we know a person had a seizure disorder, we suspect they blanked out and fell in. If he or she was depressed, we would look for a suicide."

"So if homicide was suspected, the records wouldn't be available?"

"Not until it's closed, then it's public information and you could come up here and read the record. An investigator might even sit down with you, if he or she has the time, and go over it with you."

"I might want to do that. Her mother is really upset and wants me to check into Cassie's death. Would you have time to explain things to me?" He nodded and smiled sheepishly as if I'd asked him out to dinner. "Did they think Cassie went in by the Gandy Bridge?"

"Hard to say. I'd have to know the temperature of the gulf, check the currents, that kind of thing to be sure. Bodies can go off the Sunshine Skyway and turn up at the Gandy Bridge. Once it hits the water and goes with the current, you don't know where the body went in."

"So you'll be checking all these things?"

"Not unless something happens to make this look like foul play." He motioned to me. "If you have any other questions, let's go into the library. I think there is another viewing scheduled."

"Sure." He directed me out the door first and then walked beside me in a manner that reminded me of the polite guy protecting his date.

We passed another corridor and I couldn't restrain my natural nosiness. "Where does that go?"

"Offices, autopsy room, toxicology." He seemed eager to please and proud to be showing me around.

"I heard a man in the reception area say something about a baby being back here." I hoped I wasn't pushing it, but I was very curious about the poor child.

"Yeah. There's one in there with the autopsy technician right now." He pushed open a door and I looked in. The smell of urine, blood and death was strong. I shook my head and felt a wave of nausea. A five or six-month old baby boy lay on a metal cart. He was blonde with curly hair, and no expression on his face. He was tiny thing, turned a waxy, whitish blue. He almost looked angelic, except for the dribble of dried blood that had run down the side of his head. I turned away. "That's really upsetting."

"Yeah," he sighed. "We've been getting a lot of babies lately. Sign of the times."

I wondered what kind of person murdered a child and then I remembered the poor teenagers I had seen in the Walk-In Clinic when I worked as a nurse. They were children themselves, forced to carry unwanted fetuses because they were ignorant about how babies were conceived or had been raped and did not have enough money to end the pregnancy. For them, the normal cries of a baby might have been unbearable.

Ira extended his hand to a room on the right and I stepped into the library, thankful not to be confronted with that image of inhumanity anymore. Bookshelves full of texts like *Forensic Pathology, Crimes and Punishment and Analytic Chemistry* lined the walls. A large teak table stood in the center of the room. He sat down at the end and I took the comfortable chair next to him. A sickly green ashtray sat in the center of the table with one lipstick-tainted cigarette butt in it.

I looked in the corner of the room at the stand containing a VCR and two television sets. "For your entertainment?"

He grinned sheepishly as if I had made a joke. "Nah, we don't have time for that. The bottom one's in case of a disaster and we need to watch for news bulletins. It's on it's own circuit in case we lose our usual electricity."

"And the top one?"

"That's for viewing crime scene tapes."

I referred to my notes and tried to remember what I had forgotten to ask. When I looked over at him, he was waiting patiently. "You mentioned you were here when Cassie was brought in."

"Yes, I was in with Miranda, the head secretary, going over an investigative report on one of the computers."

"Was Cassie brought in the front door?" It was a gruesome idea, but I had been put in a gruesome mood by the dead baby.

"No, let me show you how it works." He led me back down the corridor to where the secretaries hunched over their computers, fingers flying on the keys. He showed me a control panel on the wall. The quarters were close and he leaned against the edge of an empty desk to give me more room. "A bell rings and whoever is in here, looks at the monitor." One closed circuit television screen showed what looked to be a garage and another a storage room. "You push this button and the garage door opens for a delivery. The body is left in the garage cooler. We have space here for up to fifty bodies and lockers to put evidence in case of homicide investigations."

"Fifty bodies?"

His brown eyes blinked at me. "We have to be prepared in case of a disaster."

I looked at the stacked metal racks. They looked like Army cots with dark plastic bags on them. "Bodies are kept there?"

"Only until they are identified or fingerprinted or until an investigation is completed."

"Can you check for me now what Cassie was wearing when she was brought in."

He consulted a record. "Flimsy top and black pants."

"Do you keep most of your records on the computer?"

He pushed a few buttons and the screen in front of us came alive, bringing up the list of available records including protocols and FADS. I hated acronyms. They made me want to shout: "BVDs and SOB." Holding back my wry humor, I asked, "What are FADS?"

"Final anatomic cause of death. It's what goes on the death certificate. I'll show you a protocol. This is the copy of the doctor's actual autopsy. He records into a microphone while he's doing the autopsy and then a secretary transcribes it into the computer.

The screen showed me the time of the autopsy and a review of the various body organs and systems, but he moved it down too fast for me to read whose it was. "Could you tell in a drowning if there were drugs in the body?" I didn't know if Cassie was taking drugs, but she didn't strike me as the kind to commit suicide.

"Sure, we could probably find the drug. If we get them soon enough after ingestion of medication, it would still be in the stomach contents."

"What about in this case?"

"We could get it from the bloodstream, but urine is the best if it's available." He paused a minute, then said, "Anything else?" He said it as if he had all the time in the world and wanted to spend it with me.

That kind of flattery makes me nervous and I took a step toward the door. "I think that about does it. If I think of anything else, can I call you?"

"Sure." He reached into a drawer to his left and took out a business card. "Call me anytime." He gave me a warm smile that made me think he meant it. I had a sense he was single and lived alone and was probably very lonely. He handed me the card. I thanked him and tucked it in my pocket. The look on his face gave me the feeling Ira would be a friend I could count on for future questions.

"By the way," I said, turning back toward him at the door. "If I come up with any more information on Cassie's death, is there any chance you would reconsider the cause of death?"

"Of course. We're always open to information." He raised an eyebrow. "You're thinking homicide?"

"I'm thinking homicide." I had read enough mortality statistics and explanations to know that quite a few *accidents* were *suicides* and some of those were murders.

CHAPTER 8

Walking down the cement sidewalk outside the Medical Examiner's office, I thought about the description Ira gave me of Cassie's clothes. Sounded as if she might have been on one of her "dates" that night. Maybe he suffered from sadomasochistic tendencies.

I had once counseled a woman from the red light district who used to be in the business, so I found a phone booth and gave her a call. Marissa had found a john and settled down with him. Last I heard they were planning on getting married. People do change.

Marissa answered the phone. I could hear a soap opera in the background. I told her who I was and what I wanted. "There are a few guys who like to hurt girls, but I haven't heard of any lately. Course I haven't been on the streets for nearly a year now. I'll ask around. I keep in touch with a few of the girls."

I gave her my phone number. "How's things with you?"

"Darren gave me a diamond ring and we've set the date. Ain't that cute?"

"It's real nice. I'm happy for you. Don't forget to give me a call."

"Soon as we hang up I'll check."

I thanked her and hung up. It was nice to know that Marissa had found happiness. She had been sexually abused as a kid and probably turned to prostitution to continue what was familiar. I hoped her life transformation took. She deserved something better.

I went home and had a late lunch of a toasted cheese sandwich. While I washed my plate, I stared at my avocados. The darn things hadn't sprouted yet and I had tried them every way I could think of: Pointy end down and round end down. The only thing I hadn't tried was sideways and I was just about to experiment with that when the phone rang.

It was Marissa. "Jan tells me there's a nasty on the streets. He likes to hurt girls."

"What's his method?"

"I think he burned a couple."

"Toss any of them into the bay?"

"Not that I know of, but when they go bad, who knows what's next?"

'Know his name?"

"They never give their right names anyway, but I hear he's a really tall guy who's a little out of shape. Educated, but nasty."

After I hung up I thought about Rick Stetson and that he was tall and out of shape. He was also an educated lawyer and I had seen how nasty he could get with his wife. He knew Cassie, that was for sure. All I had to do now was figure out why he'd want to kill her. Maybe to keep her quiet about their "dates." It certainly called for more investigation and I knew just where Rick's office was.

It was too early to go there yet, he might still be there. Instead, I headed home and put on my sweat suit. Walking on the beach was something I did to feel good. If I already felt okay, it was more like a jaunty stroll on the hard packed sand by the water, with stops to view dolphins and talk to the sandpipers and egrets.

That afternoon I put weights on my legs and arms and tore down the beach, walking in the deep sand just to make forward progress harder. It was my way of releasing tension and Cassie's death and that poor little baby lying dead on a metal tray hadn't done much to relax me.

Gulls swooped and shrieked above me and sandpipers scurried along the beach, getting out of my way. A few diehard snowbirds lay on the sand in front of high-rise hotels, hoping to get a sunburn to taunt their neighbors with when they returned to the icy north. One or two gazed at me as if I was from another planet and I guess I looked a little strange in shocking pink sweats and red weights around my wrists and ankles and a brilliant yellow hat holding my hair out of my face.

As I chugged along, my nose took in the smell of burgers frying on an outdoor grill beside one of the hotels, stale beer from the Mugwump (a waterside thatched-roof-no-window bar on the beach) and as always, salt air. Two kids with a plastic bag from Swimsuit Heaven collected shells while their tourist father cast from lake fishing gear into the turgid Gulf waters, hoping to catch supper.

I trudged down to the Don CeSar and back, trying to force the image of that little baby out of my mind. By the time I left the beach and headed along 64th Avenue, I had almost succeeded.

Another shower and change of clothes to slacks and a shirt and I left Samantha behind. I congratulated myself on how well I had ignored her pleading eyes before heading for the Single Hearts Club.

It was housed in a two-story white frame house on First Avenue North, just off 66th Street. I parked down the block and walked up the wooden steps. The red hearts under "Single" were fading from the sun. A young man with a handlebar mustache and an out-of-date, striped suit nearly knocked me down when he came flying out the front door. "Take your money and don't do a damn thing!" he shouted, stopping to turn and shake his fist at the building.

"Not too pleased with the Single Hearts?"

"You bet I'm not. They promised to find me a mate and they didn't do it. Do you think they'd even refund part of the fee? You're darn right they wouldn't. I have rights. I'm going to sue the liars." He bolted past me and out onto the street.

I opened the front door to the club slowly, watching for any other crazed customers. The hall was empty. Attached to the oak door on the left, about waist high, was a gold plaque with the words: Gemma Fuller, Director. I knocked and entered. The place was huge, reminiscent of a ball room, with blue taffeta curtains at the floor to ceiling windows and refinished hard wood floors.

A young man with an acne-pitted face, frizzy brown hair, whittled nose and a too-short gray suit (that didn't begin to hide the extra bulges of fat around his midsection) sat in front of a video recorder in one corner of the room. He was watching tapes of women, each one giving her all to be chosen by this prized piece of humanity. While he watched, he scratched himself in places Miss Manners wouldn't approve of.

I turned to the woman seated behind a desk to the right. "Ms. Fuller?"

Mascara caked around her eyelashes and her brown hair was precisely blow-dried around her face. I could tell it was a dye job because there is no such color in nature. Only chemists could have created it. She sniffed and managed to look down her nose at me although she was seated lower than I was standing. "Ms. Fuller is in conference with a client. Are you interested in our services?"

I rummaged in my bag and came up with a business card a reporter for the *St. Petersburg Times* had given me once at a Christmas party. "I certainly am. I'm thinking about doing a story around Single Hearts for the Christmas season." I could be ruthless when I needed information and wasn't above using disguises or someone else's business card if it got me what I wanted.

Her eyes widened into a pale green that reminded me of dollar bills. She gave me a frozen smile, the kind actresses in toothpaste commercials use. "That's very interesting." She caressed the business card as if it was a fine piece of jewelry. "As soon as Ms. Fuller is finished, I'm sure she'll be happy to show you around. In the meantime, can I offer you a cup of coffee?"

"No coffee, but maybe you can answer some questions for me."

"I'd be delighted." She put two manila files back into the slotted holder on her desk.

"What kind of clientele do you get here?

"Just everybody comes here." She was exuding charm now, like a little wind up doll that had just been tightly wound.

"Could you be more specific? Mostly young people?"

"A lot are young like that man in the corner, but you'd be surprised how many retirees we get. Widows and widowers come to us." She leaned forward, letting her large breasts graze the top of the desk. "Between you and me, they're the hardest to please. No one can take their spouse's place in their mind." She rolled her eyes. "They do demand the best."

"What about the young people. Ever get any people masquerading as someone else?"

Her eyes flickered from surprise to indignation, then back to polite graciousness. "Dear me. Not that I know of and we check everyone out completely. They have to show their driver's license, give a medical history and references. We are the premier social club." She tossed back her hair.

"I'm sure you are, but I understand Cassie Saunders was a member here."

"She may be, but all our files are confidential. We never reveal any of our member's names."

"Not even to the police?"

That stopped her for a moment. A pale flush started at her throat and ascended to her cheeks. "Why would the police be interested in our little club?"

"Because Cassie Saunders was a member here and she was found dead, floating off the Gandy Bridge."

She stared at me for a moment and I could tell she was trying to figure out the best way to answer that challenge. "I don't believe she was a member here. We have an intense screening program ---"

"I'm sure you do, but she might have given you a different name."

"But her driver's license ---"

"Maybe she told you she didn't drive. Is that possible?"

"It's possible, but I don't think ---"

"Perhaps you could consult your records and see if you have a Cassie Saunders listed as a member."

She leaned back in her chair defensively, glancing to the left toward Ms. Fuller's office. "I'm afraid I'm going to have to let Ms. Fuller handle this for you. I just can't share confidential records."

"How long before I can see her?"

"I'm not sure. Just let me go check."

42

The young man at the videotape monitor had narrowed down his choices to a round-faced woman who liked to hunt grouse and a skinny woman with a mole on her cheek who made gallons of sun tea by submerging the bags in water pitchers in her back yard.

The receptionist pranced back in a moment. "Ms. Fuller told me to tell you the *Tampa Tribune* has already booked us for a story on our club and that she will be unable to see you today."

"Thanks," I said, grabbing the business card out of her hand and heading for the door. "You tell Ms. Fuller to expect a visit from the police any day now." The man at the video screen jerked out of his seat and stood staring at me with a look on his face that told me he didn't want to be there when they arrived.

CHAPTER 9

I drove over to Paula Saunders'. Rachel answered the door, poking her hatchet-shaped nose out at me. "Yes?" I hate it when people who know who you are act as if they don't.

I looked into her mud brown eyes. "Megan Baldwin. Paula's asked me to check into Cassie's death."

"Come in. She's in the kitchen." She wagged a finger in front of me. "Now don't you go and say anything to upset her. She's had enough bad news."

I pushed in and tried to ignore her eyes. They were like x-rays inspecting me. Paula sat at the table, a plate of untouched chocolate chip cookies in front of her. Even her coffee had gone cold, with a slag of long-ago poured cream lying on top in ugly ribbons.

She started to stand when she saw me. There were great hollows under her eyes and the flesh had sagged noticeably on her face. I gave her my warmest hug and sat down, taking her hands in mine. They were cold and lifeless and for some reason reminded me of the baby in the Medical Examiner's autopsy room. "I went up and identified Cassie."

Her breath hissed in. "I knew it was her."

"She looked pretty good. I don't think she suffered." I didn't have any evidence to support that, but I hoped it might comfort her. Paula nodded and squeezed my hands. I looked into her eyes. "Have you thought about the arrangements? They'll want to know where you want her---" I stopped and thought about what to say next. I could have said, "sent" or "taken" or even "prepared", but they all sounded so impersonal, so final.

Paula saved me. "I think the Wittier Funeral Home on Boca Ciega. I talked to a few friends and they've used it before. Rachel has already called them."

"Do you want me to tell the Medical Examiner's? They'll want to know."

Paula shook her head. "Rachel called." I looked over at Rachel who was eyeing me from the doorway with the smugness of the all-knowing.

I turned back to Paula. "That's good. Anything else I can do now?"

"Just find out how my girl died. I won't rest until I know."

"The investigator at the Medical Examiner's says they're planning to rule it either accident or suicide."

"Suicide? My Cassie would never do that. She was born and raised Catholic. She's committed a lot of sins, but that wasn't one of them."

"I didn't think so."

"It wasn't an accident either. How could she have fallen from a bridge?"

"I don't know. I have a few leads and I plan to follow them up."

She squeezed my hands tighter, this time to the point of pain. Her eyes looked into mine and I saw the cold, hardness of Rachel's in them. "You make sure you do. I don't want anyone saying my Cassie took her own life." I knew she meant business because she didn't even offer me something to eat, just nodded and waited for me to leave.

I got in my car and started the motor. The clock on my dashboard registered four p.m. Still too early to hit Rick Stetson's office. I decided to pay Mrs. Stetson a tea-time visit.

I drove back to the Old NorthEast. The afternoon sun glinted off the turquoise and white awnings and came through the oak and palm trees in shafts of gold. My shoes clunked up the brick steps and I waited for quite a few minutes after I rang the front door bell.

Figuring it might be out of order, I banged on the door a while. Getting no response, I started around the house. I had passed two tangelos and a lemon tree before I heard a gruff, female voice say, "Hey, get off my lawn!"

"There you are," I said, trying to look apologetic. "I rang the bell and knocked, but no one answered. I thought you might be in the back."

"I never go in the back. That's for the gardener and earth-mother types. Who are you anyway?"

I told her who I was and that I was investigating Cassie's death. Her china-doll perfect face changed from irritation to aroused interest. She motioned me to the front of the house. "Come on in and tell me what happened." Her voice was gleeful in anticipation, with a gossipy quality underlying it.

She opened the door in the same flimsy robe I had seen her in before, as if it was her daily uniform. Either she was a drinker (which I suspected from the scent of scotch on the rocks that wafted toward me) or sickly. She didn't look sick and on close inspection her perfect makeup job didn't completely cover up the track of veins on her nose and cheeks that only long years with alcohol make. She seemed to me to be the kind of woman who'd talk easily to a stranger, but never reveal herself to a friend.

I followed her along the white travertine marble floor past an umbrella and hat stand in the foyer. Huge bunches of silk flowers stood around in elaborate vases next to a grandfather clock. The living room had spotless white walls and very high ceilings. I smelled the newness of the beige carpeting. Floral over-stuffed furniture mixed in with either very good reproductions or Louis XIV antiques. Potted plants hung sedately from hooks above the old-fashioned windows.

In the formal dining room eight red brocade chairs stood around a huge oak table. We passed them and entered a small study. She sat down in a heavy armless chair next to the white fireplace. I took the chair opposite hers. A Persian cat eyed me from the corner, probably wondering why I smelled of feline. Mrs. Stetson took a cigarette from a gold case and placed it artfully in a holder, then lit it with a gold monogrammed lighter. Her movements were precise, but her carmine-tipped fingers had the slightest of tremors.

"Do you smoke?" she asked, starting to pass the case to me.

"No, I quit about ten years ago."

"Filthy habit, but then one must have one or two of those, don't you think?

"I try to keep mine to food."

She chuckled and puffed on her cigarette. "Now, tell about poor Cassie."

"She drowned in Tampa Bay."

"How grotesque. That kind of death works havoc with the body, doesn't it?"

"So they say. We did talk on the phone about her recently."

"Ah, then you're the one who called me. I'm terrible with names." She drew on the cigarette. "Tell me your name again, I've already forgotten it."

"Megan Baldwin. You told me on the phone that she was trying to blackmail you."

"Did I? See what a poor memory I have."

"If she was and if you got mad enough at her, you might have killed her." Sometimes it helped to get people moving and reacting. I read that in a detective story. That was exactly what I was doing now with Mrs. Stetson. If she was involved, she'd probably try to cover her actions around the time Cassie was murdered. If it was her husband, she might call him or alert him to the jeopardy.

She gave me a grim look. "Me? Kill her? Why would I bother with such an insignificant person?"

46

"I don't know that yet, but the police may be asking the same questions I am." That didn't seem to bother her a bit and it made me wonder if I was hounding the wrong person.

"I have friends on the police force. My husband is thinking of pursuing a judgeship, so you can see I'm not too worried about that. Besides, she was a hooker. The police do not hold women of that ilk in high regard. They probably won't even pursue it."

"What if your husband killed her? They were sleeping together, weren't they?"

"He was sleeping with half the female population of St. Petersburg. Why would he kill a prostitute? Surely she had other clients who might want her dead."

"That's what I'm trying to find out." She gave me a doubtful look and sucked on the cigarette holder. I was beginning to realize there wasn't much I did know about Cassie's murder. In fact, I wasn't even sure yet that it was murder. All I had to go on was a gut feeling, but I reminded myself when I paid attention to that in the past, it rarely misled me.

When the Persian cat began to give me sulky looks, I figured I'd stayed long enough. I mumbled a few words of thanks and left.

Since I was nearby, I drove past the parrot lady's house. No signs of life. I didn't want her daughter and son-in-law to recognize me. If they really had chased us and had a gun, I was better off snooping *in cognito*. Using my typical ingenuity, I reached in the back seat and extracted a long white box that I could tuck under my arm and look as if I was a delivery person. To complete the effect, I dug in the bag behind the passenger seat until I found the dark blue pants and jacket I had purchased a while ago at a costume shop for a Halloween party I never made it to. They were both two sizes too big, so they fit nicely over my clothes. I pulled them on, adjusted the shiny black visor of my cap and stepped out.

An elderly woman in the next yard raked leaves noisily, probably to let me know she saw me. She wore a starched apron over her flowered house-dress and the flesh in her neck and jaw had gone slack, like used wax paper. Her body was permanently stooped so she had to look up to see me. Her cinnamon-colored eyes stared into mine with a look more challenge than curiosity. I waved and pointed to the empty box I carried. She grunted and resumed sweeping, keeping an eye on me. I scurried up the walk, trying to look official.

The giant palms had already cast heavy shadows across the lawn. A dove peered down at me from the cupola above the door, then flew away. I wasn't sure if that was a comment on my costume or not. I rang the bell, trying to look nonchalant. When no one answered, I banged the gold knocker a few times and squinted against the late afternoon sun into the porch window, cupping my hands around my eyes for a better view. The neighbor's grunts got louder, but I ignored them.

The windows hadn't been cleaned recently, so I couldn't see much. Newspapers cluttered the floor and overstuffed armchairs. A cup sat on an open book on the table beside the couch. A bird cage stood by the window. It was empty. I wanted to get the key from under the straw mat by the front door, but I could feel the neighbor's eyes boring into my back so I went down the steps and headed around the side of the house.

The curtains were all pulled closed, making it impossible to see anything. In the back of the house, white wicker chairs with slightly soiled yellow cushions stood in a disorderly arrangement on the patio. Piles of brown leaves had found a home under some of the chairs and against the back door. I went up the steps and tried the knob,. Locked. I circled back to the front of the house. The neighbor had gone inside, but I thought I saw her curtain drop closed when I walked past a side window.

I still didn't dare take the key and try the front door. I'd check later. I wanted to wave to the window where the neighbor stood, but I restrained myself, got in my car and drove off. I stopped around the corner and took off the uniform, returning it to its place in my bag of tricks.

I went home, fell into a deep sleep and didn't wake up until nearly noon. After a long walk on the beach, I decided to head up to the Gandy Bridge. I took Fourth Street north and turned onto Gandy. Small businesses seemed to have sprung up overnight since my last trip. I passed the racetrack and wondered how many suckers were losing their savings that day. A little farther, bars and ticky-tack seafood restaurants stood waiting, hoping to catch a few of the racing crowd on their way home from the track.

As I neared the bridge, vans and recreational vehicles peppered the side of the road. A few men in jeans and tee-shirts and women in shorts and jackets stood by the side of the bridge, surrounded by bait buckets, coolers and extra rods and reels. Three or four pelicans waddled nearby, begging for handouts. Gulls hung suspended in the updrafts, squawking at the people below and searching the water and shore waters for fish.

I parked off the road and reached in the back for a pair of old sneakers which I traded for my gray pumps. Besides carrying clothes and shoes in my car, I also make sure I have a jug of filtered water and a few pieces of fresh fruit in case of thirst or unexpected hunger. *Be prepared* has been my motto since I was a little kid.

One thing you will not find in my car is a gun. I have heard about too many officers shot with their own guns by suspects. Then there are the civilians who shoot themselves in the foot or leg or are overtaken by their attackers and then shot. Violence, I maintain, breeds violence.

Instead, I'm sort of a self-taught Kung Fu, karate and Jui-Jitsu enthusiast. I've been to quite a few of their classes and read as much as I could. As a result, I think I can defend myself against someone physically stronger and even against someone carrying a gun or knife and maybe even from a broken arm and leg because I know how to fall without injury. Of course all this is theoretical because so far I haven't needed to protect myself from knife or gun attacks. Figuring there's always a first time, I keep my body ready.

I also keep my car tuned and packed for most emergencies. Part of my Girl Scout training, I suppose. I do the tune-ups myself, part of what happens when your father's only child is a tomboy and he's a self-taught car mechanic. I figure there isn't enough time in this short life to mess with rentals while my car is in the shop or drive back home and change or stop and buy something to eat or drink. Besides, I insist on filtered water and fresh fruit. I have a near-phobia about the heavy metals in the St. Petersburg water supply. I may die from a bullet, but I certainly won't die a terrible cancer death from my drinking water. Not if I have anything to say about it.

I even take cold showers, having read somewhere that the skin (especially during hot showers) takes in more unhealthy pollutants than you probably eat in your food or drink in your water. So most of my showers, summer and winter, are cold showers. Very refreshing after the initial shock. My neighbors have grown used to hearing my screech when I step under the frigid surge.

Turning around in my car seat, I pulled my windbreaker out of the back and zipped it on. I stepped out of my car, making sure it was locked. That was one part of my pre-Florida life that I religiously observed. As a child, living in a small town in Wisconsin, I never locked doors. Once I moved to New York, I learned to do so after someone stole my bicycle out of my friend's station wagon.

It's for these reasons I drive a Toyota (hard to get into by the coat hanger method) and have windows darkly-tinted so no one can see what is in my car and be tempted to steal it. Someone could break the glass if they really wanted to, but I usually keep an ear and eye open and so far no one has.

Tucking my keys in my jacket pocket, I started toward the water. The bay looked muddy brown. It churned below me as if it were angry, the surf pounding against the rocks and bridge supports with a vehemence that only Mother Nature could show. Across the bay, the tall buildings of Tampa gave the illusion of beauty, glittering and gleaming in the late afternoon sun.

A few sailboats skidded through the rough waters, spray splashing off their hulls. Somewhere nearby Cassie's body washed up. I looked around, but didn't really hope to find evidence. I wasn't even sure what I was looking for, maybe confirmation that she really was dead. Seeing her on that cart in the Medical Examiner's viewing room hadn't done it. I had half-expected her to blink, sit up, and ask me what the hell I was doing there.

The salt air blew brisk and invigorating across my face, making my mind click with questions about Cassie's death. Had she been there alone? If not, who had been with her? She might have driven there after a session with a john or maybe the two of them had made it on the beach in front of God and everybody. But if she had come there, what had become of her car?

I had been too shaken to ask Lou these questions when I first heard about Cassie's death, but now they swirled in my head, demanding answers. I turned from the water and went back to my car. The last of the sun filtered across the horizon and I realized I had been there longer than I had planned to be.

Driving south, I stopped at a phone booth on Central Avenue near Second Hand Sales and called Lou. His answering machine told me to leave my name and number and he'd get right back to me. I left my name and told him I'd call him back, then I headed for Rick Stetson's office.

CHAPTER 10

I drove around the block a few times and even took the alley once, making sure Rick Stetson was no longer in his office. Johnson's Cleaning Service van was parked in front, so I knew that if I waited a bit, I might be able to get in without breaking any laws.

Electra Johnson was a pleasant woman with Brillo pad hair, tobacco brown skin and perfect white teeth that stood out in a smile. When I knocked on the front door of Rick Stetson's office, her bulky body lumbered up to the door and her ebony eyes peeked out the white curtain. "We're closed. I'm the cleaning lady."

I put on my best harassed woman voice and manner. "I know. You see I've lost my keys. I'm Mr. Stetson's secretary and I have to call my husband and get a ride home. Would you believe someone stole my car keys right out of my bag?"

She shook her head, dark eyes going heavy with sympathy. "It's a terrible world these days. Ain't safe no where. Come in here then and use the phone. I'm almost finished up here." She surveyed her kingdom and pronounced it sparkling with a nod of her head.

I tiptoed in behind her, having the strongest feeling she might turn on me at any time. But she didn't. She hummed and smiled and picked up her cleaning things and got ready to leave. My eyes glanced around the office until I spied the phone, then I walked over to it and turned my back to her. Holding down the receiver, I carried on a one-person conversation.

"Honey? It's me. You won't believe what just happened. Someone just took my car keys. Would it be possible for you to come down to Mr. Stetson's office and pick me up? It would? Okay, I'll wait inside for you. No, I wouldn't want anyone mugging me again."

I replaced the phone and turned to Electra. "My husband. He's such a dear. He's picking me up here. I'll just wait inside if it's all right with you."

"I'm sure Mr. Stetson would want you to. If I didn't have a .45 in my scrub bucket, I wouldn't go out on those streets alone either. My Stanley worries about me, but I just tell him, no one's gonna mess with his woman if there's a gun in his face."

I nodded and smiled, hoping she didn't catch on that I was still wearing my sneakers. Either she didn't see what was on my feet or she was too polite to comment. A few minutes later she left, reminding me to push in the lock when I left.

I waved and called good-bye, promising myself not to make a mess and get Electra in trouble. She had been kind to me and I would return the favor. I was probably way over-stepping the bounds by doing what I was about to do, but I couldn't help it, I had gotten totally caught up in the mystery of Cassie's death.

When I was sure Electra was gone, I opened my bag and took out my handkerchief. Ross Macdonald or somebody says never leave any prints around. I took out my flashlight and turned off the overhead beams. No sense making anyone suspicious about who was inside Rick Stetson's law offices.

I pushed past the reception area, through a heavy oak door with a bronze plaque for Richard Stetson, Attorney-at-Law, and into an immense room. Brown leather was everywhere. Chairs of it stood on both sides of a huge mahogany desk and around a conference table. More brown leather in the couch and even covering the stools. The guy was a leather freak.

The heavy red brocaded curtains were pulled shut, but I sneaked a peek of his view. The back alley was not all that enthralling. Two of the three walls were lined with bookshelves filled with law books. I tried to pick up the four-volume set of contract law and found a bottle of Johnny Walker Red behind it. I wondered if he was a secret drinker like his wife or just kept it for social occasions.

Not really caring, I went back to the desk. Someone (probably Rick) had tossed ten or twelve bulging manila files into a wooden box labeled, OUT. They looked as if they had been thrown in there from several feet away. His desk matched the clutter, littered with boring papers full of Witnesseths and Party of the First Parts. I shuffled through them, but soon grew tired of their curliqued obscurity.

I sat down at his chair and pulled open the top drawer. Shoved in the front were well-fingered audiocassettes. His tastes were eclectic, running from "Relaxation Exercises for the Busy Executive" to "Silky Porn" a new album by someone named, Orgasma. The rest of the contents of that drawer included a half-eaten Almond Joy (I hate coconut) and an unopened package of Roll-Aids.

More files and folders jumbled in the side drawers along with a copy of *Penthouse* and several other magazines featuring men and women with sexual organs bigger than any I'd seen except in the bovine genus and the *Equidae* family. It wasn't until I opened the bottom drawer on the right side that I found something interesting: a matchbook for the Single Hearts Club.

I wondered if Rick had met Cassie there or if he had stronger ties to the club. If he did, there was no other sign of it. I got up and opened a door on the nearest wall. Behind it was a large clothes closet where Rick kept his tennis racket, a couple of suits and shirts and a set of golf clubs. He must have had the same motto I did.

Beyond the closet I found a huge gray-tiled bathroom equipped with everything an up and coming professional would want: a shower, sink, sauna, toilet and bidet. I flicked on the switch by the door and shut the door, even though there was no way anyone could see the light in this inside room.

Rick's medicine chest contained one well-rolled tube of Crest toothpaste, an electric razor that needed to be cleaned and the butt end of a Brut deodorant stick.

His gold-crested white cabinet drawers were full of tiny samples of men's colognes in foiled wrappers, guest bars of soap from the Hacienda Hotel in Los Fritos, New Mexico, a leather comb and brush set, and nail clippers of various sizes and shapes. Maybe he was a sadomasochist who loved to torture his women by clipping their nails until they screamed with pain.

I slammed the drawers shut and got ready to leave his office. Clearly I needed rest because my brain was starting to send me silly messages. Turning off the bathroom light, I made my way to the front door, depositing my handkerchief and flashlight in my bag before going out onto the street. The door clicked locked behind me and I looked around to see if anyone had noticed me. When I was sure no one was looking, I went to my car and drove home.

Samantha skittered through my legs and out the door when I opened it. I supposed I was in for more snubs from her. It usually took her about a week to forgive and forget.

I changed into a clean pair of sweats and completed a full set of push-ups, back bends, spinal flexors, shoulder strengtheners and floor touches. When I started to feel a little more limber, I did some hand chops on the top of my dining room table. For good measure, I did some falling exercises. Although I'd never had to protect myself, something told me I might have to in the very near future.

I was just finishing my vegetable soup and a small romaine salad when Lou called. He sounded unusually glum. "I've got some information about Cassie Saunders for you."

"Great and how come you sound so down?"

"It's this Rodgers case. Brian Taub is driving me nuts. All I keep doing is running into dead ends."

"I know how you feel."

"You're going to feel better soon. You can wrap up the Cassie Saunders' thing."

"I doubt that. What have you got for me?"

"Police have ruled her death accidental. Of course she did have a small amount of Elavil in her bloodstream, but not enough to make it a suicide attempt."

"But enough for her to be dizzy and fall off the bridge."

"So they think."

"It sounds lousy to me. I don't buy it. But I suppose they've released the body?"

"Yep, a couple of hours ago. She's probably in some silent mortuary by now."

"That means I better get myself over there. When Paula sees Cassie's body she's going to be in for a shock."

"She wasn't bloated or anything, was she?"

"Nope, but some hungry fish took a bite out of her cheek."

"That would shake up a parent. You are going to give up on the case, aren't you?"

"Not on your life."

"I thought maybe you would help me with some of the paperwork and phone calls on this Rodgers thing. I can only take so much of Brian Taub. You could use a little extra cash, couldn't you?"

I smiled, remembering how I used to help him out with paperwork. I was almost beginning to think I *was* an investigator and that kind of thinking was probably dangerous. I wanted desperately to work with him, but something made me say, "I still have a few things to check out on Cassie. Her mother doesn't buy accident or suicide."

"Okay, but let me know when you can give me some relief with Taub."

"Who's paying?"

Lou's voice took on a surprised quality. "I am. Who do you think?"

We said good-bye and I had a few fantasies that he really wanted to hire me because he couldn't bear to be without me. Samantha's return and icy looks erased those ideas and for some reason reminded me that Whittier Funeral Home awaited.

CHAPTER 11

I put my gray skirt and jacket back on and headed for the Whittier Funeral Home. If you missed the lot, you had to go around the block, so I nudged my Toyota carefully past the stop light and pulled onto the smooth-surface, following the black-and-white sign to parking.

The Whittier Funeral Home was a three-story white stucco building with gray tile roofs. It looked as if it had been a residence at one time, but the lawn had been torn up and made into a parking lot. A few Italian cypress crowded the house beyond the sidewalk, but only one tree marred the slick asphalt --- a beautifully-full pidgeon plum. How it survived there was beyond me. It was a least fifty feet high with shiny evergreen leaves and a hint of the slender spikes that would blossom pure white and abundant before bearing dark purple plums.

The night had turned cold and damp and fog was rolling in from the beach. I pulled my coat collar up and trotted to the front door. For some reason I thought of *Ghostbusters* and Annie Potts asking, "dropping off or picking up?" Funeral homes and police stations bring out the black comedy in me. I can't help it.

A few other cars were huddled in the corner of the lot. I didn't recognize Paula's, but then maybe she had come in Rachel's vehicle. I got out of my car and walked toward a doorman in a black suit who was smiling at me with a ghoulish grin. I wiped my feet on the blue-and-white mat that read, Whittier Funeral Home, and clicked up the stairs, waiting while he held the door for me. I wasn't feeling particularly gloomy, but I could see how a depressed family member would feel safe and secure from the special treatment they got here.

The doorbell softly tolled above me and I stepped inside. I was met by the smell of gladiolas and a chilly air blast. I suppose it had to be cool in there because of the bodies. A large planter with irises stood in the foyer. Above two closed doors on my right, a sign read: CHAPEL.

A pleasant-faced tall blonde man in a black suit padded down the carpeted stairs, one hand holding onto the white staircase, the other reaching out toward me as if he wanted to shake my hand from a distance. His eyes had blue circles under them and an expression that said, *You poor thing.* He took my hand, introduced himself as Donald Whittier and asked how he could help me. He reminded me of my kindergarten teacher, talking to me in short, slow phrases and bending down, looking into my face to see if I grasped his words.

I thought I smelled mouthwash on his breath, but I wasn't sure. "I'm here to see Cassie Saunders."

He nodded. "Please sign our guest book. The family greatly appreciates your visit even if they may not be able to acknowledge it in their grief."

I took the black ball-point he offered, noticed I was only the third name on the page, signed the book and returned the pen to the lectern. He leaned near my ear and almost whispered, "She's laid out in the small viewing room. This way, please."

The funeral home was much homier than the ones I'd been in up north. This one had a dusty rose carpet, comfortable powder blue and flower-patterned chairs and discreet lighting. It was also very quiet. The only sounds I heard were the whisk of his well-polished shoes over the carpet and the subdued tones of someone talking in the next room.

"You may use this space if you wish." He pointed to a small room that looked a little like my grandmother's sitting room in Washburn, Wisconsin, with substantial chairs lit by soft lamps. It was empty. He continued along like a tour guide. "Our small viewing room is in there." He pointed toward the adjoining room.

To the right of his shoulder I saw the open casket at the far end of the next room. Paula's black-craped shoulders hunched over it and Rachel stood next to her, looking like Darth Vader in a black shiny cloche hat and black floor-length cape.

He indicated some chairs in the entry room. "You may sit here if you do not wish to be in the same room with the body."

I nodded and thanked him, then went and stood by Paula. She must have felt my presence because she turned and clutched my arm. "Doesn't she look beautiful?

I winced in the direction of the casket, wondering how awful she must look with a bite taken out of her cheek. But someone had done a fine job on her. There was only the slightest hint of any disfiguration. The rest of her face looked peaceful, nearly serene. I hated to think it, but she almost looked better in death than some of the times I had seen her alive. Her blonde hair was arranged in a halo around her high cheekbones and the lighting and makeup made her look a few years younger than I knew she was.

We stood silently for a few more minutes, then Paula turned to me. "Have you found out anything?"

Rachel cleared her throat and indicated we should go in the other room if we were going to discuss business. I led Paula away, feeling the chill of her body. We sat next to each other on a mauve-colored couch. Her body had developed a slight, but continuous tremor and sitting next to her made my body hum as if I was on a railroad car zooming across the Arctic.

After a minute, she turned to me. "What have you found out?"

I chose my words carefully. I didn't want to tell her, "hardly anything," because I knew how much it meant to her, but I really knew very little. I finally settled on, "I do have some leads."

"Good. Then you can prove she didn't take her own life or fall into the water?"

I hedged on that one. "Possibly ---"

"I can get some money to pay you. I have some bonds ---"

"Maybe you'd better not get your hopes up. There seems to be something with the Single Hearts Club and possible Rick Stetson, but I can't tie it all together yet."

Her eyes had gone shiny, like a beetle's. Maybe from associating too much with Rachel. Her voice sounded rough and uneven. "You don't believe what the police say, do you?"

"You mean about it being accidental?" She nodded. "I don't know yet. It does seem pretty far-fetched for her to fall in. What was she doing up there anyway?"

"That's what I'd like to know. Cassie was a night owl and was likely to be up all hours, but bridges were not the kind of places she liked. She had a fear of heights and didn't want to be in situations that are open like that. Closed in like elevators was all right, but steep drops like that scared her. Always had. Ever since her father pretended to push her off the balcony overlooking the Museum of Science and Industry."

She had started to rattle on. I was still back at fear of heights. If that was so, it did seem strange that she was there, alone and had fallen. "You never told me Cassie was afraid of high places."

"I guess I forgot. This whole thing has me coming unglued."

I put my arm around her. She felt cold and stiff. "I know, but it will get better."

"If I can just get through the funeral. You are coming, aren't you?"

I hated funerals and tried to miss as many as I could. When her hand clutched my arm, the only thing I could do was say, "I'll try." Every now and then I let someone have the power over me to make me feel guilty. This was one of those times.

The front doorbell chimed someone else's entry and I thought I might escape, but Paula stood up and pulled me along with her. She looked relieved that at least someone beside the three of us had come.

The man and woman lumbered in together, eyes staring ahead. They looked enough alike to be brother and sister. Both had fine eyebrows and hair pulled back over their foreheads. From the creases alongside their noses and mouth and the hooded look of their eyelids, I judged them to be in their late forties. The woman wore a polyester dress of a nondescript color that sat almost off her shoulders, revealing the white of her bra strap. She had ungainly hips, a roll of fat around her waist and large, flapping breasts. There was nothing about her that was attractive, even her facial expression was cold and bitter.

The man beside her wore a black velour shirt under his gray sport coat. A gold cross lay on a mat of graying hair on his chest. He wasn't quite as overweight and out of shape as the woman, but almost. The look on his face was more lost than cold. The woman strode over to us, her thick heeled shoes whistling across the carpet. The man hung back, but finally followed.

Her cheery, singsong voice surprised me. It was the kind that's pleasant at first, but can drive you crazy if you have to listen to it all day. "Mrs. Saunders? We're Mary and Dennis. Friends of Cassie's. Our sympathy goes out to you absolutely."

Paula's face lit up and her arm moved from mine to Mary's. I watched them walk toward the casket, Mary chattering away and Dennis lumbering behind. I hurried out the front door and down the steps, thankful to be leaving the Whittier Funeral Home.

While sashaying toward my car, I couldn't help thinking that Mary looked familiar. I must have seen her somewhere, but I couldn't remember where. I told myself it was only the stress of the evening. A few more cars pulled into the lot and I felt a stream of relief that Paula would have someone else to sit with besides Mary and Dennis. I really didn't have anything to base my suspicions on, but something told me those two were trouble.

CHAPTER 12

I was cold and tired and should have gone home, but I turned my car in the direction of the Old NorthEast. For some reason, being at the funeral home reminded me that I still hadn't contacted the parrot lady.

The fog grew thicker the closer I got to Tampa Bay. It seemed to be skirting across the ground like shaggy corridors of white. Fog usually gave me a feeling of security and softness as if it was protecting me from outer events. That night it gave me the creeps.

I pulled in front of the parrot lady's house and went up the walk. A small light burned somewhere near the back of the house. I thought I heard Buck say, "Hey, good lookin,'" but it could only have been wishful thinking.

The lawn looked eerie with fog and I could barely make out the jacarunda and palms. The fruit trees concealed themselves behind a white cloak of low-lying cloud. My heels clicked up the brick steps to the front door and I rang the bell a few times before I heard Buck say, "Pretty girl, pretty girl." Then he whistled and gave a squawk or two.

"Buck?"

His voice got louder and more insistent. "Pretty girl! Pretty girl!"

When no one answered the bell, I banged on the heavy door and shouted, "Veronica? Are you in there?" I heard the panic in my voice and wondered why I needed to see her so badly just then.

A car roared up the block and I waited for it to pass, but it only slowed. I turned. It was the blue Ford Festiva, the one that had chased me and the parrot lady.

I clattered down the stairs shouting, "Wait!" Through the fog I could only make out two figures, but I couldn't see who they were. The driver stepped on it and the car skidded into the cloudy mush before I could see the license plate.

I rushed to my car and jammed the key in. My Toyota is usually cooperative at times like this and that night was no exception. I heard the Ford turn the corner and remembered the next street was a cul-de-sac and the next a dead end, so the Ford would have to turn left to go anywhere.

Gunning straight ahead, I turned right on the next street and nearly rammed into the side of the Festiva at the next corner. The driver swerved, rode up on the sidewalk and screeched away, leaving nice deep furrows on a few peoples' lawns. If there was that much hurry to get away, there was a reason and I wanted to find out what it was.

59

I followed as best I could, but had to swerve from hitting the curb. By the time I had turned my car, the Ford barreled off toward Fourth Street. The driver led me on a merry chase around Mirror Lake, down Ninth Street, past the Fire Station and Boyd Hill Nature Park in the Lakewood Estates. The road twisted and turned around and I thought I'd lost them on Cortez, but the Ford turned up again on Granada Circle.

I closed in on them by the Bay Pointe Plaza Shopping Center, but the driver slowed at the yellow, then made a quick left turn, leaving me with the choice of stopping at the red light alongside a police car or getting a ticket for running it. I chose to wait. That car would turn up again. At least I knew it traveled the Old NorthEast. Tomorrow I'd take some alleys and see if I couldn't find it again.

I went home and had a hot bath and some peppermint tea. Even Samantha wasn't interested in going into the pea soup outside. Sometimes cats are wiser than humans.

I wanted to call Lou and talk to him about my work like I used to in the old days. He wouldn't mind if I did, but I felt a little silly, as if I were afraid of the dark and needed reassurance. But I reminded myself of what the paper had said about particle bombardment and decided this was a special case. There was something very funny going on, but I couldn't quite get a handle on what it was.

Susan answered. She sounded tousled and a little too relaxed. I hoped I hadn't broken up their lovemaking. On second thought, I hoped I had.

After our usual greeting and a few niceties, the phone clattered down on the counter until Lou picked it up. "What's up?" he asked.

"I've just been to the funeral home and seen Cassie Saunders laid out and been pursuing a Ford Festiva. What's new with you?"

He sounded alarmed at what I said, but I told him about the parrot lady and reassured him I knew what I was doing, even though I wasn't sure I did. Finally he said, "My evening has been tranquil compared to yours. I'm still chasing my tail around with this Rodgers case."

"Nothing's broken then?"

"Only that Nancy Rodgers may not be the beneficiary of her daughter's estate."

"Who is?"

"That's what still is a mystery. The insurance company is driving us nuts on this."

"No legal recourse?"

"Brian's been leaning on them, but the wheels of the law grind exceedingly slow. How's Cassie's mother taking things?"

"She's a little wild-eyed and still wants me to pursue things."

"What about you? Are you ready to hang it up? You shouldn't be investigating anything, you know."

"I was just about to give up until Paula told me her daughter had acrophobia."

Fear of heights. Chances of her getting close enough to the edge of the bridge to jump or slip in are miniscule. You think someone pushed her?"

"Exactly. I just can't prove it yet."

"What about this maniac in the blue Ford?"

"I don't know. I went to see the parrot lady and the car pulled up in front of the house. Could be coincidence, but I doubt it. Why would they take off like they did?"

"Maybe you terrified them. Your driving leaves something to be desired."

"Thanks. I'll remember that when you need a lift."

"Okay, I take it back. Now will you re-consider helping me with this Rodgers case?"

"Not yet. I was thinking about asking you to help with the parrot lady thing."

I thought about it for a minute. "I withdraw my offer. If anything else breaks, I'll get back to you." I hung up and wished I, not Susan, had the benefit of his warm and tender body, not just his voice over the telephone.

As a consolation prize, I curled up with a Sue Grafton mystery and stayed up half the night finishing it. Then I must have fallen asleep on the couch because the next thing I knew, the sun splattered down on me from the living room window in warm bursts of light.

I got up, groggy and grumpy, and decided to take my usual walk on the beach. The wind had turned warm and the smell of orange blossoms drifted toward me on my walk toward the Gulf.

Even at seven a.m. ten or twelve people strolled the beach or bent over near the water, searching for shells. The sky looked like a silk tapestry of pinks, blues and grays. I took a deep breath and tried to clear my head.

A few tourists were making "ohs" and "ahs" about two dolphins swimming 100 feet out in perfect synchronization. I loved dolphins, but each year saw fewer. The beautiful sea creatures were caught by tuna fishermen and were left to die in their nets. I had already written to the canned tuna people, the government and whoever would listen to me. As a last resort, I boycotted the grocery store tuna bins. It didn't make me a favorite with Samantha, but then what do cats know about inter-species protection?

For me, dolphins have almost a mystical quality. On one of my walks, two of them followed me along the shoreline, keeping perfect rhythm with my pace. It almost seemed as if they were trying to communicate with me, but being a dummy on dolphin-human language, I wasn't sure what the message was.

Completing my circuit for the day, I turned toward home, feeling more peaceful than I had in a while. All that changed when I walked in the door. Samantha gave me a strange look when I went toward the shower. Even with the water running, I swear she was up the curtains trying to shred them to bits. The cat had a perfectly good scratching post in the garage. All she had to do to get out was push the special little door I had put in, but when she was mad at me or in a strange mood, she refused to use it, preferring to find something else to mangle.

One day when I came out of the shower, I found her eating the leaves of my spider plant. Remembering that, I left the bathroom dripping and ready to scold her. I found Samantha with big, friendly eyes, lying quietly on the window sill. I swear that cat has ESP.

That scene made me feel twice as bad. Can one sink lower than falsely accusing a feline?

I went back to my bedroom and pulled on one of my better pair of jeans and a cotton shirt. Over that I draped a cotton blazer. The effect was casual but hip. At least I thought so. I looked pale as hell, so I put on some blusher, squeezed a dab of Panthenol conditioner on my bangs to give them some height and pronounced me finished.

I was just squeezing the last of the juice out of a half pink grapefruit when the phone rang. Audrey Lang had a high, screechy voice and she was using it at the highest decibel imaginable, so I held the phone out about two feet from my ear, which turned out to be the perfect distance. The woman was hysterical, so it took me a few minutes to piece together what she was talking about.

She turned out to be the parrot lady's neighbor and long-time friend. Evidently Veronica May had given her my card after I dropped her off and Audrey had decided to call me. Visions of a new subscription to my newsletter danced in my head. "What can I help you with?"

I could hear the panic in her voice. "It's Veronica."

I tried to stay calm for both of us. "Something wrong with her?"

"Yes. She's dead."

CHAPTER 13

"Dead? Veronica May is dead?" I shouted it at her, half out of anger and shock and half because I didn't think Audrey would be able to hear me from two feet away from the receiver if I didn't.

"Yes, there was a terrible fire. Well, not so terrible. Only Veronica's bedroom was seriously burned."

"My God. That poor women."

"Isn't it awful? I don't know what I'm going to do. We were so close."

I knew how she felt. I had only spent a few hours with Veronica and I had an ache in my chest the size of Utah. "How did it happen?"

"That's what I want to talk to you about. But not on the phone."

"Not on the phone?" I hoped she wasn't one of those paranoid types who believed her phone was being tapped by Russian agents or a resentful son-in-law.

"No, I want you to come here. They're gone now and we can talk."

Who's gone?"

"Her daughter and son-in-law."

You don't like them."

"Of course not. Who would like them? Wait until you hear what they did to poor Veronica."

I supposed I was in for a whole lot of gossip and very few hard facts, but I felt I owed it to Veronica to at least hear her out. Besides Audrey kept telling me she was going to hire a detective to check into the fire, and I was already entertaining ways of pulling Lou Rasnick into the case.

Audrey Lang lived in the Mediterranean stucco on the right of Veronica's. It was painted a peachy pink and had two golden shower pudding-pipe trees in front. I knew what they were because Paula Saunders had taken me on a tour of St. Petersburg's flora and fauna and once in a while would quiz me about them. The golden shower trees were impressive, thirty feet high with light green oval leaves. They would be even more spectacular in August when their bright yellow, foot-long pendant clusters are so profuse they seem to radiate sunshine.

Driving up to the Lang residence, I saw the charred portion of Veronica's roof and smelled the odor of past-burned wood. Portions of the lawn were singed, probably from flying embers and the grass looked smashed down by more than a few vehicles and large-sized feet. It wasn't a pleasant sight.

Audrey met me at the door in a pink A-line dress that covered her considerable girth quite nicely. Fine white hair curled around her sun tanned face. She wore no makeup except for light pink lipstick, yet she was attractive and might have been beautiful if she was thirty pounds lighter. "Ms. Baldwin?" I nodded. Her voice rumbled in her throat as if she was just getting over bronchitis and her gray eyes had a wild quality to them. Otherwise she seemed to have calmed down considerably since our phone call. She had a triple chin and when she talked, white creases separated the folds between them. She stood about four-feet-eleven to my five-five and made me feel tall, a rare experience for me. For that alone, I decided to give her the benefit of the doubt and followed her inside.

Walking in her low-heeled white polyester patent shoes in a step somewhere between a funeral dirge and a docent's tour, she led me in the pink door, across a pink carpet and past pink walls to a pink settee. I guess her favorite color was pink. I heard a squawk from the kitchen and then the words, "Hiya cutie, why don't you come up and see me sometime?" followed by an irresistible wolf whistle.

"Buck?" I inched around the corner. Sitting in a metal cage, feathers a little droopy and singed, was Buck.

"I'm a ladies' man," he said, lifting a foot gingerly and replacing it on the wooden rod he sat on.

Mrs. Lang touched my arm and her eyes flashed. "That's the first time he's spoken since the fire." She pulled me aside and whispered, "They found him wandering around in the back yard. Had to put a towel over his head to capture him he was so upset. Guess he escaped before the fire. Poor thing, he really misses Veronica. I don't know how long I can keep him. It's almost time for me to visit my daughter in Michigan and then I'll have to give him up." Her arm tightened on my wrist. "You wouldn't take him, would you?"

I shook my head. "No ma'am. I have a cat. Can you imagine what would happen with those two in the same room?"

She looked up at me. Her eyes had flecks of burnt umber in them. "You could keep them separated until they get used to each other. My brother had a cat and a dog and they were okay. Even became friends. Yes, Fluffy and Codger used to lie on the floor together."

"I think that only works if they're raised together from a very young age."

She pinched her lips together and her eyes narrowed in her wide face. "Don't you believe a word of it." She coughed a wet cough that shook her body. She grabbed for a glass of water and downed it. "Darn cough. I just can't shake it. "Now where was I? Oh yes, Codger and Fluffy. That dog was nearly three years old when Fluffy

64

wandered by, torn and tattered, a victim of someone's nasty prank." Her eyes pleaded with mine to take Buck.

I gently extracted my arm from her hand. "No. I can't consider it."

"Just asking." She pulled away, a hurt look on her face. "I suppose you wouldn't want to take tea with an old lady either."

"Tea would be fine. Something decaffeinated if you have it."

That brought a hint of a smile back to her face. "I have just the thing. My daughter sent me some herbal teas for my birthday. What about Raspberry Delight?"

"Sounds wonderful." I spoke to Buck while she made the tea. He seemed pretty chipper, but I didn't know a thing about birds.

She led me into the living room and put down the tea things on a rattan table in front of two white wicker chairs. She placed a biscuit on my saucer and poured the steaming red liquid into my cup. It smelled wonderful and had a tangy raspberry taste.

She took two biscuits for herself and chomped on them noisily. When she took a breather from eating I asked, "Tell me about the fire."

"Oh, yes." Her eyebrows went up in a doubtful arch. "The police said she suffocated and probably never knew what hit her." She frowned.

"You don't believe them."

"No, I sure don't. How would a fire start in her bedroom anyway?"

"Did she smoke?"

"Veronica? Of course not. Dennis and the boys did, but she hated the smell. Claimed it made her sick."

"Maybe it was faulty electrical wiring."

She glared at me as if I'd said something too stupid to be answered. Then she sighed loudly and gazed toward Veronica's house. "She just had an electrician in there last year fixing things up. Even I know wiring doesn't go bad in a year."

"Maybe he was working on another part of the house."

"I don't believe the police. Maybe they're covering up something too." I was beginning to get the impression Audrey didn't trust anybody. Her face was dark with indignation. "It wouldn't be the first time they took the easy route. No siree. Those people over there---" she gazed toward Veronica's house again, "wanted her out of the way and I think they finally succeeded."

65

"So you don't think it was an accident." The word hovered on my tongue and I realized it was the second *accident* in three days.

"No, not even with all those bigshots over there."

"What bigshots?"

"I don't know. Cars pulling in every which way. Sirens blaring. No one could sleep with all that noise. Policemen, firemen and some other cars."

"Must have been the Arson Task Force." I said, shamelessly trying to impress her.

"I don't know who they all were. The firemen pulled their hoses all over the place and the others tramped around the house." Her eyes turned dark brown. "Nearly ruined my oleanders." I got the impression someone could do a lot of things, but nothing worse than step on her flowers. "They were here a couple of hours, then they left. It would have broken Veronica's heart to see what they did."

"Did they take anything out with them?"

"Not that I noticed. The ambulance took poor Veronica's body, but that was all that left the house."

"Then they must have determined the cause of the fire.

"A rather nice young policeman told me it was an accident, but then his superior dragged him away and told him not to talk to civilians. That seemed rather fishy to me." She glanced toward Veronica's house. "Course it was nothing unusual considering the goings on over there."

"What do you mean?"

Audrey took another bite of her biscuit and chewed it nervously, then swallowed. "There's Veronica's son-in-law. He isn't much of a man if you ask me. Acts like Mary's doormat and even after they were married he spent more time with the cab driver friend of his than one would think proper."

"What cab driver?"

She shrugged. "Misty, he called her."

"Know her last name?" Audrey shook her head. "What cab line did she drive for?"

"I don't remember, but that blue-striped car was forever pulling up. And she drove like a maniac. Nearly took down one of my oleanders with her front wheel."

"Shoreline drives blue-striped cars. I'll check with them." Audrey nodded and took another bite of her biscuit before she went into a coughing spell that turned her face purple.

"You want some water?"

She picked up her tea and downed it. "I'm all right," she managed to gasp before she coughed a few more times, swallowed and then sat back.

"You were telling me about Veronica's family."

She nodded, cleared her throat and said, "One of the worst is Veronica's ex-husband. And of course, Mary, her daughter. She's a nasty person, even told me to mind my own business once when I suggested they be nicer to Veronica."

"Was there something wrong between Mary and Veronica?"

"They argued. Day and night. That girl had no respect for her mother. She nagged Veronica constantly. Then when she married that door mat, Dennis, the arguing got even worse."

It struck me then that Mary and Dennis were the names the two overweight people gave who came to the funeral home. "Did they know Cassie Saunders?"

"I wouldn't know that. More tea?" I signaled *no* and she re-filled her cup. "Who is this Cassie person?"

"A young woman who drowned off the Gandy Bridge."

"Sounds like their kind of people." She sniffed, then took a sip of tea.

"What were the arguments between Mary and Dennis about?"

"Dennis was always after Mary's boys. Course they were lazy and got into a lot of trouble, but a least they didn't argue.

Mary's sons lived in Veronica's house too?"

"Off and on. When they weren't in trouble with the law. When they were at Veronica's, it was likely they'd have their friends over too. That house fairly rocked with noise. Neighbors used to get annoyed and call the police."

"Did you?"

"Once or twice, but I think Mrs. Yoder on the other side called every night. She'd call the police if anyone watered on the wrong day or turned up the radio."

She said the last sentence in a challenging way, as if she wanted me to argue with her, but I refused her offer. "Do you know Mary's sons' names?"

"I believe she named them John and Joseph, but she called them Itty and Bitty. They are skinny and small. It would take two of them to make one of her. But then Mary was always a big girl. She sure liked to eat. French fries and potato chips. I think she existed on them while she was growing up. Veronica never could get her to a decent meal." Audrey clicked her tongue like a judgmental nutritionist.

"Is Dennis big, too?"

"As big as Mary. Like two peas in a pod they are. They could pass for brother and sister."

"Two hefty people in a blue Ford chased Veronica and me at the beach. And two people calling themselves Mary and Dennis came to the funeral home where Cassie Saunders was laid out."

"You don't say. Isn't that strange?"

"That's what I thought. Anybody around here own a blue Ford?"

"I don't think the boys have a car, but I believe Mary's car is green. Pea green." She took a bite of biscuit and stared out the window.

"That's what Veronica said."

"She was right about that. Poor thing." She shook her head in disgust. "Cars used to come and go at Veronica's at all hours of the day and night."

"Did Mary or Dennis or anybody work?"

"I believe Mary made meals at Bayview Hospital. But she quit that."

"How long age?"

"Sometime earlier this year. Lately all she did was lay around and eat. I think she took on another ten or fifteen pounds.

"What about Dennis or the boys?"

"Dennis used to work at Bayview, too. Doing what, I'm not sure since he didn't seem to know much about anything."

"What about Veronica's ex-husband?"

She grunted. "He never worked anywhere that I know of. Inherited some money from somewhere. Always yelling at me to prune back my trees or some other nonsense."

"What else do you know about him?"

"Not much. I think he's been in prison too, but I'm not sure about that." She shook her head. "I just don't understand it. Veronica is---was such a sweet person." Her lower lip quivered and tears sprang to her eyes.

I know." I gulped back a lump of sadness that had invaded my throat. "Anything else you can tell me about her ex-husband?"

"He was a brute. I think he hit her a few times. He used to get drunk and start yelling. Even threatened to kill her once or twice." She looked at me with big eyes. "You don't think he set the fire, do you?"

"Possibly." I took out a notebook and wrote down all the names she had mentioned. "Is there anybody else who would benefit from her being dead?"

"Not a soul. Who would want to kill Veronica?"

"I don't know." We sat in silence for a while. I thought about the last time I had seen Veronica and what she told me about her friend, Selma. "Do you know a woman named Selma Wyberg?"

"Veronica's childhood friend? I never met her, but Veronica used to go on and on about her."

"Do you know where she is?"

"No, but if she finds out about Veronica, maybe she'll come to the funeral." She sniffed into a pink handkerchief she had pulled out of her pocket. "I don't know how I'll get through that. Veronica was the last of my friends." She stared through her tears at the wall behind me. "They're all dead now. Every one of them." She gulped and looked at me. "Don't get real old if you can help it. You'll be left alone with no one to talk to."

I nodded and tried not to think about dying. "Maybe you should keep Buck. He'll be company for you."

She gave me a crooked smile. "Maybe I will. Buck's a good bird."

From the kitchen Buck's voice said, "Buck's a good bird, a ladies' man."

Audrey smiled and I said, "See, he'll be good for you."

Her face toughened and a few more wrinkles came out. "The only thing that will be good for me is finding out who did this to Veronica." Her words came out sudden and raw and very angry. She reached across the table and grabbed my wrist. "You'll find out, won't you?" With her other hand she wiped some perspiration off her upper lip.

"The police are still investigating."

Her mouth curled into sullenness. "Why not just take a look around her house? Can't hurt, can it?"

I shrugged. I knew I was probably deluding myself, but I couldn't help it. My mind kept trying to figure out what Lou Archer would do in this position, but then Lou had an investigator's license. What if he'd lost it? That would make us pretty much equivalent, wouldn't it? Of course there was that little matter about Lou just being a figment of Ross Macdonald's mind in all those mysteries, but still, it was the closest I could get to a logical argument at that moment. Boy was I mixed up!

Audrey's lips moved into the faint beginnings of a mischievous smile and she handed me a key. "This is to Veronica's house. Maybe you could start there."

I took the key. "Who knows," I said, turning to leave, "Maybe I'll even find out something." I left then, feeling the two *accidents* weighing heavily on my shoulders and not giving a twit about my illogical thoughts.

CHAPTER 14

I walked across Audrey Lang's lawn to Veronica's house. The smell of smoke and burned wood got stronger. I didn't see any car around or hear any noise inside, but I rang the bell, just in case.

Sure no one was there, I shoved the key in the lock and hurried in the door. I didn't want her neighbor, Mrs. Yoder, calling the police on me for breaking and entering.

Newspapers no longer cluttered the floor and overstuffed armchairs. Mary or one of her boys had done a quick clean-up job. The calico-covered furniture was frayed and carried soil stains. Someone had been putting their feet up on the coffee table with boots or hard shoes, creating scuffs and scratches and the wood looked as if it hadn't received a coat of wax or oil for sometime.

A dusty, over-sized brandy snifter on the side table caught my eye. It was about half-full of matchbooks. I started through them, stopping when I came to one for the Single Hearts Club and tucking it in my pocket.

Could Mary's boys be customers there, too? It made me wonder if they knew Cassie Saunders. It also sent a slight sliver of guilt through me because I was now concentrating on Veronica's death and had let Cassie's slide. I wondered if real-life investigators ever felt that way.

In the kitchen I found some singed rags in the garbage can, along with empty economy size cans of Campbell's beans and soups. Veronica's family were not gourmet cooks. All the cupboards were open, making me think somebody had been there before me. A set of St. Regis white china sat chipped and cracked on the upper shelves, collecting dust, while only a few generic paper plates remained in a plastic bag on the bottom shelf.

Gray and pink fingerprints (of greedy eaters who were too hungry or thirsty to wash their hands before opening it) covered the area around the refrigerator door handle. Inside the chilly receptacle, Budweiser six-packs, salami, cheese and other fast food items cluttered the shelves. Three half-gallons of chocolate-chocolate fudge ice cream and some frozen meals (the kind my mother used to call TV dinners) resided in the freezer.

The sink contained dirty dishes covered with a scum of cold water and unfoamed soap. A collection of last notice billings for the phone and utilities hung on a clip under the black wall phone. It looked as if Veronica and her family lived on the edge of disaster.

I hate being in places I'm really not supposed to be and this house gave me the creeps. I wasn't sure if it was because I knew it was where Veronica May had died --- or something else --- but I made a mental note to myself to hurry along.

Not finding any sure signs of fire, I followed the smell of smoke, scorched wood, and the chemical odor of household objects reduced to their simplest components down the hall. I guessed the bedroom at the end was Veronica's because the extreme heat had blackened the walls and floors.

In one corner by the door, only the inner springs and metal mattress stand remained to identify it as a bed. A brass lamp turned black from flame lay on the floor, its lampshade completely burned.

Badly burned batiste white curtains hung from the windows. Someone had taken a swatch from one of them. Either Veronica liked to walk on bare floors (which I doubted) or the fire had destroyed the rugs.

There didn't seem to be enough ash. I wondered if the fire department had taken some samples for further testing.

The wooden closet door was charred and gave off a sickly odor. The dresses inside were half-burned. The only remains of her shoes were two thick heels, the metal core beneath the sole and some black ash. Her white polyester wig had melted onto her black straw hat.

I closed the closet door and went over to what must have once been a dresser. It sat in a heap on the floor, its legs burned off. In the corner by the bed I found what looked to be the remains of a hand-crocheted glove.

I eyeballed the walls, but I couldn't see any pattern of burn consistent with an electrical malfunction. The Fire Department must have come to the same conclusion. If I didn't know better, I would have concluded Veronica was smoking in bed and started the fire. But I did know better, so I kept searching.

In the far corner, a pearl comb and brush set sat on a crisp doily atop a maple dressing table, apparently untouched by the fire. In the drawers I found a large jar of Apner's cold cream, a big box of off-white powder and ten or twelve tubes of lipsticks.

I stared at a picture of a man in a gray suit with smiling eyes, that somehow had survived the blaze, wondering where Veronica had kept her important papers. They certainly hadn't been in the closet, unless the police had removed them, which I doubted.

Veronica must have hidden her papers somewhere, but I didn't see a place in her room where they could be. I went back to the closet and poked around until I found a loose piece of plasterboard. My fingers traveled along the inside until I hit pay dirt. Lodged way back there was a metal box.

I inched it way through the opening, pulled the box out, and sat down on the dressing table chair to examine its contents. It wasn't locked with a key, but had a metal latch holding it closed. When I opened it, I found papers of every imaginable kind, including Veronica's marriage license, a death certificate for an Elise Orga, flood insurance and home owner policies for the house.

The last thing I found was Veronica's life insurance policy. I read through it quickly, looking for the beneficiary. It turned out to be Audrey Lang. I didn't think Audrey had started the fire and then called me to come and investigate. Yet, I had read about investigators being hired by guilty clients before. I think it was in a Lou Archer detective story.

The only thing I knew for sure was that I had to talk to Audrey Lang soon about her newly-acquired ownership of the May house, but I had a few things to take care of first, nosy person that I am.

CHAPTER 15

When I left Veronica's house, I headed north toward Bayview Hospital. If I could find some of Mary or Dennis' co-workers, they might tell me something interesting about those two. On the way up, I munched on a Granny Smith apple I had in my back seat.

Traffic was relatively light and it wasn't long before the Bayview Hospital sign came into view. The complex must have been built in the '60s and had that ugly look I associate with the decade. It was the kind of blue-gray stucco that always looks dirty. An American flag fluttered by the circle drive next to the sign that announced in big red letters, *Reserved for Emergencies*. I pulled into one of the spots and hoped they'd think I was an emergency.

Before I got out of the car, I dug in my bag behind the passenger seat and pulled out an expired press card I had found somewhere. It was faded enough that no one could make out the date unless they were inside the car. I stuck the card inside my window, like I had seen Jim Rockford do once on the "Rockford Files," got out and clunked up the cement to the front entrance.

The hospital smelled of medicine and disinfectant. A pink-cheeked, grandmother type sat behind the reception desk looking as if she should be knitting one and pearling two instead of directing traffic. Her bright blue eyes glanced up at me, eager to help. A name tag on the white sweater over her navy dress read: Mrs. Almans.

"I'm trying to find food service." I dug in my bag, pulling out a business card from the health department, one of my nursing colleagues who worked there had given me.

Mrs. Almans read the card, smiled and pointed a finger to the right. "Just take the elevator down to the basement. Mr. Strothers is in charge of food service."

The back hall was chilly and ill-lit. Tapping the business card against my chin, I waited for the elevator. When it finally showed up, a dark-faced man with a goatee stood there with a food warming cart. "Is there room for me?" I asked, half wishing there wasn't.

"Sure, miss, just scoot on this side." His voice had a monotonous whine to it. I scooted where he pointed, the elevator door closed and we creaked downward.

He let me off the elevator first and I turned right, following the signs until I heard voices. Two women in white uniforms and hair nets huddled over large stainless steel bowls, pouring canned fruit cocktail in the mammoth containers so fast it plopped and splashed.

Their voices echoed off the ivory tile walls. "And I told them that they knew what they could do---" said the tall one with a harelip, broad cheek bones and skin so pale it looked as if it never saw the light of day.

"They ain't got the sense they was born with," said the shorter, plumper one in a lilting voice that sounded Jamaican.

"Excuse me," I said, "do either of you know Mary Dwyer?"

The shorter one looked at her co-worker and laughed. "You talk to this one. I don't have the time." Feet squeaking across the well-waxed floor as she moved, she pranced to a large stainless steel refrigerator on the other side of the gigantic room and opened it, nearly disappearing in the opening.

The woman with the harelip looked at me. Her eyes were a fragile gray. "Mary Dwyer don't work here no more."

"I heard that. Did you work with her when she did?"

She picked up a large ladle and stirred the Jell-O. "We worked together sometimes. Who's asking?"

"I'm Megan Baldwin. Her mother was a friend of mine. She died in a fire and I'm trying to find out what happened."

"She died? That's too bad." She looked genuinely sorry. "I'm Rosalind. Mary was an all right person."

"You liked her?'

"Sure. When I first came here no one would talk to me but Mary. She was outgoing and friendly. She was my friend when no one else was."

The plump brown-skinned woman pranced back and said. "Mary Dwyer? I knew her. She had an air about her."

"Come on Dolores, she was all right and you know it."

"Girl, you don't know the whole story." Dolores turned toward Rosalind, hands on her hips, head trust out in a challenge. "She had this air about her, like she had a million dollars." Dolores looked at me. "When for sure she had only two cents in her pocket."

Rosalind's face turned pink. "You don't know that. She told me she inherited some money and that's why she quit working here.

"Girl, she got champagne tastes and Kool-Aid money." Dolores stomped off, a loaf of bread under each arm.

Rosalind turned toward me. "Mary didn't like Dolores. That's why she's so mean, but Mary was fine to me. A real friend."

"Did you know her husband, Dennis?"

Rosalind shook her head and gave me a frantic look. "My supervisor's due to come by now and I got to do my work. If she catches me talking again I'll probably get fired.

I nodded and turned. "Thanks for your help. I really appreciate it. I'm sure Mary would too."

I left Rosalind cutting up a vanilla cake big enough to feed two hundred people. The dark-faced man with the goatee was still in the elevator. I wasn't sure if he'd captured another food cart or was still trying to get the same one out. I took the stairs up and headed for the phone booths.

On a lark I looked up the Wybergs, the name of Veronica's great and true friend. Selma wasn't listed, but a Hector G. was, so I dialed the number. A tinny machine voice told me the Wyberg's weren't home just now, but if I'd leave a number, they'd get back to me real soon. The woman's voice sounded friendly, so I decided to take a chance and copy down the address. Then I drove off in the approximate direction, heading for I-275.

The Wyberg's lived in a trailer park across from the county garbage incinerator. I hadn't been near Gandy Boulevard in a while and it had changed. A brand new commercial park filled much of the north side opposite the boulevard and it looked as if the road had grown a lane or two. Someone had even removed the sign for the incinerator and re-routed the street so there was no discernible entrance to the toxic fume monster, but the smell of burning garbage layered the air.

The Wyberg's rusty brown mobile home sat on a stingy square of poured concrete and peeked out from under heavy, power lines and a few dusty, sad-looking oaks. I pulled in front of their home. A banged up yellow mailbox carried scraggly red paint letters that spelled out *Wyberg Residence*. A plastic flamingo grazed on a patch of browning grass next to a dented Ford truck that had seen better days.

From inside I could hear the sounds of Lawrence Welk and his champagne boys playing a lilting, too-sweet melody. The window was open an inch or two, releasing a delightful smell of garlic and oil. I knocked on the door. No answer.

I knew someone was there, so I stood on tiptoe and leaned to the left to peek in one of the dingy curtains. The interior was "neat as a pin" as my mother used to refer to her mother's house. A lavender, freshly-ironed table cloth sat proudly on a well-polished pine table already set for lunch. A lavender throw carefully covered the brown-and-yellow plaid couch which I suspected was worn and soiled. Plastic roses decorated a blue vase in the corner next the kitchen.

I could just barely make out the shape of a woman in purple polyester slacks and matching sweater. Her body was heavy, sturdy and hard, bursting with energy as she chopped onions and dumped them in a sizzling pot.

I banged on the door again and saw her turn and scramble for the door. It gave with an unpleasant creak and she showed me a face smudged with flour and history. A red plastic rose was pinned to her white hair behind her left ear. Small lines of pride flickered around her thin lips when she flashed me a smile. She'd been through a lot and her face showed it.

Her brown eyes were wise, bright and bemused when she said. "Sorry. I just love Lawrence Welk and I'm getting a little hard of hearing. Hope I didn't keep you waiting too long."

"Not at all. Are you Mrs. Wyberg?"

"That's me, Sorita Wyberg." Her voice had a sweet edge to it.

"Sorita. That's quite an exotic name."

"My mother visited Mexico once when she was pregnant with me and so she named me after a woman she met there." She clicked her fingers like a Spanish dancer.

I laughed and then handed her my business card. That sure made her smile vanish. "Not trying to sell me something, are you?" she said refusing to take it.

"No. I'm looking into the death of Veronica May. Your sister, Selma, may be able to tell me something."

"Veronica dead?" She looked apologetic that she hadn't been more hospitable and invited me in. "Coffee?" she asked, then trotted into the kitchenette before I could answer. From behind a neatly-hung hand towel she sing-songed, "I was just about to have lunch. Homer just called to tell me he wouldn't be home. Maybe you'd like to join me?"

"I wouldn't want to intrude---"

She sidled back into the living section. "No intrusion, especially if you like Italian squash and egg salad."

"Sounds good to me." She seated me at a wobbling chair and set a plate in front of me. It smelled wonderful and the egg salad was just the way I like it---not too heavy on the mayonnaise.

She sat down, buttered her bread with egg salad and took a giant bite. Then she poured us each some coffee and asked, "What's this about Selma?"

"I thought maybe she could tell me a little more about Veronica May. She seems to have died under suspicious circumstances, at least according to her neighbor.

She shook her head. "Veronica dead. So many of them gone now."

"How well did you know Veronica?"

"I lived next door to Selma. She and I and Veronica used to play act together as kids. It was only a few years later the Selma ran off with Lucas somebody or other. She kept in touch with cards and gifts now and then. Homer's her brother, you know. Younger brother. He idolized her and always told me she was going to be a big movie star." She took another bite of egg salad and savored the basil in it. "Of course she never was, but then that's what dreams are for, aren't they?"

I nodded, gazing around her small domain, wondering what dreams she had and lost from childhood. "Do you know how I could get in touch with Selma?"

Sorita bounded out of her chair and flew to a tiny cupboard in the corner. She knelt down and pulled out the drawer which threatened to stick until she gave it a good whack and it slid open. Her fingers minced through a pile of browning letters and postcards. "I think the last one we got was last Christmas. No, it was Easter. She was in Tucson, I believe."

"Selma travels a lot?"

"You bet. That woman never could stay in one place more than a few months. Here it is. The Tucson Arizoner." Her eyes scanned the message. "She says here she is on her way to San Diego to visit her cousin, Clara."

"Do you have Clara's phone number?"

"Should be in my address book." She stood and went to a phone hanging by the kitchen counter. "Clara lives in Rancho Bernardo in one of those retirement communities. Maybe I should call Selma and tell her Veronica is dead. She'd probably want to get here for the funeral."

"That's a good idea. Maybe you could mention that I'd like to talk to her whether or not she comes here."

"Sure, glad to." Sorita picked up the receiver and dialed. She stood a few minutes, then raised her eyebrows in impatience. "No answer, but I'll try later."

"I'd sure appreciate that." I handed her my card. "Call me if you have any luck."

"I sure will." I left, hoping she meant what she said.

CHAPTER 16

I found a pay phone outside Ronald's Hair Care on Fourth Street and called Shoreline Cab. They told me Misty wasn't on duty until seven p.m. I decided to call on Mrs. Yoder. The sun was beating down and the temperature must have been about 80 degrees by the time I reached the Old NorthEast and pulled up on Veronica May's street.

Mrs. Yoder was in her yard again, still wearing a starched apron over a flowered house-dress, this time a blue print one. Her cinnamon-colored eyes stared at me as I strolled up the walk toward her, hoping she didn't remember me.

I handed her my card, which she refused, glancing at my name and face and then back at the ground again. "I saw you."

"You did?" My face got that hot feeling, the one I used to get in third grade when Mrs. Whopfers caught me passing notes.

"You were over at Veronica May's house the other day."

"So I was."

"You deliver things, too?" She cast a doubtful eye over me.

"Not usually," I mumbled.

She grunted and went back to her work. Her gnarled hands worked in an ordered rhythm with her rake to push oak leaves into small piles. I followed her around the yard, asking her questions.

"You know Veronica May is dead."

"Yes, I heard."

"Were you here that night?"

"I certainly was."

"What did you see?"

"Fire trucks, police cars, men tramping all over the place. Good thing they didn't come over here or I would have called the sheriff."

"I understand you have called the police before when it gets too noisy."

79

She stopped raking and looked at me. Little lightning bolts of anger shot out her eyes. "You bet I do. People should be more considerate of other people's rights."

I had to agree with her on that, but I didn't say so. "What else did you see. Did you see anything before the firemen and police arrived?"

"Not much. Just the usual."

"And what was that?" I felt like a dentist trying to extract a wisdom tooth from a resistive patient.

"A car."

"What kind of a car?"

"A blue car."

"A Ford Festiva?"

"I wouldn't know about that. The last Ford I got excited about was the Model A."

"Did you see anyone get out of the car or get back into it?"

"No, I must have dozed off. I was watching the eleven o'clock news and that's about when I started to nod off."

"Do you know Veronica's ex-husband, Edward?"

"No, but I saw and heard him a few times. He was a loud and nasty man."

"What about Veronica's daughter, Mary?"

"She's all right. She gave me some grapefruit from her tree once. She used to take out the garbage now and then and chat with me about her yard."

"You like Mary?"

She gave me a look that told me she didn't like anyone too well. "She's all right. That's more than I can say for her boys."

"You know her boys."

"I only know they tried to hurt my dog once. Caught them trying to choke him by his collar."

"Nice people. Both of the boys did that?"

"One egged the other on. I told them if they ever touched my dog again or came near my yard I'd fill them full of buckshot."

"Did you?"

"No, because they stayed away after that."

I gazed toward the house and wondered if she had an arsenal of weapons inside. "Then you didn't see anything the night Veronica May died?"

"Only Dennis and Mary."

"Her daughter and son-in-law?"

"That's them."

"What were they doing?"

"Hollering as usual."

"Did you hear anything they said?" She gave me a disgusted look as if I had let loose some foul gas. "I don't listen in on neighbor's conversation."

"I know that. I just thought maybe ---"

"Well you thought wrong. I didn't see anything and I didn't hear anything. Now if there's nothing else ---" She clanked her rake down on the sidewalk and pulled it across, making screeching noises like chalk on an old blackboard. It was enough to get me moving toward my car. That woman sure knew how to make people feel welcome.

I found a phone booth on Fourth Street and gave Lou a call. I left a message telling him I could sure use some information on Edward May, the ex-con, figuring that would get his attention.

Feeling a little guilty about ignoring Cassie's plight, I called Paula. Rachel answered. The Spider Woman told me the funeral was tomorrow if I cared to go. I hoped I didn't groan, but I really do hate funerals. Rachel gave me the details before I said, "Tell Paula I'll see her there." She hung up before I could say good-bye. Lovely woman.

I looked up Veronica's physician in the yellow pages. Stephen Oakes, M.D. had an office nearby. My air conditioner wouldn't work, so by the time I arrived at the stone fortress, I was overheated and irritable. My mother always used to say, "Feed Megan, keep her warm and dry and don't overheat her and she's a pleasant girl. Otherwise, she's liable to tear the heart right out of you." I sharpened my claws on an emery board while I waited in his reception room.

The man was bald with a fringe of white hair around his ears, square-shaped spectacles and a deep tan. The guy probably played golf every Wednesday and all weekend while the rest of us were trying to make a living. "Ms. Baldwin, I understand you're a friend of Veronica May's." I had told his nurse she had recommended me and

81

that I was having trouble sleeping. I was getting devious as hell and it was beginning to bother me.

He escorted me into his conference room. Leather chairs, imposing desk, degrees and plaques on his walls. All the comforts of home. "What seems to be the problem?" He took out a form and readied his pen to start writing.

"I understand you gave Veronica some Valium. Helped her to sleep."

"Umm hmm. And just what are your complaints?"

I didn't really know what I was doing there. Maybe I just wanted to pick a fight with someone and I've always considered doctors fair game since they usually try to keep nurses in their place. "Did you know Veronica May is dead?" I said it for shock value and I got the expected reaction.

His face turned a shade somewhere between cardinal red and Congo rubine, and I had the distinct feeling his mind was already ticking away about malpractice concerns . "But she was in fine health---"

"Died in a fire. Burned to a crisp. Poof!"

He coughed and loosened his necktie which looked as if it might be too tight anyway. Then he cleared his throat and repeated my words: "Burned? That is sad. Of course she was getting on in years---"

"She wasn't even a smoker. And no faulty electrical wires."

He regained his composure and his authoritative tone. "Why are you telling me this?"

"Because the police think she took the medicine and then drifted off to sleep and wasn't able to smell the smoke."

"It was a small dosage."

"I'm sure they'll be around to quiz you."

"I assure you, Ms. Baldwin---"

"You don't need to assure me. On second thought, I could use some reassurance. What with Veronica dead and Cassie Saunders, too."

His next words came out of his mouth slowly as if he was afraid to hear himself say them. "Cassie Saunders?"

"That's right, she died under mysterious circumstances, too. She didn't happen to be a patient of yours, did she?"

His face was now a mottled gray. He stood up, nearly knocking his leather chair into his expensive intercom system. "I'm afraid I have no more time to chat with you Ms. Baldwin." He directed me toward the door. "No charge for the consultation."

I left feeling I had accomplished my mission --- shake up a physician a day. Dr. Oakes acted like a man who had something to hide. I also had the distinct impression that Cassie had been his patient, but what the connection was between the two women totally escaped me. I'd have to talk to Paula about that.

CHAPTER 17

I went home for a little food and some solace. All Samantha gave me was a sour look, then she went back to licking her paws. Cats sure do spend a lot of time grooming themselves. I shoved some carrots in my juicer and made some juice. I do that so then I can eat anything I want and still feel like a healthy person. Tonight was one of those eat-chocolate-until-you-puke nights. I could feel it coming on. To ward it off, I ate a tofu burger sandwich, sans sprouts and stuffed some fruit juice sweetened cookies in my pocket.

Shoreline Cab was located in the south side of town, across the street from one of the two million strip malls in St. Petersburg. Blue-striped cabs lined up neatly in front of the place, waiting to be called to various points in the city. I stuck my head in the first cab and asked for Misty.

"She's at the end. That gal's always the last one in."

I nodded and went to the end of the cab line. A cigarette hung out of Misty's heavily-lipsticked mouth. She had been to the hairdresser recently and obtained a dye job that reminded me of the carrot juice I had recently consumed. The false eyelashes attached to her lids were so long they touched her face every time she blinked. Three bangles of gold clinked on her brown-spotted wrists. Jeweled earrings swung above her purple sweatshirt. She was somewhere between forty and sixty, I just couldn't pin down her age.

"Where to?" she said in a disinterested voice that had deepened with years of smoking.

"No where. I just want some answers."

"Gotta charge you anyway. Better if we drive somewhere or else Neddy will think we're passing drugs or something."

"Okay, just drive up Thirty-Fourth street." She started the engine and we roared off into the humid evening. Most of the shops in the malls were already closed, except for the yogurt shop, K-Mart, movie theaters and Chinese restaurants.

"What kind of questions you need answers to?" She looked in the rearview mirror and the street light glistened off her liquid green eyes.

"I want to know about Dennis Dwyer. I understand he is a friend of yours."

"Who's asking?"

"A friend of his mother-in-law."

"Veronica? How is that old biddy anyway?"

"She's dead."

The car lurched and careened to the curb. "Dead? Veronica? I thought the old broad would live forever."

"Accident the police say. Fell asleep and didn't smell the smoke of the fire."

"No kidding."

I couldn't see much of Misty's face, but she looked truly shaken. "You knew her pretty well then?"

"I spent a lot of my free time at her house. Used to play hearts with her. She cheated like a bandit, but we laughed like hell. I'm gonna miss her."

"What can you tell me about her son-in-law?"

"Dennis? Where does he come in on this?"

"No where that I know of, but I'm trying to check things out. I'm sort of a free-lance detective."

"Free lance?" She whooped with laughter. "That means no one's paying you, right?"

"Right." Her words echoed off the walls of the sedan and I began to realize just how ridiculous my mission was.

"Forgive me for laughing. It's really refreshing to know people are out there doing a good deed and not asking for payment. How can I help?"

"Tell me about Dennis."

"He's an okay dude. Got a short fuse, but who hasn't? He was happy with Bobby Jim for years."

"Bobby Jim?"

"Bobby Jim Watson. A driver for Shoreline. The three of us used to be real thick. At least around the station. Whenever Dennis had free-time, he'd hang around Shoreline."

"What was the attraction?"

"You kidding? Bobby Jim was a hot number if you're into gay guys."

"Gay guys?"

"Sure. Dennis has always been gay."

"Then why did he get married?"

"Search me. Especially to Mary. She's one bitter bitch. And pushy! I warned him about marrying her, but he wouldn't listen. Said they had a lot in common. I told him, 'You've been gay too long. It'll never work!'"

"What did he say?"

"He told me to mind my business and he married her anyway. I just never could feature it, but who knows about these things."

I nodded. Who knows indeed. What kind of attraction did Mary have for him. Not her looks. Or her personality.

Misty pulled back out into traffic, raising her fist at a Trans Am leaking rap music into the street. "Kids. Don't they know that's not even music?"

I had to agree with her there, but I kept my opinions to myself and continued my search for useful information. "Do you know Veronica's neighbor, Audrey Lang?"

"Oh, sure. Audrey. Always sticking her nose where it don't belong. She was more worried about Veronica's front yard than Veronica was."

"Were they friends?"

"I guess so. Veronica didn't speak ill of anybody. She was one unusual broad. Always a kind word. Even for her grandsons and heaven knows they aren't much to brag about."

"You know them."

"Sure. Joe and John. The Bobbsey twins. When they weren't in jail, they hung around Veronica's. I always kept a keen eye on my jewelry when they were there. Steal you blind if they get the chance." She snubbed out her cigarette, jammed another between her lips and lit it in one smooth motion. Probably one she'd repeated a million times before.

"Would they have a reason to kill Veronica?"

"You kidding? Veronica used to give the boys money on the sly." She took a deep drag on her cigarette and released it into the air above her. The smoke lay above her head like a gray wreath. "I don't know where Veronica got the bucks, but she gave them a five or a twenty now and then. Don't think they even appreciated it, but she felt sorry for them. Can you imagine that?" She shook her head sadly. "How they ever came from her stock I'll never understand."

"Were any of them patrons of the Single Hearts Club?"

"Not that I know of. Dennis sure wasn't unless they have a gay clientele. Mary? I always thought of her as asexual, sort of like those one-celled animals that reproduce by themselves. The boys? Possibly, but I never saw either one of them with a woman."

"Were they gay, too?"

"Could be, but I never saw them with men either. Took after their mother."

"You don't by any chance know a woman by the name of Cassie Saunders, do you?"

"No. She in on this?"

"I'm not sure. She's dead too, and she knew about the Single Hearts Club."

"That must be some club. You talk to them?"

"Yeah, but I didn't find out much." I'd about exhausted my questions so I asked her to drive me back to Shoreline Cab.

We drove back in silence. She let me off by the station and refused to take my money. "Honey, if you find out what happened to Veronica, that will be payment enough for me. Keep me posted." I got out of the cab, waved to Misty and headed for my car.

When I got home there were two messages on my machine. I hate using the thing but sometimes it does bring good news. The first message was from Lou. My heart did that funny little thing it does when I hear his voice. The second recording was from Ira Wickstein, the investigator with the Medical Examiner's Office. He wanted to know if I wanted to have dinner with him tomorrow night. A date? I hadn't had a date in over a year. My God, what would I wear?

I calmed myself down and called Lou. He picked up the phone on the first ring. "Where have you been?" He reminded me of my mother when she used to scold me for coming home late from a date.

"Trying to find out who murdered my friends." I was angry and I could hear it in my voice.

"That's what I want to talk to you about. I think you better drop the whole thing. You know, you really don't have a clue about what you're doing."

"Thanks a lot. I don't make fun of your work."

"Investigating is not your work. Writing is. When you going to accept that?"

"Listen, I found out a lot of good stuff and I'm not stopping. Besides, people are depending on me." I didn't tell him one was a grieving mother, another the possible murderer and the third, a gravel-voiced cab driver. While I had his ear, I wanted to find out about Veronica's ex-husband. "Did you get my message about the ex-con, Edward May?"

"Yes." He sounded like a little smile had crept into his voice and I could almost picture the dimples coming out on his cheeks. He began to recite as if he was reading a police memo. "Edward May. Convicted on two counts of assault and one of robbery escaped from prison two weeks ago."

"For real?"

"For real. There's an all-points out for him, but so far no sign of him."

"Any address on the guy?"

"You kidding? Guys like that don't give real addresses anyway. Besides even if I had it, I wouldn't give it to you." He paused. "Megan. You're not planning to look for the guy, are you?"

"Who me?" I could be excruciatingly noncommittal when I wanted to be.

"Yes, you."

"I have no plans." More double-talk. I loved it. Besides, it gave me time to think.

I savored what Lou had just told me about Veronica's ex-husband for a moment. If Edward had been out when Veronica died, could he be her murderer? I searched my memory banks, trying to remember what Audrey had told me. "Threatened to kill her..." were the only words I could retrieve. But what possible connection could he have with the Single Hearts Club?

Although I didn't know the answer to that yet, I put him on the mental list of suspects I had been collecting, along with Audrey, the Stetsons, Dennis Dwyer and Veronica's grandsons. I recalculated. Maybe Selma Wyberg deserved a place on that list, too. I just didn't know yet. There might even be a few others I hadn't even considered, but then I was new at this.

I tuned back to Lou's voice. Somewhere in the interim, he had settled into a harangue. "I'm warning you. Lieutenant Johnson is on to you."

"What do you mean?"

"Some doctor called him up and swore you were harassing him."

"Some doctor?"

"Oats or Oakes or something."

Don't mess with doctors. They have more power than nurses. I never seemed to learn that lesson. "I didn't harass anyone. I just asked him a few questions, that's all. Jim Rockford ---"

"Who?"

"Jim Rockford on the *Rockford Files* always goes around---"

"Megan, are you out of your mind? Do you honestly believe that garbage you see on T.V.?"

"Sure. I've found some of that stuff very useful."

A long, frustrated sigh. "Megan. What am I going to do with you?"

Five minutes earlier I would have told him. But by that time, I just thanked him for his concern, said goodnight and hung up. Then just to show naggy old Lou, I called Ira and told him I'd be delighted to have dinner with him. No more than two seconds after I hung up, my feet automatically rushed me to the closet. I figured it would take about three hours to try on every piece of clothing I owned. I had a wonderful time dressing up and deciding what to wear on my date. Not once during that entire time did I have even a brief fantasy of some old ex-cop named Lou.

CHAPTER 18

The next morning I put on my sweat suit, did a few yoga stretches calculated to make anyone look like a pretzel, completed some hand jabs and leg blocks, then wound my shocking pink weights around my wrists and ankles. I neither heard from nor saw Samantha. I suspected madam was sleeping in this morning.

I grabbed my whistle and key out of the wicker basket hanging by my front door and left. I always take my whistle when I feel in danger. Not that there was much to be afraid of on the beach, but the deaths of two people I knew made me feel like checking behind trees and peering behind cars for any murderers who might be lurking there. I figured a loud whistle was a good deterrent in case I did see anything out of the ordinary. I read in a community police memo that if you make a loud noise, criminals are apt to be scared away.

The whistle was also a good idea that morning because it was foggy as hell. White mist hung down, making everything look unusually spooky, like a set for a Vincent Price movie. To be extra-careful, I decided to make a shorter than usual loop this morning, cutting through a resort hotel rather than walking across the deserted parking lot behind the liquor store. A few seagulls shrieked above me, but except for three cars on Gulf Boulevard, the streets were deserted.

As I padded along the asphalt, alert for any suspicious types, what I was doing chasing after maniacs in Ford Festivas struck me as slightly illogical. By the time I reached the beach I had it reasoned out. Trying to find that car fell under the categories of risk-taking and helping out friends. In my mind, mixed up as it was, security measures took a back seat to finding Cassie's and Veronica's murderer.

That settled, I completed two miles, sharing the beach with an elderly man with a metal detecting device. Digging for buried treasure under the beach chairs in front of the resort hotels seemed like a ill-rewarded task to me, but then maybe he had a lot of free time on his hands.

Rushing toward home, I made great time and had plenty of time for my cold shower. It was cool and it was damp in the bathroom, so I turned on my little heater. I didn't mind freezing in the shower, but I like to be warm while dressing.

I put on my gray skirt and jacket. It was sure getting a workout these days. I put on my last pair of pantyhose and figured I'd better buy some more. If I snagged them (which I almost always did), I'd have nothing for my date that night. Pantyhose were invented by somebody who hated women. They take a contortionist to get on, always slip down off your waist, making an uncomfortable bunch between your legs and they don't give you adequate ventilation. Despite all these traumas, on special occasions, like funerals, I submit to them.

Finally dressed, it was time for one of my quickie breakfasts. I dumped a banana, some frozen strawberries and a cup of plain yogurt in my blender. It made a heck of a noise, but gave me wonderful drinks. Samantha wandered into the kitchen, gave me a pleasant look for a change and snuggled against my legs. "You're very friendly, miss," I said, taking a long slurp of my drink before reaching down to scratch behind her ears. "What's gotten into you?" She didn't answer, just walked majestically to the front door and waited for me to open it. Samantha was a formal cat. She only used the back entrance in emergencies.

I finished my drink and let her out. Then I cleaned up my breakfast mess and sat down at my desk to consult my finances. My money market account was in pretty good shape, but was slowly inching its way down. Then I remembered the un-cashed check I'd hidden under my socks. With a little rummaging around in my dresser, I came up with payment from a health and fitness workshop I'd presented for the nursing staff of a medical center in Indiana.

Strange occasion. They were less interested in what I had to say than in fighting among themselves and with me. But the pay was good so I put up with the fun and games of being a consultant on occasion even though I hate to travel and wake up alone in a strange bed in some nondescript hotel.

I tucked the check in my purse and was about to leave for the funeral when the phone rang. Sorita Wyberg's sweet voice came softly across the wire. "Selma's coming to Veronica's funeral."

Selma. Veronica's girlhood friend. Maybe she could shed some light on the parrot lady's death. I certainly hadn't done much to illuminate it. "I'm so glad she's coming," I said. "Did you mention I might want to talk to her?"

"I did and she would be happy to speak with you. She wants to find out as much as she can about poor Veronica's death."

"That's terrific. When will she be in town?"

"Late tonight."

I remembered my date with Ira and had a vision of coming home late and slightly plotched on good wine. My talk with her would have to wait until tomorrow. "Good, then I'll see her at the funeral home." I said a courteous good-bye and sat down to leaf through the *Times*, looking for the announcement of Veronica's funeral home. I couldn't believe it, but it was the Whittier Funeral Home, the same place Cassie had been "shown" in. The coincidences for these two women were increasing geometrically. I knew that meant something. I just wasn't sure what it was.

I put the phone on machine-answer and headed toward the door. A couple of rings of the phone and Audrey Lang's bronchitis rumble roared in my ear. "I saw her. I swear it was her."

"Saw who?" I rushed back and picked up the receiver.

"Veronica."

"Veronica's dead." I knew the grieving sometimes heard their loved one's voices and sometimes even saw their faces. I didn't take the college course on death and dying for nothing.

Audrey's voice sputtered at me. "No, she was here. She came right into my house and took Buck. I was in shock the whole time. She didn't say a word, just took the bird and left."

I was totally lost for an answer. Should I jump into her delusion and pretend Veronica had been there or maintain the parrot lady was dead? Neither one sounded like a red hot idea, so I said, "I'm going to a funeral now, I'll come by to see you after that, okay?"

Audrey gave me a very unconvincing, "Okay."

"Have some tea and rest. You've been through a lot." I chattered on gaily, figuring I had to cover all exigencies, real and imagined. She babbled something in return and I hung up.

The fog had lifted, turning the morning beautifully warm with a breeze that blew clean, orange-blossom scented air into my lungs. Definitely not a day for a funeral. I felt like playing hooky and going to the beach again like some school child. But I knew Paula would be waiting for me at the church, so I crawled into my car and navigated across the bridge into St. Petersburg, making a stop at a drugstore for an extra pair of pantyhose and at my bank to deposit part of the workshop check.

Cassie Saunders' funeral service took place in St. Anthony of the Flowers Catholic Church, a two-story beige stucco building that covered nearly a square block in mid-town. The faithful provided well. It was well-maintained and well-landscaped with some floss silk trees still dressed in glorious pink blooms.

Part of the parking lot was cordoned off and was being asphalted. At least sixty cars had done battle with the church staff over the remaining spaces; some had overspilled onto the grass beside the walkways.

I looked at my watch and confirmed the fact of my lateness. I should never have stopped at that drugstore, but sometimes I think I'm capable of jamming more things into fifteen minutes than any normal person possibly could. I nosed into a spot a block away and ran back toward the church. Organ music and muted voices drifted toward me from the closed doors. I hate being late and doubly hate it when I have to enter a public place and everyone sees me doing it.

I nearly knocked down an usher when I pushed open the heavy door. He muttered something and moved way out of my way with an accusing look on his face as if he thought I might try to bump into him again. A few other latecomers shuffled in behind me and quickly took seats.

The congregation was already kneeling on prayer benches while a priest dressed in a black vestment offered prayers. His voice was reedy and full of sin and repentance. I took a seat in the back pew, looking around the church for Paula. Somewhere mid-church a little girl screamed in a temper tantrum and her father flung her over his shoulder and ran for the door, her petticoats and feet kicking up in the air.

I had been raised Lutheran, but hadn't been in a church since my marriage five years ago, so I didn't feel exactly comfortable with the proceedings. In fact, I had no idea what I was supposed to be doing, so I tried to follow whatever the woman next to me was doing. Later I figured out she was deaf and mute so we must have looked pretty strange to anyone who might have been watching.

Paula was sitting up front beside Rachel. Both wore black. In front of them was a closed casket draped in a white pall with three lit candles on each side of it. More candles flickered on the alter. Huge statues of saints or somebody important looked down at me. They were intimidating enough until I glanced at the stained glass windows. The physical and spiritual torments depicted there made me want to rush up to the confessional box and reveal all, but I restrained myself. I wondered what kept the true believers in tow.

The smell of incense wafted back toward me. After a while, my mind wandered and so did my eyes. I watched a man in the row in front of me unroll a peppermint Life Saver and shove it in his mouth. He sucked on it so loudly I thought the priest might ask him to be quiet, but everyone else ignored him, making me think I was the only one there who wasn't deaf.

"Oh, Lord," intoned the priest, "We ask forgiveness for Cassandra Saunder's sins and commend her soul to Almighty God. Bring her home safely to her Heavenly rest." He was pretty far away, but there was no mistaking the martyred look on his face. He must have been in his fifties, still he was vaguely handsome. Even two cherubic alter boys noticed it, looking up at him adoringly.

They made me think of a mystery I had seen on Channel 3 about a priest who was caught sodomizing alter boys and throwing them off the church roof. I gazed back at the priest, but he didn't look the type. But then, you never know.

More music. Some holy water (at least I think that's what it was) got sprinkled on the casket. More music and a rather noncommittal eulogy followed. I wondered how the priest was going to get around the fact that Cassie had spent a number of years as a prostitute, but he managed fine, making some comments about her graciousness and quoting some mystical piece of scripture.

Before I knew it, six pall bearers shuffled by, pulling the casket along on silent casters. One of them was a woman realtor I'd seen at Paula's a couple of times. She was a hefty woman who looked like she might have been pulling the brunt of the weight, judging from the age and puniness of the others.

I waited for Paula to pass by. She had pulled a veil over her face, but she still looked terrible. "Megan," she mumbled, grabbing onto me with a death gripe. "Ride to the cemetery with us."

Her sister, Rachel, gave me an evil Darth Vader glare, but didn't say a word. I nodded and fell in beside Paula. In a minute we stood on the curb, watching the casket disappear into the hearse. The others hurried for their cars, started them almost simultaneously, adjusted their seatbelts and revved their engines as if they were getting ready for the Indianapolis 500. Either they were in a hurry to join the procession or were already late for other appointments.

A man in black beside us opened the door for the first limousine and helped Paula inside. Rachel stepped back, letting me crawl in next. Maybe she did have a heart after all. Well, half a heart anyway.

Paula's breath was very bad, but then I supposed she hadn't eaten anything for days. Judging from the way her clothes fit, I suspected my supposition was correct. "Have you found out anything else?" she asked, her words nearly overwhelming me with odor.

"Not really." A quiver of guilt stole up my insides. I had been spending most of my time on Veronica's demise. "Her death may be connected to another woman's death. There are too many coincidences to be coincidental." Rachel glared at me.

Paula patted my hand. "Anything you can do will be a blessing. Do you think the mass went all right?"

What did I know of masses? I found myself reverting to pat phrases which I always said I'd never do. "It was beautiful. Just beautiful." Trite as it was, it seemed to comfort Paula and she held my hand all the way to the cemetery.

It was one of the larger ones in town. The name, *Royal Palm* was etched in the stone markers by the road next to the words, *established, 1920*. Spanish moss hung from many of the oak trees. The brownish-green grass was peppered with tall palms. An American flag hung near the entrance. Flowers in vases came out of the ground and sat on top of bronze plaques.

A white statue of Jesus with outstretched arms gazed down at our cortege. Farther up, a huge white stone bible marked a turn in the road. Benches with family names sprung up here and there. Our little procession passed the cemetery office and turned right on the circular drive. A heron watched us from a white bridge walkover. Reeds grew in the lake beneath him. We stopped before we got to the yellow one-story building housing urns of ashes. It made me wonder what it might be like to be suspended above ground, cemented in space next to vases of pink and red roses, with your name on a little wall plaque. I guess it wouldn't be any worse than being buried under a ton of dirt.

Paula grabbed a fistful of tissues from the box the driver extended to her and then crawled out of the limousine. I swear I saw a blue Ford Festiva on the other side of the lake, but the mind can play tricks after a couple of days like I've had.

Paula grabbed my hand and pulled me out behind her, then leaned on me with her full weight until we reached the casket. The priest gave a few more short prayers and Paula sobbed all over my gray jacket. We watched the casket being lowered into the ground, then someone handed her a shovel and she dumped a load of earth onto the casket.

A car started on the other side of the lake. It *was* the blue Ford Festiva. I made a run for it, dragging Paula behind me. "It's them. The ones who chased me all over St. Petersburg!"

Her veil fell off on someone's grave and I lost a shoe on the way. She seemed to pick up energy and by the time we reached the lake, she was ahead of me. "Who is it?"

"I don't know who exactly, but they have something to do with the death of Cassie and the parrot lady. I'm sure of it!" I watched the blue car careen out of the Royal Palms and take a left onto the street.

Rachel caught up to us at the cemetery office, thrusting a veil and a mud-splattered shoe into my hands. "Paula! Have you lost your mind! Grief is one thing, but running out like that ---"

By that time I was feeling a little silly, realizing there was no way we'd ever catch the Ford on foot. But Paula had gained the spirit that had left me, oozing out like air from a deflatable raft. She turned on her sister and did something I never suspected. She thrust her red face into her sister's and shouted, "Shut up! Just you shut up."

CHAPTER 19

I disentangled myself from Paula with a promise to try to drop back to her condo later that afternoon which both of us knew I wouldn't keep. Rachel gave me a guarded look that said, *I know you instigated this fiasco,* but I did my best to ignore her. Jumping in my car, I headed toward the Old Northeast and Audrey Lang's house. There was no way she could have seen the parrot lady, but I was very curious to find out how Buck had disappeared. Despite myself, I was quite fond of the little guy.

Even with the air conditioning cooperating today, the November sun beat down relentlessly so I pulled off my jacket at a stoplight, unbuttoned another button on my shirt sleeve blouse, and wished to God I hadn't worn pantyhose. I pulled over at a gas station, elicited the women's room key and removed them. It may not be the ladylike way to dress, but the Florida heat wasn't made for stockings. Good thing I carried a lot of powder with me. I dumped a goodly amount in my gray flats, slipped in my over-heated feet and drove off. Much better.

Audrey met me at the door. Her starched apron looked wilted and she seemed to have gained a few more pounds. Maybe she was one of those people who eat more when they're sad. Or maybe she was responsible for Veronica's death and was the kind who at out of guilt. I followed her into the living room and decided her gait was definitely funereal.

She poured me some ice tea, then picked up a green Japanese fan and fluttered it in front of my face. "I sure wish winter would get here. This heat is very tiring."

I took a sip of my mint tea and then said, "Tell me about Buck."

Her voice rumbled at me. "One minute he was here and the next he was gone. She just whisked in here, took the cage and left."

"What did she say?" I had decided to humor Audrey about talking to deceased persons.

"Nothing. She didn't say a thing."

"How did she look?"

"About the same. Her gloves weren't as clean as usual, but otherwise I can't say I noticed she had been dead for a few days."

I stared at Audrey, feeling my mouth drop open. Even I couldn't believe we were having this conversation. "You do know, Audrey," I said, patting her hand as if that would soften the blow, "that Veronica died."

"Of course I know it. I'm the one who told you!" Her jowls shook and the flesh in her neck trembled with anger.

We sat silently for a few minutes sipping tea, neither one sure what to say next. Finally I said, "Do you have any idea how Veronica could have gotten here?" I had visions of angels flying her down and depositing her on an unsinged patch of grass by her house.

Audrey dispelled any such notion. "She came here in a blue car."

"Blue car? A Ford Festiva by chance?"

"I don't know what *kind* of car. Who pays attention to those kind of things?"

I held my breath and asked, "Did you see who they were?"

"Couldn't make out any faces. Looked like a man and woman, but I can't swear by it."

That damn Ford Festiva again. I supposed it could be the man and the woman who chased us first day. But who were they? "You didn't get a license plate, did you?"

"As a matter of fact I did. I was in shock after I saw her, but whoever was driving took his time pulling away so I had time to run out and copy down the license."

"That's terrific!" Show it to me." Audrey got up and shuffled over to the kitchen counter, retrieved a piece of paper and handed it to me. I took it, my eyes scanning its contents. "I'll look into this right away. If it holds up --- I mean when we find out who owns the car, maybe I can find Buck."

She shoved her lower lip out. "What about Veronica?"

"Veronica?" I still had my doubts she had seen her. In fact, I was leaning toward the theory that this whole thing was a wild goose chase to keep suspicion off Audrey as the murderer, but I didn't tell her that. I just smiled, finished another cup of tea and left with a promise to find out who the car was registered to.

Then I went home and called Lou. He wasn't there so I left a message. That left me plenty of time to get ready for my date. So what if it was only three o'clock and Ira wasn't picking me up until seven. These things take time. First I took a long walk on the beach. Nothing like salt air for making the skin glow. Then I soaked in a bubble bath until the skin on my fingers wrinkled. I wondered if my unsprouted avocado pits felt as relaxed as I did. I came out pink-cheeked but more frizzy-haired than I went in.

I had decided on a rayon turquoise skirt and white embroidered blouse. I pulled the freshly-ironed clothes over my head, feeling their coolness against my skin. Sort of the peasant look. I draped a white sweater over my shoulders, dabbed on a little Jean Nate, pulled on a pair of low-slung heels, and dangled some wooden earrings from my pierced earlobes. The doorbell rang and I went to answer, scrutinizing my reflection in

97

the full-length mirror in the hall. Ira seemed to like the effect. He gave me an approving smile and stepped inside.

He looked like he had just gotten a haircut and may even have had his hair blow-dried. A tiny band-aid decorated his neck. I guessed he'd cut himself shaving. Probably from trembling at that thought of being out all night with all my loveliness. Or else he was a clumsy oaf. I suppose there were other explanations, but at the moment I couldn't think of any.

He smelled clean and musky, like some aftershave I had admired in one of the department stores in the Tyrone Mall. The pink in his shirt made him look more casual than he had seemed at the Medical Examiner's. But then anyplace away from sharing space with dead bodies would tend to lighten one up. He wore a pair of tan slacks. He wasn't as well-muscled as Lou, but then you can't have everything.

He took me to B.J.'s. I swear I didn't even mention the place, but B.J. was having a special on grouper and a long line of diners waited patiently to be seated, sipping their drinks on the steps or deck beneath the blue awnings and between the red-geranium window boxes. Pleasant conversation and cigarette smoke wafted toward us. We took our places in line. When the wait got too long, some couples wandered off, past the seagrape bushes and onto the beach, where they stood amid seaoats, ogling the water. I guess the word about B.J.'s specials had gotten around to Ira too, because he chatted away about the unique touch the chef had with fish.

I just hoped we didn't run into Lou. After thinking about that for about one second, I reversed my decision. I hoped we *did* run into Lou. It would serve him right for marrying Susan and not me.

Either through blind luck or the exchange of cash, Ira got us into a back booth more quickly than I would have expected. The bar was full of young things in tee-shirts and short haircuts --- some male,some female --- all sunburned and noisy. I didn't see Lou.

"What would you like to drink?" Ira asked, eyeing the wine menu.

"Chablis."

B.J. clunked over in his cowboy boots and stood eyeing me. He was wearing his usual western shirt, faded jeans and boots. His mustache twitched in amusement. "Megan. I would say long time no see, but you were just here a few nights ago." I thought he might mention who I was with, but he didn't. Instead, he conferred with Ira about our drinks.

Ira seemed almost handsome in the subtle light although I've never gone much for redheads. Who knows, maybe I'd go gaga over him before the night was over. The track lights picked up the copper in his hair, reminding me of a scouring pad my mother once had.

He turned to me with a serious look and said, "I'm divorced. My wife left me for the tennis pro at her father's club. We were married nine years but it was never any good. My daughter's eight. Ruthie lives with me."

I'd always been too involved with a career or something to take time out for kids. Or maybe I was just too scared I would repeat the mistakes my parents made. Now I wondered what I had missed. I pictured a little red-headed, pale-skinned beauty named Ruthie. "Who's watching her?"

"My mother. She lives in Largo. She's been a big help. I don't think I could have managed alone. When Becky left, she just took off and never looked back."

B.J. sauntered to the table with a chablis for me in one hand and a burgundy for Ira in the other. He set them down in front of us, then left. "I'm divorced too." I sighed. What were we doing together? I'd been out of my marriage long enough to have my head on straight, but he looked vulnerable and ready to leap at the first available warm body.

B.J. stared at us from the bar with a happy look on his face. He could tell it wasn't going that well between us. Dirty old man that he was, probably still thought I had eyes only for him.

I looked into Ira's brown eyes. There was something there beside thoughtfulness. Maybe sadness. "So, how long you been apart?" I asked.

"A year." He took a sip of his wine. "It tore me up for quite a while."

"I know how that is. Sort of like having all your fillings fall out at once."

He laughed a deep, warm laugh and I felt a little fondness toward him building inside me. A man who can laugh at his own troubles is not half-bad. "Are you still trying to prove Cassie Saunders was murdered?" He asked it good-naturedly and without malice.

I liked that, too. Especially since Lou's voice seemed to be full of accusation and criticism lately. I didn't know why I was comparing the two men, but I took another sip of wine and vowed to forget all about Lou. "Yes, still trying to prove it. She didn't commit suicide," I said. "Did you know that Cassie Saunders had a fear of heights and probably wouldn't be caught dead anywhere near the Gandy Bridge?"

"But she *was* caught dead."

It was my turn to smile. He did have a sense of humor and here I thought he was only pleasant and thoughtful. This date was starting to look like it might turn out to be a good thing after all.

When B.J. came back, I ordered the grouper with pasta on the side and an arrugala salad. I was suddenly starving to death. Ira had the grouper too but chose a baked potato and a cup of chowder. B.J. took his time writing everything down, as if he was waiting to hear part of our conversation. Neither one of us said a word until he clumped away.

"Friend of yours?" said Ira, taking a hard roll and cutting it in half before he buttered it.

"Not exactly. I come here a lot. Guess he's a little protective."

Ira smiled. "I can understand that. What about you?"

"What *about* me?"

"You haven't said a thing about yourself."

He was right. Maybe I *was* a little protective of myself. I watched Ira take a bite of his roll. I didn't want to open any gaping wounds that I knew were still buried there, deep inside me. Finally I said, "I was married too. It lasted about three years."

"He didn't leave you."

"Nope. I left him. He lied a lot. When I caught him in a big one, I left."

"Another woman?"

"Probably. But it was more than that." B.J. arrived with our food. Ira gazed at his admiringly. Although B.J. was a drag sometimes, he always served a great meal.

After B.J. left, we dug into our food. When there was nary a scrap on either of our plates, he said. "So what was it with your husband?"

"Ex-husband." I know there was irritation in my voice, but I didn't want to be linked with Ned in any way. I considered what he did immoral.

"Ex-husband. What did he do to you?"

"He didn't do it to me, exactly. More like to millions of other people."

"My God. He must have been a bastard."

"He was. Is. He sold guns to both sides in Middle East skirmishes, sold a faulty nuclear power plant to some South Americans and who knows what else? Those were only the things I found out about."

"He didn't tell you what he did for a living?"

"He told me he was a banker. I suppose he could be classified as that. But I just couldn't stomach his doing anything he could get away with for money. I'd rather starve."

"Some things are hard to take," he said, setting down his fork.

"My mother loves him. Thinks I should re-marry him."

"Really? Doesn't she care about how you feel?"

"He has status, money, sends her flowers on her birthday. That's what impresses her."

"Parents are funny. Mine can't understand my divorce either. They've been married for forty years and fight like cats and dogs. They'd never dream of splitting up. Probably afraid they'd never find anyone else who could stand them."

I finished my wine and nodded. Parents were strange. We would never understand them and they probably would never understand us. Generation gap.

After dinner we took a stroll on the beach, walking almost to the end of Pass-a-Grille. I took off my sandals and walked barefoot, loving the cool sand feeling between my toes. His sneakered feet moved soundlessly alongside mine. The moon lit our way and the surf splashed up on the sand, making shushing noises.

Then he took me home, seeming as relieved as I was that neither expected physical intimacy yet. He hugged me at the door, but it was a tender, warm thing, like a small, sleepy child might give. We must have stood there for five minutes, then he released me, kissed my cheek and said, "I'll call you."

CHAPTER 20

The phone rang early. It brought me up out of my dream. A blue Ford Festiva was chasing me through the streets of St. Petersburg. I was on foot and the car bore down on me like something out of a Stephen King horror story.

I struggled to my feet and padded barefoot to the phone. Samantha eyed me. I just knew she was thinking: You had one too many wines last night, didn't you?

She was right. My head had that stuffy, tight feeling. Not quite a hangover and yet not its usual, bright self. "Hello," I mumbled.

"You called?"

It was Lou and he sounded nice. Concerned. At least for a minute or two. "Yes, I tracked down that Ford Festiva I told you about. The one that chased me and the parrot lady. I got the license plate number and I wondered if ---"

"Oh, no. I'm not getting into that."

I tried guilt. "You do owe me a favor."

"From when? Seems to me I'm the one always doing you favors."

"Need I remind you of the Witherspoon case?"

Long silence. "Okay, but I paid you back when I found out about Cassie Saunder's cause of death."

"Pah! Ira told me about that."

"Who's Ira?"

"The investigator with the Medical Examiner."

"So you're going to other people for your information now."

He sounded vaguely hurt, but I didn't feel like giving an inch. "Only when I can't get what I need from you." The sentence hung in the air like double entendres often do.

After a long silence he said, "Sorry Megan, but I can't help you with the license number. Jamey Henders called me to say they're clamping down on the kind of thing. It's not like I work for the police department any more."

"What about asking Jamey Henders to look it up?"

"Megan, enough!"

"All right. I suppose it is asking a bit." I said a cordial good-bye and hung up, my mind already trying to figure out how I was going to find out for myself. If the Ford was linked to the two murders, wouldn't it show up at the second funeral or maybe even at the funeral home? If I stationed myself in an inconspicuous spot I might just hit the jackpot.

I did some stretches and took a long, fast walk on the beach to clear my mind. Some barefooted couples in shorts strolled the beach near the water, stopping to pick up shells or point at dolphins. I felt a twinge of envy, wondering if I'd ever find someone to walk with again. An image of Ira flashed before me, then I superimposed Lou's face over it. I guess I still hadn't given up on him yet. Dreams are hard to kick, even when they turn into nightmares.

When I got home, I took a shower, sprinkled some uncooked oatmeal on my yogurt and ate it while I caught up with my newsletter work. It's amazing how many stupid letters I got every day. Some were from subscription services asking me to renew or cancel subscriptions they had never even ordered. Others were in response to an ad I'd placed in *FREETHINGS*, stating they would receive a free "Healthful Living Booklet" if they sent in a stamped, self-addressed #10 envelope; fifty percent of the replies presented a too-small envelope and another twenty-five percent did not carry an address or a stamp.

I read in the paper that kids' reading skills were declining. Perhaps they have been for many years or maybe in the stampede to receive something free, people's brains get addled.

After I cleaned off my desk, I dug in my file and took out the press releases and journal articles I planned to use in the next newsletter. I managed to finish two pages by eleven a.m. Then I put that away, made sure Samantha wasn't into some devilish behavior, locked the house and drove to the Whittier Funeral Home.

The parking lot was full of compact and mid-range cars. No blue Ford Festiva. I walked up to the three-story white stucco building. The cypress trees looked familiar and so did the doorman in the black suit. He was still smiling that goulish grin and still holding the door open for me.

"Ms. Baldwin," said a woman's voice with a deep southern accent.

I turned and nearly bumped into a tall woman wearing a black wide-brimmed straw hat over her wavy red hair. Her cornflower blue eyes looked down at me. They were full of energy and a little mischief. She was about Veronica's age, but dressed younger, as if she used every means available to ward off aging. Her face had that pulled back and up look of a rubber mask that I associated with face lifts. Even then her skillfully made up face couldn't conceal the fact that her chin sagged and her eyelids drooped as if she had neglected diet and exercise and counted on the plastic surgeon to see her through. Diamond earrings (or very good imitations thereof)

103

dangled from her tiny earlobes. Her too-short black taffeta dress rustled against her withered thighs and her three-inch patent leather pumps clicked up the steps. A satin belt cinched in her tiny waist. Her fingernails were long and tapered and painted a brilliant red. A black satin handbag was tucked under her arm and she projected studied grace as if she'd taken acting or modeling lessons.

I took the hand she offered. "Yes, I'm Megan. You must be Selma."

She nodded and gave me a warm handshake. Her smile was glorious, as if a high-powered lamp had been turned on inside her. "Sorita said you wanted to talk to me."

"Yes. Come on inside. There's a sitting room we can probably use."

She followed me, bringing her lavender scent with her. I turned at the iris planter and led her inside a room with a dark roll-top desk, two chairs and a ivory-and-plum-flowered couch. The room was softly lit with table lamps. A walnut stand clung to the wall next to the desk. It contained small brochures telling me how to chose between cremation and ground burial and how to set up a living trust. I averted my gaze.

Selma sat down and sighed. "I never thought Veronica would go first. She was always so full of life."

David Whittier's face poked in the door. His eyes still had blue circles under them and his face still wore a *You poor thing* expression. "I know you," he said, reaching out his hand.

"Yes, I was here for Cassie Saunders' showing.

He clicked his tongue against his teeth. "Sorrows often come together." He looked at Selma. "Perhaps I could direct you to the appropriate room."

Selma flashed him a brilliant smile. "We're here to see Veronica May, but we thought we might sit here a moment and talk."

"That's perfectly all right. When you're ready, please sign the guest book. Mrs. May is in the small viewing room. Is there anything else I can do for you at this time?"

I shook my head. "No, we're fine." He propelled his tall body out of the room as if he couldn't wait to be free of us.

"They said the fire was an accident," said Selma, taking out a lace handkerchief in case she needed it. She turned her blue eyes on me. "But you don't believe it, do you?"

"No. There are some pretty funny things going on. Have you been in touch with Veronica over the years?"

"Of course. We spoke on the phone and we used to send cards on Christmas and birthdays. She never complained, but I know that ex-husband of hers made her life hell. And her sons took after their father."

I stared at her. I thought I had remembered Veronica saying she hadn't spoken to Selma since she ran off with Luke Pesco, but after all that had happened in the last few days, I wasn't sure. "She spoke very fondly of you. She said you ran off with Luke Pasco and were destined to be a movie star."

Selma sniffed into her handkerchief. "That was Veronica. Always wanting the best for everyone. Yes, Luke and I ran off. He promised to marry me. Instead he stole my money and took off. I never heard from him again. I was too embarrassed to go home so I got a job and worked my way to Hollywood. The best I could manage was hairdresser to the stars, but it was exciting work. Of course now I'm retired and time passes slowly. "She looked down at her hands lying on her lap as if she was waiting for a reply from them.

"Can you think of anyone who might want to get rid of Veronica?"

She gave me a nasty look. "Besides that criminal husband of hers?"

"You think he might have killed her?"

"He didn't have a big brain, but he was capable of great violence. Even when she didn't tell me, I kept tabs on what happened to her."

"How did you do that?"

Her look turned mysterious. "I have my ways."

What ways were those I wondered. Mental telepathy? Private investigators? Delusions of grandeur? For some reason I thought of Audrey Lang and so I said, "Her neighbor swears Veronica is still alive."

She leaned back on the couch and crossed one leg over the other, showing a hint of black nylon petticoat. "Which neighbor is that?"

"Audrey Lang. She says Veronica came back yesterday and took her parrot, Buck."

"I wouldn't put it past her. Veronica always was a survivor." She stared up at the ceiling for a minute, then laughed a low, guttural laugh. "Wouldn't that just show them all?"

"Who would it show?"

"Whoever stands to gain anything from Veronica's death."

"And who would that be? Did Veronica have a will?" I was testing now, staring at her eyes to see if she flinched or showed any sign she might know something. I couldn't read anything in them, but then if she was an actress, she might be very adept at keeping whatever she wished to herself.

She gave me a sincere look. "I wouldn't know that, but I imagine we'll all know that very soon."

"Is there anything else you can tell me about Veronica?"

"Only childhood memories and I'm afraid those wouldn't be much help."

"I guess not." I stood up. "Shall we go in and pay our respects."

Selma nodded, stood up in one easy movement and accompanied me to the guest book. The page was full. Veronica had many friends. More than poor Cassie and for some reason that made me feel sad.

The front door opened to the sound of a bell. Audrey Lang's voice rumbled at her companion, Mrs. Yoder. "I know you don't feel comfortable in funeral homes, but who does?" Audrey caught sight of me and gave me an embarrassed smile as if I had caught her without a pass in the grammar school hall.

"Ms. Baldwin. I didn't expect to see you here."

"Veronica was a friend of mine." Mrs. Yoder mumbled something. "What's that?" I said.

"Thought the neighborhood should be represented." Even though she didn't have her rake in her hands, she stood as if she did, with her hands in tight fists. She wore a non-descript dress and had smeared some pink lipstick across her lips.

I turned to the two women. "This is Veronica's childhood friend, Selma Wyberg."

Audrey brightened. "Veronica will be so happy to know you're here."

"Would have been," I said through gritted teeth.

Audrey grabbed Selma's hand and shook it as if it was a water pump. "Ms. Baldwin doesn't believe I saw Veronica yesterday, but I did. I don't know who they have in the casket, but it's not Veronica May."

David Whittier bounced into the hall. "My goodness are you all together? Where can I direct you?"

"We're going to see Veronica May," said Selma.

"But it's not her in the coffin," said Audrey, grinning. She had a foolish look on her face and I wondered if she hadn't had a few sherries before she came.

"Not her in the coffin, did you say? Of course it's her. Who else could it be?"

Audrey giggled and handed him a newspaper clipping. I looked over his shoulder as he read.

WRONG BODY FOUND IN FAMILY CASKET

The children of a St. Petersburg woman had gathered at the funeral home to mourn the death of their mother, 65-year-old Isabel Sommer. They asked that they be given time to be alone with the body before friends arrived. Their grief turned to shock when they opened the casket, because inside was the body of a stranger.

A mistake had been made and 80-year-old Vanessa Rachett was shipped to San Diego where Mrs. Sommer's family had gathered for her funeral. "We knew it wasn't her right away, said Mrs. Sommer's daughter. My mother had heart surgery last year, but there were no scars on this woman. Besides the faces were different. The funeral director tried to tell us people change in death, but we didn't believe him. How could an 90-pound woman alive become 230 pounds in death?"

The Medical Examiner's Office issued a statement saying they handle hundreds of bodies every year and this is the first time this kind of thing has happened. They're supposed to put a toe tag on at the scene of the crime, but someone must have slipped up.

Mrs. Sommer's daughter, Lynn, told reporters, "I wouldn't wish this on anyone. A death is bad enough, but a mix-up, too! This should never be allowed to happen."

David Whittier's hand began to shake, then his breath came out in little gasps. "This is terrible. Nothing like this could ever happen here. It's outrageous." He let go of the clipping as if it carried the plague, then he backed away from us until he stepped inside the chapel. Once there, he closed the door firmly. The look on his face made me wonder if he was thinking about the bodies lying in state in his funeral home and worrying they might not be the right people.

Audrey reached down and snatched the article back from the floor, then she stuffed it in her purse. "I told you! That isn't Veronica in there. Let's go see!" She rushed forward toward the viewing rooms, fist raised above her head. I half-expected her to draw out a bugle and blow the cavalry charge. I've never seen an elderly woman move over that amount of dusty rose carpet so quickly.

She pushed her way into the small viewing room, with the rest of us on her heels. Two matronly types stood by the closed casket, making appropriate sad noises.

"It's not her in there. I can feel it!" Audrey shouted. Their heads whipped around and their faces stared at her with a blank look.

107

Now I was sure Audrey had been drinking. Her eyes were small and pink and her lipstick had smeared onto her teeth. The flesh in her jaw rumbled with her voice. "It's God's will that this coffin be opened for inspection!" She banged on the casket with her fist.

Mrs. Yoder jumped back away from Audrey and started to scurry in the other direction, head down, mumbling something like, "I knew she was crazy the first time I met her. Yes, ma'am. Crazy as a bed bug."

The skin on Audrey's face had turned splotchy and tears were running down her cheeks. I wasn't sure if it was due to drink or helplessness. Selma and I glanced at one another, then we each grabbed one of her arms. "It's okay, Audrey. We'll have this checked out. Let's go now," I said through clenched teeth.

Audrey bolted and kicked like a heifer about to be branded. "I'm not going anywhere until I know my friend isn't in that box."

I made shushing noises and smoothed her tangled hair, while I tried to lockstep her toward the front door.

David Whittier lunged into the room, tie askew and blonde hair looking as if he'd just waged a battle with it and lost. "What's happened? What's going on here?" His reassuring vocal tones had amplified to pandemonium voltage.

I gave him what I hoped was a we've-got-this-under control look. "It's all right. Mrs. Lang is very upset about her friend's death. We'll just take her outside for a breath of air."

"Are you sure? Do you need help?" His arms waved ineffectually in the air and he looked as if he couldn't help a flea at that moment.

"We're fine, just fine." Selma and I dragged Audrey outside and stuffed her in my car.

Just then the blue Ford Festiva screeched into the funeral parlor parking lot. "It's them. It's the car I saw the night Veronica was killed," shouted Audrey, struggling to get out of my hold.

They must have heard her because I turned around just in time to see the driver throw the car into reverse and turn the car around. "Get In!" I shouted to Selma. She was more quick-footed than I would have suspected. By the time I had the key in the ignition, she had buckled herself in the passenger seat and locked her door.

Audrey screamed at me from the back seat. "Don't let them get away! Follow the---" My Toyota screamed out of the parking lot, jamming Audrey up against the front seat and losing her next syllables (which I knew just had to be swear words) in the blue vinyl of the seat cover.

By the time I got to the street, the Ford was just disappearing around the corner. "Hold on, back there," I said, feeling like Luke in *Star Wars*. (Audrey did remind me a little of R2-D2 in some ways, especially around the belly area.) Now this was getting to be just like a Jim Rockford mystery with a car chase and everything. I only hoped I could keep up and that I would know what to do once we caught up with them.

CHAPTER 21

Later, I probably would have claimed that if I would have known what was good for me, I might have turned around and driven Audrey home instead of chasing after the blue Ford Festiva. But if it's one thing I never seem to know, it's what's good for me.

We zoomed along, Selma giving directions like the police in some high-speed car chase and Audrey bumping and gurgling in the back seat, occasionally shouting out an obscenity when she bounced against the seat or car roof. I kept my eyes on the Ford Festiva, swerving through traffic, half-losing it in the many turns and twists it took.

By the way the man was driving, I was sure he knew we were after them. Down a one-way street and two alleys later, we pulled up with Audrey panting and waving. I'd never been in that alley before, but the sign on top of the building was unmistakable: Single Hearts Club.

I took my foot off the gas and coasted by. "There!" shouted Audrey. "Their car is parked behind that club."

"I know, Audrey," I reassured her. "But we don't want them to see us, do we?"

"Why not? It's just getting exciting." She grabbed the front seat and pulled her body forward. "What do we do now?"

"I don't know what you do, but I'm leaving. That guy has a gun in his car and who knows what he might have inside the club?"

"But we can't leave now, not when the fun's starting," moaned Audrey, spraying her sherry-breath in my face.

"I'm taking you home. Enough excitement for one day. Why don't you take Selma home with you for company?"

Selma nodded. "I could do with a little freshening up." She examined the run in her hose and straightened the front of her dress.

"That's settled then." Audrey started to protest, but I jammed down on the accelerator, made a quick turn and she slid across the seat and had to hold on for dear life. We headed in the direction of Audrey's house. I dropped them off promising to pick them up again before I returned to the Single Hearts Club. Another small lie. They were getting easier and easier to make. If the road to hell is paved with good intentions, then the road to investigating must be paved with little white lies.

It was too early to go into the Single Hearts Club. I didn't want to run into the driver and his snub-nosed .38. Instead, I camped out in the alley about a block down and waited. I pulled out that book on the empresses of Constantinople I'd gotten on inter-library loan and soon was deep in 4th century palace intrigue.

A couple of hours later a motor revved up and I saw the blue Ford Festiva pulling away. I verified the license plate Audrey had given me. It never hurts to check up on things, except sometimes I get really obsessive, worry if I left the teapot turned on the stove, necessitating a five mile ride back home to make sure it wasn't on. It never was, but if I hadn't checked, I would have worried all day.

It was starting to get dark and chilly. I pulled on a jacket and waited a little longer. I had to go to the bathroom real bad, but I figured better safe than sorry and waited a little longer. I inched the car into the driveway next to the Single Hearts Club, got out and crunched along the stones to the back door. A white Dodge was still parked there. I figured it must belong to the receptionist. Gemma Fuller must surely drive at least a Mercury or some other huge gas-guzzling beast.

Turning the handle, I found it open. It made a hell of a noise squeaking wide enough to the slide inside, but it didn't appear anyone heard me. At least no one came rushing at me, shouting, "Stop or I'll call the police!"

A small sliver of light came at me from under the closed door ahead. I ducked into the first hallway I came to. Luckily it turned out to lead to the restroom. I relieved myself, crept back out into the hall and waited behind a pile of boxes.

Ten minutes later the receptionist made her way past toward the back door. Her high heels clickety-clacked unsteadily along. Even in the dim light I could see how thick the mascara caked her eyes. She must have been in a hurry because she didn't stop at the john, just rushed out, letting the door slam locked behind her.

I must confess I breathed a sigh of relief that I was at last alone in the place. Although I didn't think the receptionist was capable of any violent moves, you never can tell.

I pulled out my flashlight and made my way along the narrow hallway toward the front of the building. I opened the door I had seen the receptionist leave. The letters, GEMMA FULLER, had been painted in a sparkly script. I stepped inside, closed the door and took a look around. A scratched, but substantial oak desk stood on the other side of the small room. Hideous red velvet curtains with black tassels covered the windows. I waded across the thick red carpet to the desk and sat down in the squeaky swivel chair behind it.

The desk was clear except for a photograph of three adults. They grinned back at me, their eyes like quicksilver in the flashlight beam. I recognized two of them: Dwayne and Mary Dwyer. The third was a cheap-looking woman in a red-sequined dress, rhinestone earrings, and platinum wig with more make-up on her aging face than her receptionist wore. I guessed it was Gemma Fuller.

111

The pieces were starting to pull together. I also guessed the blue Ford Festiva belonged to the Dwyers. Hands shaking with this new knowledge, I pulled open desk drawers, probably expecting the rest of the information to fall into my hands magically.

It did.

From the top right-hand drawer, I pulled out a red leatherette appointment book and started paging through it. Nearly every week for the past year Gemma Fuller had an appointment with R.S. The times varied, but were all after five p.m.

R.S. had to be Rick Stetson, prominent lawyer whose wife said he was bedding every woman in the Tampa Bay area, including the now-dead, Cassie Saunders. I had figured out a few days ago that he was tied to the Single Hearts Club, but still didn't know how.

Sniffing like a bloodhound nearing the catch, I dug through the top drawer, past coffee-stained and cigarette smoke-smelling piles of files full of written applications from applicants to the Single Hearts Club. It amazed me how much intimate information the hopeful customer would give up in order to have an evening out with someone they probably wouldn't be caught dead with if their mother suggested a blind date.

The second drawer wasn't much more interesting. It was jammed with videotapes labeled with applicant names. I had a flashback of the acne-pitted man with frizzy brown hair I had seen watching videotapes in the ballroom. I hoped I never got that desperate, but maybe I'd surpassed that. Who was I to be critical of these folks when I was lusting after the husband of a friend and dating a man who spent his days looking at dead bodies?

The bottom drawer contained a box of half-used tissues and a huge make-up kit. Gemma Fuller owned only the best and most expensive. I took another look at her photo and decided it was because she needed it.

The middle drawer had the usual stuff, paper clips, half-chewed pencils, leaky ball-point pens, some white-out, a well-used emery board, rubber bands and a roll of stamps. The left top drawer was empty except for a key. It was taped to the back of the wood. I gazed around the room looking for what it might open, but didn't see anything it might fit. I closed the drawer and opened the next one.

It was full of expensive vitamins, wrinkle creams and a gross of condoms. I didn't know whether Gemma used them or dispensed them to her customers. The bottom drawer contained a pair of extra-high heel silver slippers with ankle straps. Gemma like to dress up. I closed the drawer and stood up. I hadn't really found anything significant except the appointment book. There had been nothing to match it in Rick Stetson's office, but then I didn't remember finding his appointment book. Maybe his secretary kept that or maybe he carried a small one in his pocket.

I got ready to leave, making sure I hadn't left any tracks behind to follow. When I was convinced, I pulled the door shut with my handkerchief and headed out the back. On the way home I tried to figure out the connection between Rick, Gemma and the Dwyers, but nothing occurred to me.

I pulled into my driveway and was halfway to the door, planning just what delicacy I'd have for dinner when I heard a squawk, then the words, "Why don't you come up and see me sometime?" I stopped in my tracks, then ran to the metal cage that stood under my mailbox.

No mistaking Buck. He was perched in his cage on one foot with his head cocked to the right. "How you doing, sweetie?" he said in a low voice, then gave a wolf whistle.

"I'm doing fine. What are you doing here?"

"Read the note, read the note," he said, then gave a squawk for emphasis.

"What note?" I looked at the cage. Taped on the backside was an envelope. I ripped it off, tore it open and read:

Dear Megan,

I know you and Buck are fond of each other
so I wanted you to be together. Besides, I think
he can help you solve my murder.

Good luck investigating!

Veronica May

I felt as if I'd just been struck by lightning, as if I would know what that might feel like. I slid to the step and sat there staring at the note. Who was playing tricks on me? Audrey? She had gone a little off the deep end, claiming Veronica was still alive. Maybe it was Audrey. After all, she was high on my list of suspects for Veronica's murder. She did stand to inherit what remained of the parrot lady's house.

Then again, maybe it was someone connected with Single Hearts. Rick Stetson. Nah, I doubt he even knew about the parrot. Veronica's daughter and son-in-law. They certainly knew about the parrot, but why would they want to throw suspicion on themselves.

Buck squawked, yanked at one of his tail feathers, then said, "Time to end this thing."

"You're darn tootin' it is. Come on inside young man and meet your stepsister." I knew I was in for nothing but trouble, trying to put a bird in the house with Samantha, but for some reason I just didn't care. I unlocked the door and peered inside. No sign of the feline. I tiptoed in, birdcage in tow.

The little creature was not in any of her usual spots. She must have gone out the back door on one of her adventures. Just as well until I figured out what to do with Buck. For now, the best place was on my shoulder. I opened the cage door and stuck out my hand. He cocked his head, bit at my finger gently with his beak, then stepped onto it. "That's a good birdie," I said, holding my breath.

"You're darn tootin'," he said, then whistled.

I set him on my shoulder and put the cage on top of my refrigerator. It was the highest spot in the room. Not safe from a cat, but safe enough. "Is Audrey in on this?" I asked, half-expecting an answer.

Buck gave me a disinterested look and preened a feather or two. I could see he was going to be just as uncooperative as human beings. I made some camomile tea. It's supposed to be calming. Come to think of it, it did help me decide that the best way to find out if Audrey was the one who sent the bird was to confront her about it.

I washed my cup and swiped a bran muffin from the peach-colored glass jar etched with the words, Products de Campaign. I loved that jar, having bought it purely for its beauty. Then I found it was useful for housing brown rice, dried beans or muffins, depending on my mood.

Buck ate the muffin crumbs from my hand and settled into my shoulder. He might come in handy after all. I might be able to do away with garbage disposal entirely. We went out the door together. He was a little fidgety when I started the car, making some squawks and trying to jump off my shoulder, but by the time we were headed for Audrey's he settled down, staring straight out of the front window like a driving instructor intent on finding something wrong with my driving.

By the time I pulled up to the Mediterranean stucco on the right of Veronica's, Buck was active again, sputtering a few words, blinking and switching from one foot to the other. Veronica's house still smelled of past-burned wood.

Audrey came running out to meet me. Her elderly, heavy, slightly stooped body seemed to fly through the air by sheer will. The flesh hanging below her neck and on the underside of her arms jiggled along in a flip-flop rhythm. Her cheeks were nearly purple and her eyes had that I-had-too-many-sherries-to-drink look. "We've been waiting for you! When do we go back to the Single Hearts?" She jerked at the locked door of my car and looked as if she might jump up on the fender if I didn't open up. Then she spied the bird. "Buck! I knew it! I knew I wasn't crazy. She did bring that blasted bird back. Come here little birdie, give Auntie Audrey a kiss."

"Bug off," said Buck, in a disinterested tone, extending his foot in a stay back gesture.

Undaunted, Audrey gushed, "He's just bashful, you know. Shy. Bring him out. Wait until he sees me. He always liked me."

I opened the car door and stepped out. "I'm sure he likes you, but remember, he's been through a lot in the past few days." She smiled a pasty smile, but I don't think she believed me. Buck remained silent on the issue. She looked hurt that the bird was giving her the brush-off.

Audrey grabbed my arm and jerked me up the walk behind her. "Come inside and tell us everything." She burst into the front door of her house dragging me in behind her. Buck started to do weird little jumps on my shoulder and emit distressed squawks.

When he saw Selma, I thought he was going to fly off my shoulder and attack her. "Look out! shouted Buck, swooping off my shoulder toward her.

"Cover your head, he's coming for you!" I shouted. Luckily Selma still wore that silly hat. Buck took a bite out of it then cruised around the room, flapping his wings furiously.

Selma gave me a look somewhere between anger and terror. "Go hide somewhere. Try a closet and shut the door!" I shouted. "I better get Buck out of here. He doesn't like Selma at all." Selma made a run for it while Audrey and I cornered Buck by holding up some newspapers in his flight path. It took a few minutes, but he finally calmed down. Feathers askew and mandibles yapping with excitement, he agreed to be coaxed onto my finger and then onto my shoulder.

"Bad! Bad!" he screeched, then clamped his beak shut.

"I guess I'd better get him out of here," I said, heading for the door, and wondering if Buck knew something evil about Selma I hadn't discovered.

Audrey followed me out onto the walk. "I never saw him act like that. And with a total stranger, too. What do you suppose got into the little birdie?"

I had a few ideas, but I didn't want to stop to chat. I doubted Selma was going to talk about what just happened, but her sister, Sorita might have some very useful information.

CHAPTER 22

I drove up I-275 toward the county garbage incinerator. To the northeast, a gray plume of toxic waste hung against a perfect blue sky. Why we couldn't conserve more and burn less was beyond me. I figured I did my part by keeping a little compost pile of vegetable skins in a jar (until I found time to plant them under my fruit trees) and by carrying my own shopping bag to the grocery store. Although the newspapers claimed environmental concerns were top of the list for most Americans, I hadn't seen much sign of it in St. Petersburg. When I talked to people about composting, they gave me a sick smile. Some even laughed out loud. Maybe my public relations skills leave something to be desired.

Buck gazed out the window and I could have sworn he shook his head in dismay, but I did have to keep my eyes on the road so I could have been wrong. A few minutes later I pulled into the Wyberg's trailer park. The delightful smell of burning garbage tingled up my nose. The withering oaks were still there, looking as if they could use a good watering. The plastic flamingo lay twisted and fallen in the grass like a wounded swan, probably the victim of some uncaring driver. Buck let out a squawk. I wondered if his sympathetic clucks were in mourning for his plastic cousin.

I got out and tried to get the deformed bird to stand up, but it crumpled to the ground when I let go of it. Its plastic eye stared up at me, reminding me of Cassie Saunders lying on the Medical Examiner's cart.

Sorita was still playing the heck out of Lawrence Welk. The champagne music drifted out of the rusty brown mobile home and down toward my Toyota. Buck perked up and whistled along. I guess he knew the tune.

No garlic smells in the air and no sign of Sorita but the music. I didn't bother peeking in the window this time. I felt a little guilty when I did that to people I knew. I reserved that kind of thing for strangers.

Sorita opened the door before I banged on it. "Ms. Baldwin." She smiled and the plastic rose behind her ear slid down an inch or two. She was wearing a polyester slack set again, only this time it was an apricot shade. It made her brown eyes glow, then glitter when they fell on Buck.

"Megan. Call me Megan. This is Buck, Veronica's parrot."

"How nice to see you." Her smile faded and she took a step backward. "He doesn't bite or anything does he?"

"No, no of course not." All right so I lied. But he did only bite a hat, not a person.

Sorita kept her arms carefully out of Buck's reach and her eyes on his claws. "You did find Selma, didn't you?"

"Oh yes, definitely. Can I come in?"

She glanced at the bird, then back at me. "Is he house broken?"

"Oh, sure." I hadn't the slightest idea if that was true. So far he hadn't landed any droppings on me so I guessed it was safe.

Her sturdy arm held the door open. "Excuse me. I don't know where my head is. My husband, Homer, is in the hospital and I'm at odds and ends." The lines around her thin lips looked more helpless and sad today.

"Nothing serious, I hope," I said, stepping into the neat interior. It was neat, except for the cerise table cloth on the pine table. A few grease marks decorated it. I was surprised to see that, but then you can't blame a lady whose husband is ill. It takes something out of your housewifery skills.

"It's some minor surgery, but you always worry when they put them to sleep. You never know if they'll wake up." Traces of goose bumps flickered up and down her arms. She sniffed. "He's a big baby about things like that."

"Bucky's a baby, what a big baby," said Buck, blinking his eyes and rocking his body back and forth.

I giggled and Sorita smiled. "I hate to bother you when you're so busy---"

"Pah!" She waved a disclaiming hand at me. "It'll do me good to think about something other than Homer. How about some coffee?"

"Delighted." I sat down on the couch and sunk into the lavender throw. It was soft and spongy and reminded me of my grandmother's house for some reason. Maybe it was the clean smell.

Sorita cocked her head in Buck's direction. "Does the bird want something?"

I looked at the bird. "What'll you have, Buck?"

"Give the bird some food, give the bird some food," Sorita shook her head, smiled and headed for the kitchen. She came back a few minutes later with a pot of coffee and a plate of toffee bars. My favorite. My mother used to make them for me when I was little, when I was good, which wasn't too often.

Sorita poured me a cup of the dark liquid and handed it to me. When she passed the toffee bar, I took the biggest one I could see. She smiled. "My son, Todd, always did like these, too." She sat down and nibbled at her fingers. "What is it you wanted to ask me?"

I broke off a piece of the sweet and handed it to Buck. He put it in his claws and gave it a pretty good working over with his beak. I looked at Sorita. "Have you ever seen this bird?"

"No."

"It's Veronica's you know."

"Really, I didn't know she had a bird. Does he have something to do with her death?"

"Audrey Lang, Veronica's neighbor, claims Veronica isn't dead at all."

"Isn't dead? But then who is that at the funeral home? I distinctly remember Selma saying she was going there to view Veronica."

"Yeah, well, Audrey may not have all her screws on tight." I didn't tell her I was beginning to believe Audrey. Of course there just wasn't much evidence that, Audrey was right, unless you counted Buck and the letter attached to his cage.

"You know Buck didn't take to your sister very much."

"Really? I didn't know birds were like that."

"You don't know Buck. He tried to attack her at Audrey's house."

Sorita pushed her chair back a few inches and stared at Buck. "Veronica bought a crazy bird?"

"No, nothing like that. Buck is a very sane parrot. Smarter than some people I know. It wasn't his typical reaction."

She gave the bird a suspicious glance. "Then I wouldn't know why he'd go after Selma. She's an animal lover. Has two dogs she loves dearly."

"Do you think she might have seen Buck before?" I hesitated to say the night Veronica died because I didn't want to point any fingers, especially not at Sorita's sister.

"I really wouldn't know if Selma had seen the bird before." Her face seemed to blanch to a sick white, but it could have been my imagination. She took a nervous sip of coffee. "Did you ask Selma about that?"

"No, I didn't. There was such an uproar after Buck flew at her hat that I didn't have the chance." We chatted for a while after that, but I had the distinct impression Sorita didn't want to tell me anything else about her sister. That made me very suspicious of Selma and even a little suspicious of Sorita. I thanked her for the toffee bar and accepted a doggy bag of them to take with me. That made me feel a tad guilty, especially since I now had grave doubts about both sisters, but that didn't stop me from taking the bars. Great food is great food.

I drove home. Samantha still had not returned. Either she knew about the new family member and was pouting or she was off on some adventure of her own. I was almost glad she wasn't there and I tried to pretend the two would never have to have a confrontation, even though I knew that wasn't true.

I put Buck in his cage and spent the afternoon at my computer working on my newsletter. About 4:30 Ira called. He invited me to dinner and I agreed to go. I'm no dummy. I don't pass up free meals from eligible (and nice) bachelors.

Feeling much more confident this time, I only tried on half my wardrobe. After all, it was our second date and I could assume he liked me well enough to try again. I settled on a pair of white pants and a long cardinal red knit top. It made me look pretty spiffy if I did say so myself. Even Buck whistled when I checked on him before I went to answer the door.

Ira hadn't injured himself shaving this time. No band-aids of any kind visible. His thoughtful brown eyes gave me the once over. "Megan. You look great," he said, stepping inside. His tall thin body was clad in gray slacks and a mint green wool sweater. Kinky, copper hair stood out around his eager face.

I was really glad to see him. He didn't make my heart leap the way Lou did, but he did make me feel warm and gushy inside. Warm and gushy isn't half-bad.

"Don't mess with the woman," squawked Buck from the kitchen.

Ira cast a worried look in the bird's direction. "Who's that?"

"A parrot. Veronica May's parrot. She left it for me. I mean someone left her bird for me. I'll explain it all over dinner."

He nodded, took my hand and walked me to his car. "I wouldn't have expected you to have a parrot. A dog or cat maybe, but not a bird."

I let that comment pass because I had a feeling he was going to say something that might make me mad. I had a razor-sharp temper when people pressed the right buttons and I was in no mood to fight. Lou and I had done enough of that. Now I wanted peace and quiet.

We drove to an Italian restaurant north of St. Petersburg Beach, where the tablecloths were red and the smell of garlic and fresh bread hung in the air. Carriage lamps on the stucco walls illuminated paintings of Raphaelesque women picking grapes and carrying casks of wine.

I could tell Ira knew his way around the place because he led me right to a booth in the back. I slid my legs in under the red-checkered tablecloth. A white candle stuck out of an old chianti bottle next to the jar of red pepper. Many candles had burned their way to oblivion in that bottle, leaving layered accumulations of colored wax. Very picturesque.

A waiter in black pants, white shirt and short red jacket appeared from behind a column. He and Ira exchanged pleasantries and the waiter set a velvet-tasseled menu in front of each of us before he left. There were only two other couples in the place and I thought it might be because the food wasn't good. I was wrong. The food was fantastic.

Ira ordered cold antipasto and we ate our way through that, dipping our bread in the tangy oil and vinegar and sipping wine with peaches in it. He told me about his daughter, Ruthie. "She's eight going on forty," he raised an eyebrow, then smiled, "but she's a good kid. Thinks she has to take care of me since the divorce."

Ruthie sounded like my kind of person, a creative female who didn't hesitate to question adult authority and stick her nose in where it didn't belong. Sort of like me. "I'd like to meet her," I said between sips of wine.

"And she you. She's already pumped me for information, asking a million questions---what do you look like, what kind of work do you do. I think she's probably running a credit check on you at this very moment."

"Sounds like my father when I first started to date. I guess she's having a little trouble with your dating."

"That's an understatement. She even told me what time I had to be home. Talk about role reversal."

"At least she cares. Sounds like a great kid."

By the time the waiter cleared our plates away, I was feeling pretty mellow and I told him a few things about Lou. Not much and certainly not that I still had the hots for him.

The waiter came back and set the food we'd ordered down. I made a pig of myself, eating up half the platter of hot and sweet peppers, potatoes and chicken, leaving the veal chops and sausage to Ira.

I hadn't eaten better since I left New York and the Italian Village around Mulberry Street. When we were done, we sipped expresso and anisette. Ira was sensitive and didn't push me about Buck. After my second anisette, I volunteered the information.

He gave me a doubtful look. "And this woman, Audrey, really thinks the parrot lady is still alive?"

"That's right. At least that's what she claims, but then maybe she's involved with Veronica's death. To tell you the truth, 'The Rockford Files' never had a case like this, so I'm a bit stumped." He laughed when I told him that was one of my primary sources of detective information, but it wasn't a derisive laugh like Lou's. I appreciated Ira for that.

When a three-piece band started up in the corner he touched my hand and motioned toward the dance floor. I hadn't danced in years and it felt strange to be out there in Ira's arms. He was a good dancer and the music was soft and gentle. The lyrics were about being in love and it swept me back in time to my high school days when things were simple and uncomplicated. He smelled of that musk aftershave and I snuggled against him, humming to the music.

We danced a whole set, then left and took a long walk on he beach. He kissed me softly on the lips when he dropped me off and I wondered if things would be simple and uncomplicated with Ira.

CHAPTER 23

I unlocked the door and was about to start inside when Samantha skittered through my legs. It was at that very instant that I remembered Buck. "Stop! Don't go in there!" I screamed, as if the cat was going to obey.

Ira's voice shouted from his car. "You okay?" His footsteps pounded across the gravel and up the walk as I burst in the house and rushed into the kitchen. Samantha was already up the refrigerator clawing at the cage.

I grabbed her by the nape of her neck and pried her off. "Don't hurt the birdie, be careful of the birdie," screamed Buck," trying to hide under his tray of water.

"What the---" Ira came running around the corner, charging like a pit bull. He grabbed the cat out of my hands and ran toward the living room.

"Lock her outside," I shouted at him. A few foot scruffs and flying paws later I heard a door slam.

"She's locked out," he said. His face had drained of color, but his kinky red hair was perfectly in place. Guess that's the advantage of thick hair. By that time mine was straggling across my face and my red knit top had scratch marks in it.

"Good." I looked back at Buck. "It's okay, Buck. Bad old Samantha is all gone."

"Take care of the birdie, take care of the bird," he mumbled in a nearly inaudible old man's voice.

The phone must have rung then, but I wasn't paying much attention. Buck whipped his wings up and down like an enraged ostrich and made strangling noises as if someone was throttling him.

I was distracted, but not enough to miss Ira say, "Yes, she's here I'll get her for you." I turned and took the receiver from his hand. "It's some guy," he said, trying to look unconcerned, but not being able to stop the slight band of pale pink concern tightening his cheeks and chin.

No matter how distraught I am, I never mistake Lou's voice. This time it was angry and the scolding tone had become one of panic. "Where have you been, for God's sake?"

"I do have a life after Lou Rasnick, you know."

After a grunt and a long silence, he said, "Who answered the phone?"

122

"Ira Wickstein, a friend of mine."

His voice turned suspicious. "Friend of yours?"

"Part of my new plan to start a social life and not just count on running into old flames occasionally at favorite restaurants."

Another grunt. "Yeah, well, I suppose."

I had him and I was ready to hoist him on his own petard. Using my most sarcastic tone, I said, "Now that you have me on the line, what did you want?" I was enjoying playing with him and was probably getting a little unbearable, but I just couldn't help it.

A sound of disgust, then, "It's about that car license number you left on my machine. I wish you'd quite leaving me weird messages and stop with the investigating---"

"You found out something?"

"I did, but I don't know if I should tell you or ---"

I winked at Ira and put on my haughtiest voice. "Then why'd you call?"

"Well --- there was something of a --- personal nature I ---"

Lou never talked like that. Terms like "personal nature" and "like I say," were the kind of phrases he used to secretly wince at when he heard them from others. From that I deduced something was really wrong with him or he was more jealous than I suspected. Settling on the latter, I drove home my point without the slightest concern for his feelings, a trait that has been known to get me in hot water before. "What did you find out about the license plate?"

He answered with only the slightest hesitation. "That the car is co-owned by a Mary and Dennis Dwyer."

"Aha!" I shook a fist in the air as if I had single-handedly stopped all offshore drilling for oil along both coasts.

"Aha?"

"I knew those two were trouble the first time I laid eyes on them, I ---"

"Don't get too cocky. There may be more to this than you think. I don't want you going off ---"

"Don't worry, I wouldn't think of doing any more investigating. At least not tonight. I still have a brandy or two to drink." It was mean and it was petty, but it felt so good coming out. I said goodnight and hung up and didn't give Lou a second thought.

But even after two brandies and Ira's doting attention, I still couldn't forget about Dennis and Mary Dwyer.

Buck had settled down and only soft sounds of ruffling feathers and clicking mandibles emanated from his cage. I had the slightest fear that it was all a ruse. Dare I leave him there with Samantha's return a real possibility?

Ira kissed me with more than a little fervor at the door, but my mind was focused on the Dwyers. The sound of his car zooming down the avenue still hung in the humid evening air as I ran toward my Toyota and headed for Veronica's house. Maybe Samantha wouldn't come home at all that evening, or hopefully, at least not until I returned home.

Veronica's house was quiet. Not a single light flickered inside. I pulled into the driveway, my wheels making a shussing sound as they caught the edge of her rock-lined drive. A shiny FOR SALE sign gleamed back at me from its new found home on the singed lawn. Grabbing my flashlight from the floor behind me, I rushed to the front door and peered in the window. No more calico-covered, frayed furniture. No more scuffed coffee table. No more anything. The place had been swept clean of any remembrances of the Dwyer crew. I tried the door. No give. A lock box dangled from the knob. No doubt Mary and Dennis had moved and left the place for the realtor to sell. I copied down the name and phone number from the FOR SALE sign just in case someone there might be able to tell me something.

I gazed over at Audrey Lang's house. A light burned in the kitchen, but otherwise her house was dark, too. I trotted across the lawn and rang her bell. After four rings and five knocks I gave up and went back to my car. Had Audrey gone with them? Was she really in on the whole thing? I shuddered to think how friendly we'd been, sipping tea in her parlor. Gullible is as gullible does.

When I got back home I placed a call to Marian Dowlings' Professional Realty Company. A female voice with a nasal twang told me, "There is no one in the office at the moment. Would you care to leave a message?"

I thought of a few choice words I'd like to say to someone, but instead I replied, "Ask Ms. Dowling to call me when she gets in tomorrow." I left my name and phone number and hung up. Just for the heck of it, I looked up Dennis Dwyer's phone number and dialed it. A recording told me in a tinny voice that "that number has been disconnected."

Sighing, I covered Buck's cage with a towel. My parents had had a slew of parakeets and I'd watched my mother do that every night of my childhood. The parrot dozed on, but I required two strong cups of Sleepy time Tea before I could even get my eyes to shut. It was going to be a busy day tomorrow and I needed my wits about me, but my mind didn't seem to want to slow down. I tried a little self-hypnosis and it worked. Without at least seven hours of sleep, I'm a zombie.

When the sun woke me in the morning I rolled out of bed and tramped into the kitchen for a drink of water. Samantha eyed me from her perch on the windowsill in the

Florida room. Her eyes seemed to ask me, *Just what do you think you're doing bringing a bird into the house*, but she made no move to follow me into the kitchen.

For a second I had the distinct fear Samantha had swallowed Buck and left only a few feathers in the bottom of the cage. When I got up the courage to take off the towel, Buck's clear eyes stare back at me. "Give the bird a drink, will you?" he said in a southern drawl.

I heaved a sigh of relief and filled his water dish. Then I cut up a Granny Smith apple and gave him a few pieces, munching on the rest myself. Had the cat and parrot made some kind of truce while I slept? I shook my head in disbelief, but that looked exactly like what had happened. Maybe non-humans really are smarter than what we give them credit for.

A shower, some oatmeal and a cup of tea later and I was ready to face the world again. I glanced at the morning paper and read it was going to be near ninety that day. I pulled on a white cotton sundress and a pair of well-worn white sandals. One should at least be comfortable at work.

On the off-chance it might be there, I looked up Edward May's number in the phone book. It was listed to a residence on Fourth Avenue North in Saint Petersburg. I couldn't believe my good fortune. I checked to make sure Buck had enough seed and made a mental note to purchase some before returning.

He gave me a look only a bird who is about to get the best of you can give. "Take the birdie with you. The birdie can help." His voice was half-Audrey Lang, half-Veronica May. I pretended to ignore him and rounded the corner toward the front door. "You'll be sorry, Pilgrim," he called out in a very good imitation of John Wayne.

I giggled. It felt so good to laugh a little that I went back and opened his cage. He flew onto my finger, then stepped up on my shoulder. "You won't regret this," he mumbled.

I headed toward the door. "I'd better not." Ignoring Samantha's disapproving look, I went out the front door, locking it behind me. At least the bird gave me a laugh or two. Try to get any humor out of a snooty cat.

It felt like my lucky day. Even the bridge to Pasadena was down. How I hated getting caught waiting for some tourist in a yacht to cross under while dozens of us poorer car owners sweltered above. Only a few curious drivers craned their necks to see the bird on my shoulder. Buck was so silent on the ride I nearly forgot he was there.

Traffic was slight and I made good time to Fourth Avenue North. Edward May resided in a newly painted apartment complex that had seen better days. The shocking pink paint barely covered the eroding plaster beneath it. Metal signs screwed into strategic places on crimson columns under the steps of the two-story building announced: Private. No Trespassing. No Soliciting. No sitting on Balconies. No Loitering. No Drugs. No Prostitution. New Owners Will Prosecute.

Even in the bright sunlight, all the porch lights were on, as if to ward off the evil forces the management believed lurked out on the street. There weren't any cars parked in the newly-asphalted parking lot either and most of the apartments looked empty. I walked up the creaky steps to 2D and knocked. No answer.

I heard the laughter of youthful voices and turned to see school children playing tag on their way home, backpacks of books swinging from their shoulders. I turned around and tried the door. It opened with a slight click and I jumped back, startled. Buck ruffled his feathers and clicked his mandibles. The smell of old clothes, sweat and cigarette smoke hit me like the slap of an angry parent. I wondered if some violence had recently taken place on the premises.

"Mr. May?" I could hear the schoolgirl in my voice. "Mr. May?" I said again, trying to reassure myself with my own voice. Clothes lay in disorderly piles on the filthy plaid rug in the living room. Stacks of dirty dishes stood in the sink in the corner kitchenette and a bucket of unfinished Chicken Delight sat at the table as if waiting for its owner to return. Either Edward May had left in a hurry or the chicken had been more disgustingly greasy that I remembered. "Don't cook tonight," sang Buck.

"Shush," I said, hoping he would.

I stepped inside, feeling my heart thud in my chest. What if Veronica's ex-husband was there? What if he came running at me with a knife in his hand. Or a gun? What protection did I have except years of Kung Fu and Jui-Jitsu? I talked my heartbeat down until it only boomed softly and didn't feel as if it might poke its way out of my chest.

An old racing form lay across the pea-green sofa next to a pile of even older newspapers. Several menial-type jobs in the classified section on one yellowing page were circled. An angry hand had scribbled obscenities next to the entries as if the writer had tried to find work and had been rejected.

No more than five steps away a closed door at the end of the hall beckoned. Was Edward May in there? Dead? Dismembered? Hanging from an exposed light fixture?

Amazing what horrors the mind can conjure up when it's frightened. My heart speeded again and I had the distinct feeling I might lose consciousness. Buck's claws dug into my shoulder. That was when I wished I hadn't shushed him. Some sound from another source besides my terror-filled body would have been reassuring.

I forced the air out of my lungs and lunged for the door. It fell open and I almost tripped into the shower. It was an ugly thing with a ripped plastic curtain. Layers of body hair and skin crusted on the cemented floor. The man was not a good housekeeper.

Except for an empty tube of toothpaste, a graying towel, a stub of Life Buoy soap and fingernail clippings, there wasn't much else to see. "Look around," said Buck bolting to alert posture and pointing his head toward the bedroom.

"Good idea." It wasn't until the words were out of my mouth that I realized Buck was probably just spouting some words he heard someone say and not really making a suggestion. Yet when I squinted into his eyes, he still had the look of confidence about him as if he knew exactly what he was saying. Unnerving.

I veered down the wavy green linoleum toward the room in the middle of the hall. The door was open and a mildewy smell caught me. Taking a deep breath, I stepped into the room. Gold drapes hung unevenly from the high windows and a filthy brown spread with black tassels bunched up on the bed. Cigarette butts and candy bar wrappers crammed the fake gold wastebasket in the corner.

An open bird cage dangled from the floor lamp by the closet. Buck flew from my shoulder to the metal container for a closer look. "Feed the bird," he said in a high-pitched voice that sounded angry. The seed tray was half-full of a disgusting mixture of dried seed, bird droppings and feathers. Buck turned away in disgust and so did I.

"Is that your cage, Buck?" In answer, he shook his head (or maybe he was just rearranging his feathers.) "But did you ever live in it?" Buck's eyelids flickered shut and he turned away, refusing to answer. It was as close as a bird could get to taking the Fifth.

I turned and nearly jammed my thigh into a heavy maple dresser. Although scratched and carved with hearts and initials, it was the nicest piece of furniture in the apartment and looked quite out of place. Resting in a undisturbed layer of dust was a silver-framed picture of two young people. The woman had the unmistakable smile of Veronica May.

The man must have been Edward May. He looked angry and hurt as if someone had just scolded him and he didn't like it. Veronica wore a white dress and veil and a shiny gold ring on her third finger. Head inclined toward Edward, Veronica's violet eyes shone with a look that reminded me of adoration, but could have been lust. His tall, stocky body encased in a too-tight dark suit, Edward's eyes glazed straight at the camera, ignoring his bride.

I didn't know why, but looking at that picture made me feel good. Maybe it was because I had seen Veronica again and I really missed her. Or maybe I was going off the deep end. Either one held distinct possibilities.

I grabbed for the drawer handle and jerked it open. A few balls of dust were keeping company with a stack of old envelopes. I picked up the pile and shuffled through them. They were addressed to Ed May and carried a downtown hotel address. My eyes traveled to the upper left hand corner. Two were from Joe May, one of his sons. The address was reminiscent of the state penal institution. The words were barely legible, but smacked of self-importance and braggadocio.

Two of the letters were from Veronica. They were peaceful, but firm. No, she didn't want to take him back. No, there was no way he could live with her and get a job to pay his share of room and board. The last letter, with a recent stamped date, was from Mary.

Dear Dad,

Dennis and I are selling Mom's house in the Old
Northeast. After the fire, it needed too much repair
and we just weren't up to it. We have signed a contract
for a new house on Shore Acres. As soon as the sale
is final, we'll let you know. Maybe we can all have a big
celebration then.

Take care of yourself.

Your Daughter,

Mary

As I finished reading the letter, I remembered something important. How could Mary and Dennis sell the house when Veronica had willed it to Audrey? Could Veronica still be alive or had they killed her after extracting a new will?

Questions were popping into my brain. Questions I had no answers to. I wanted Lou and I needed his help, but I was too proud to ask. I wanted to go back to my car and drive away. Maybe that would uncloud the fuzz that had collected in my mind.

I folded up the letters and replaced them in their envelopes. For all I knew Ed might come back to claim them. Starting toward the door, I heard the sound of feet pounding up the steps in our direction. "Time to go," squawked Buck, punctuating his words with fervent shakes of his head.

"That's for sure." I raced across the rug, nearly tripping on its rumpled edge.

A key grated in the lock. My heart started doing strange things, making the entire percussion section of the Boston Symphony Orchestra seem soundless by comparison. "You in there, Dad?"

The man's voice was crude and had a hint of evil to back it up. My eyes scanned the apartment for another exit. Besides the window and a ten foot drop to the asphalt, there was none. I reversed direction and pedaled toward the other wall. A yank or two and I discovered what I should have already known: the windows were painted shut.

The door flew open and an Edward May replica burst in. "What the hell ---" He was big and he was ugly and his huge torso cast a menacing shadow across the doorway. He may even have had a weapon in his hand. I wasn't sure and I didn't wait to find out. A shriek of a banshee and Buck flew at him, ripping at his nose and jerking on his ear before swooping out the door behind me.

128

Wild howls of pain and anger echoed behind us. Angry heels pounded down the steps. His voice forced my feet to run faster. "Stop!" he shouted, "or I'll call the cops!"

I doubted that. Besides, I wasn't stopping for anything or anyone. I dove into my car and started it up. Buck hopped in the window and took up his seat beside me, casting fearsome glances toward the steps. A massive hand reached inside my window just as I snapped the door locked. "Who do you think you---" The rest was lost as I roared forward, yanking his heavy body alongside the car. "Stop!" He shouted and tried to reverse the roll of the car, but even his strength couldn't do the job.

I jammed the stick into reverse and squealed back. The crunch of bone against the pavement told me we had lost our unwanted visitor. The nurse in me wanted to stop and see that he was all right, but the survivalist in me kept going. I thought we had gotten clean away until I spotted a hopped up red VW following us down First Avenue North. He wove in and out of lanes, beeping and screeching, trying to catch up. The VW followed us south on Pasadena until the tourist with Michigan plates cut him off, leaving him steaming, swearing and shaking an angry fist at a red light.

I turned right on Gulf and drove as fast as I could toward Madeira Beach, just in case he was following. He wasn't. I pulled into Tony's Ristorante and waited for my breath to slow. That was more excitement than I'd had for awhile and my body was showing the effects.

When my breathing slowed, I turned toward the bird. "How about some lunch, Buck?" The parrot glared up at me as if he was a driving instructor and I was the proverbial bad lady driver. "Come on, lighten up. We got away, didn't we? Thanks to you, by the way. You're a good bird, you know that? A damn good bird."

Buck nodded and continued preening his feathers. I guess parrots have their aloof moments, too. I got out of the car and got a cold antipasto to go and lots of garlic bread. Buck and I had a feast in my car, then rinsed our feet in the Gulf of Mexico while I tried to think what I should do next.

We got back into the car and I started driving south, stopping at Captain Ahab's Aviary for some more bird seed. I wondered if I should have brought Buck inside. Maybe some of the residents in the cages were his relatives. When a cockatoo nearly bit me, I made a swift retreat to the car and forgot all thoughts of bird reunions.

It came to me then that my next move ought to be to find out about Dennis and Mary Dwyer's new house. I found a phone booth and called Marian Dowling, but she wasn't in. Exactly how I was going to track down the Dwyers was a bit fuzzy in my mind, but I thought Paula, my realtor friend, might have some ideas.

CHAPTER 24

I stopped at home and gave Paula a call. Having no idea how she'd been since the funeral made me feel a little guilty, but I pushed that away and waited for her to answer. Unfortunately for me, Rachel picked up the phone. She was still giving me the holier-than-thou treatment. "Paula is taking a nap and can't be disturbed."

"All right. Tell her I'll stop by in a couple of hours." I hung up before Rachel could argue with me. I took Buck home and put him in his cage. Samantha barely lifted her head to look at us. She had her eyes peeled on a gray heron who had landed on my patio. "Fat chance, my little feline," I mumbled, but the cat ignored my words and stared outside, body taut and ready.

Buck started to snooze as soon as I put him on his perch. "Been a busy day, hasn't it, pardner?" I closed the cage door and went into my bedroom. I had left in a hurry, forgetting to hang up my robe. Being a stickler for neatness, I put that away first, then stripped and climbed into a pair of shorts for my walk.

There is something about walking outside that helps me think. Maybe its the fresh salt air or the sandpipers skittering along the beach so purposefully or maybe its just that my mind wanders and makes connections I don't allow it to make when I'm engaged in other tasks.

I didn't even have a chance to cast a regretful eye at the hotels and condos that were crowding onto the beach because I didn't notice them. My mind was busy trying to decide who was the most likely suspect in Veronica's murder---if there was a murder. No. There must have been a murder. Lou would certainly have told me if the body hadn't checked out. Or would he?

My feet ground a little harder into the soft sand and I passed a bevy of seagulls (or is it a flock?) all nestled into their feathers, beaks pointed into the wind. One or two squawked at me, most just stepped out of my way or sat still, hoping I wouldn't come any closer. I continued on, my mind focused on suspects. Right now, Edward May's son figured pretty high on my list, but I had no evidence at all.

Before I knew it I was standing by the volleyball net in front of the Don CeSar and I knew I had better scurry back home, shower and get over to Paula's before it was too late to check out anything about the Dwyer's new home.

Buck didn't let out a peep on my return and Samantha had taken the back exit out, probably checking out that gray heron. I put on a pair of white cotton twill deck pants and a tee-shirt and pulled a khaki blazer over it. One does not go to county buildings in tee-shirts.

Rounding the corner of Paula's condo, the undeniable odor of fresh baked chocolate chip cookies tipped me off that she was home. I stepped to the window by the kitchen and saw her. Her head was bent over a tray of the delightful things. She was using a spatula to scrape them off onto a strategically-placed piece of waxed paper. Paula is one of the few living souls I know who still uses waxed paper. Maybe that's because she's one of the few people I know who still bakes all her own cookies, spurning the frozen-microwavable goodies in the supermarket.

I thought maybe I had lucked out (or is it in) and Rachel had left the condo or maybe even the state. But no, her hatchet-shaped nose appeared around the corner just before her hand made firm contact with the door knob and held it closed. "Oh, it's you. I thought maybe you'd changed your mind."

"Good afternoon, Rachel." Forced pleasantness sometimes works. "No, I haven't changed my mind. Can I see Paula?"

Long sigh punctuated by raising of the eyebrows. "Yes, she's in. I'll see if she can see you." She let go of the handle and I turned it and pushed inside.

"Is that you, Megan?" Paula's foghorn voice and ample body came closer. She had exchanged her black mourning clothes for a bronze cotton dress that made her cheeks pink. A glint of late afternoon sun made the smudge of flour on her nose look like it belonged there. She pulled me into her arms. "Give me a hug, will you? I could use a good hug." I complied. She pulled me into the kitchen. "Now come on in, you look like you could use a few cookies and a glass of iced tea." I could never fool Paula. Skirting past Rachel I took a seat at the maple table next to the pile of glistening cookies.

Paula's able hands picked up three of the sweet things crammed with more chocolate chips than I would have thought possible and deposited them on a plate she pulled out of the cupboard. Before I had downed one, a tall frosty glass of iced tea with a quarter of a lemon perched on the edge slid next to my hand. I glanced up at Paula gratefully. "You look pretty good. How do you feel after all that's happened?"

"I'm doing all right. Soon I'll send Rachel packing and get back to playing cards with the folks next door and finding out where the best sales are around the Bay."

"Good for you."

She sat down, took one of the cookies and balanced it on the edge of two fingers, looking at it approvingly. "I do bake good cookies, don't ?"

"Best ever."

"If I had it in me I'd open up a little tea room on Gulf Boulevard and put my baking expertise toward financial gain."

"You should. It would be just the thing ---"

"No. Not really. I'm fine. I don't need to forget anything, if that's what you were going to say. Cassie lived her life on the edge and she paid for it. Now it's time to go on. I hope you weren't coming here to tell me more bad news about her." She raised an eyebrow and set the cookie back down on her napkin.

"Not at all. I'm coming to pick your brains about house titles and such. You are my resident real estate expert."

She clasped her hands together as if she might be getting ready to sing a ballad and gazed earnestly at me. I wasn't sure, but I think a glimmer of her old spirit shone in her gray eyes. "Of course, I may be a little rusty, but I was in the Million Dollar Club."

"Then tell me how I would go about finding out where a property is."

"Who owns it?"

"Dennis and Mary Dwyer."

"Good. As long as you know that, you can find out the rest. What you have to do is ---" She turned and squinted at the cuckoo clock on the wall above the stove. "You'd better hurry. I think they close soon."

"Who does?"

"The Federal Building or whatever it's called." She waved her hand and gave me an impatient look as if names were of small consequence in the big game stakes of selling houses. "Anyway, it's off First Avenue North, near Mirror Lake Library. You know where that is, don't you?"

I nodded. Paula knew I frequented every library in and around St. Petersburg, spending many hours in each, either researching articles, devouring popular magazines or browsing through novels. She was one of the few people I had told I was working on a novel. I looked up at her. "Is it by the place where you get marriage licenses?" When I had been more sure of myself with Lou, I had checked out the license bureau, sure we would be married someday.

"Right across the street! Now let me think ---" She tapped an index finger against her lips. You ask someone in information, if you can find a place to park. There is a parking lot, but it's very small and usually is full. You'll probably have to take what you can find on the street ---"

I'll find a place to park. Thanks for the ---"

She went on like a tightly wound clock that had just been waiting to unwind with information. "Once you're parked, go inside and ask someone in the information window. They'll direct you to titles and deeds. When you get to the room, just tell the clerk you only know the names of the people who own the house, but not the address. Everything's computerized now. She should be able to find it." She stopped for breath, but only for a second. "Maybe I should go with you, I always know how to extract the information about these kinds of things ---"

"No, no," I said, standing to leave. I didn't want Paula and maybe even Rachel tramping around with me, increasing suspicion. I wanted to play this low key, like I'd seen Jim Rockford do. Even then I was planning exactly how I would approach the clerk.

"But you haven't finished your iced tea." I grabbed the glass and downed it in one noisy chug-a-lug. "And the cookies. You've only eaten one." I scooped up a bunch and placed the delicacies in the folds of a paper napkin.

"Gotta go, Paula. I'll come back and see you when I have more time." I gave Paula's cheek a brush with my lips, then squeezed past Rachel's belly. She gave me a look that said, *I'm so pleased you didn't stay long.*

"If that doesn't work," Paula shouted from the kitchen, "you can go to the Post Office and pay them $l.00 or so and they'll look up the Dwyer's change of address forms."

"Okay," I shouted back, then slammed out the door. I was back in my car and on the street headed toward downtown in seconds. They weren't going to lock the door on me today. I was determined to get to the Federal Building before it closed.

Paula's razor-sharp mind was getting a little fuzzy. I had crossed Arlington and was almost to Mirror Lake before I realized there was no Federal Building, only a County Building. I turned left heading toward the library when I let out an audible gasp. The most beautiful tree in St Petersburg, a 80-foot, silky-trunked Banyan (whose aerial roots used to dip to the ground and thicken to form innumerable props for the massive top of downy evergreen leaves) had been shorn. No more aerial roots and no more shimmering leaves. It reminded me of a gawky kid who had been caught with head lice.

I wanted to go in and complain and rant and rave to someone about it, but I convinced myself I didn't have the time and besides it wouldn't have done any good anyway. The damage was already done.

I turned my eyes toward the old mint-colored building that housed Mirror Lake Library. Even it had been accosted. Dark green platforms peppered its exterior and a big black and white sign that had been driven into the earth announced the Mirror Lake Public Library Restoration was being completed by C.F. McCoogan, General Contractors. I only hoped they did a better job than whoever had hacked away at the Banyan.

I turned my back and headed toward the County Building. I stayed in the shade under the orchid trees. Their blooms hung down nearly to the ground, keeping me from the heat of the sun. I moved past the memorial garden. I couldn't see much behind the curving cement wall except the upper torsos of two concrete cherubs holding baskets of fruit on their shoulders. Sounds reminiscent of the dentist drill or an angry lawn mower came over the wall at me and I hurried along. Neither of those noises is music to my ears.

I crossed Arlington and walked up to the off-white building with black panels above its high windows. Parking meters edged the street and huge trees provided shade. Some drooping petunias bordered the sidewalk. Metallic letters stood on top of the lower roof: County Building. Above me, thick ropes fell to the ground and two young black men in white uniforms swung from a lift, paint buckets hanging at their sides.

The automatic door slid open as I approached it. The smells of coffee, floor polish and a man's heavy cologne came at me. Legal Notices hung on a cork board on the left wall opposite a silver plaque announcing that this was the County Building. I glanced at the Directory, but it wasn't much help. The Information window was closed and and the office was vacant.

Straight ahead a man in a black uniform and the kind of shiny black shoes you don't have to polish patrolled the hall between the elevators and the food service counter. A badge on his arm read: Sheriff. The only action there for him to watch was a little black girl with braids who was clapping her hands and waiting for her mother to buy her an orange juice.

I turned left, thinking I'd go by the marriage license/passport bureau and ask there. My white sandals clicked along the smooth tile floor, past the pale pink marble walls. The clerk behind the passport counter smiled and directed me to the adjacent room.

There the paneling was fake wood and the rust carpet on the floor industrial grade. Trees and street were visible behind gold curtains and tinted windows. Men in jeans and short-sleeve shirts punched in names and addresses in rapid fashion on computer keyboards. Instructions for use of the microfilm index hung on the wall by the door above a table holding a huge book of public records. Two clerks sat behind imitation wood desks. Both were women, one very thin and black, wearing glasses, the other plump with red hair, pink cheeks and a pale complexion.

"Can I help you?" asked the pink-cheeked one.

I stepped up to her desk. "I hope so. I know the name of the people who own a house, but I need to know exactly where the property is located."

It must have been an odd request, because she pushed back a strand of hennaed hair and contemplated the ceiling for a second. "What exactly are you looking for?"

"The address and description of the property."

She nodded. "Name of owner?"

"Mary and Dennis Dwyer."

Her fingers moved across the board of her computer. She consulted her monitor. "How long ago was the property purchased?"

"I'm not sure. Recently."

"This year?"

"Yes."

I strained to look at the screen when she stood up. "No sense in you not being able to see, too." She walked over to one of the computers by the wall and stood next to a man in Levi's. He was still going through his list of addresses and owners. She punched in the information and the black screen came alive with orange figures. "There it is," I said.

Tucked between Dennis Dunston and Douglas Dwyer I found the house. Name: Dennis Dwyer   O/R: 6274   Page: l5ll   Inst: deed   T/F: T   Descr: 3 Blk 3 Palm Point Sect 5Pl   57/82   Filing Date: ll/l3/90

The clerk returned to her desk and I scribbled the information in my notebook and left. Three Palm Point was on St. Petersburg Beach, not far from where I lived. Now all I had to do was go there and I'd soon find out what I needed to know. That or I'd be in deep trouble just like Veronica.

CHAPTER 25

There was one thing I had to do before I was ready to confront the Dwyers. Samantha and Buck were both waiting for me when I came bursting into my little bungalow. "Well sports fans things are coming along," I said, probably rubbing my hands together like some slick car salesman.

Samantha seemed her usual unconcerned self, but Buck rocked back and forth from foot to foot, then beat his mandibles before exclaiming, "Go get 'em girlie!"

"I will, I will." I opened the refrigerator and grabbed for the peanut butter jar and a loaf of seven-grain bread. If there was to be a confrontation, the least I could do was be well-nourished. My mother taught me that, though you'd never know it from the regime she fed me when I was growing up. Ketchup or Karo syrup sandwiches on Wonder Bread (brown sugar and butter made do if neither of these were available) do not add up to a nutritious meal. But then I guess we were poor. Later on, when we were better off, such questionable nutritional choices were replaced with chocolate cake, brownies, french fries, steak, pot roast and a bevy of fresh pies.

Although my mother was very fond of baking (and God knows she was good at what she loved), it was cholesterol-heaven at our house. Not one to miss a trick, she also subscribed to *Prevention* magazine and sent it to me when I was away at college. Although she never embraced its philosophy, I took its principles to heart and only splurged on baked goods in Paula's company.

I finished the last of the sandwich and washed it down with a large glass of V-8 juice. Then I changed to my confrontation clothes: jeans, tee-shirt and sneakers. Who knows what physical dangers I might encounter? I did a few arm jabs and leg kicks to warm up.

As I pondered that thought, the phone rang and took me away from the ideas too terrible to mention. "Hello, this is Ruthie Wickstein," said the businesslike, but still little-girl voice on the other end.

"Ira's daughter?"

"Correct. I'm calling to invite you to lunch tomorrow."

I was speechless. I'd had lunches with men and with friends, but never with the daughter of a man I was seeing. "Lunch?" I think I mumbled.

"Yes. The meal between breakfast and dinner."

Confirmed. She was a smart-ass just like you-know-who. "I'm not sure about that, kiddo. I'm in the middle of an investigation and---"

"Ira told me about it. Something to do with a double murder."

Ira? She called her father, Ira? Well, why not? She seemed precocious as hell. I held back a giggle. "Yeah, that's it, a double murder. I'm just about to tie the whole thing together."

"You mean you're going to arrest the gang?"

"No, sweetie. I'm not a policewoman. I'm just going over to do a little spying." Although I'm not usually a blabber mouth, I couldn't resist trying to impress the kid. "You know it's all tied to the Single Hearts Club."

"The Single Hearts Club?"

"It's a place you never want to go. Ask your father about it."

"Gee, then you really are a detective."

"Umm hmm," I mumbled, realizing I was bragging a bit too much. "So now I gotta go."

"Yeah, I understand. But about lunch."

"I may be in the thick of things by lunch tomorrow."

"But you have to eat."

I giggled. Who was the kid and who was the adult here? "You're right. Why don't you come over here tomorrow about noon and we'll see what we can find in the refrigerator."

"I've already made reservations at the Ship's Captain. Will one o'clock be all right with you?"

"Fine. Shall we dress?"

"I usually wear a dress, but the maitre d' will seat you in slacks if you're with me."

"How about I meet you in the lobby?" We agreed and hung up. I could hardly wait to see the body that went with that overly-sophisticated voice. I could feel an attack of trying-on-all-my-worldly-belongings-to-find-the-right-outfit coming on. Maybe I was losing it, wanting to look my best for a little kid.

I had barely replaced the receiver and the phone rang again. This time Lou's panicked voice burst in on me. "I want to talk to you."

"I want to talk to you, too."

He grunted, then, "Okay, you first." It was uncharacteristic of him to let me go first at anything, but then he did have his sensitive side.

"I think I've figured out this double-murder-Veronica-May-Cassie-Sanders thing."

Long pause, then a taunting laugh. "Come on, Megan. The police don't even have all the pieces yet."

"Then they do have some."

Another pause. "Well sure. I told you they had the Single Hearts Club under surveillance."

"No, you didn't, but since they have, maybe you'd let me see the reports."

"Of course you can't see the reports. Even I can't see them."

I'll bet your friends at the station let you read the blanked out pages."

"Not this time."

I could see I was getting nowhere. Time to try a little bombast. "I know Rick Stetson and Gemma Fuller are in on something with Dennis and Mary Dwyer. And they've been having their meetings at the Single Hearts Club."

A wolf whistle. "You really did find out something. How did you do that?"

"I'm not stupid, you know."

"Course you're not stupid, it's just that you don't exactly have the skills of a trained detective."

"I'm learning," I muttered.

"What?"

"Nothing. Maybe you could meet me at the Dwyers' and we could---"

"Oh, no. You're not going over there. I need you over here."

"You need---you need me over there?" All thoughts of Three Palms Point flew right out of my head.

"Yes, I need you. I've got to see you. Can you come over right now?"

Do birds fly, is the air humid in Florida, does it always rain right after I wash my car? He needed me. I started to feel all warm and gushy. Those were the words I'd been waiting to hear from him for so long. Part of me wanted to drive over there at breakneck speed and tear his clothes off. While the other part of me, the more paranoid part, was cautiously advising me what happened the last time we tried to work things out.

I sputtered in the phone. "What's happened?" A true paranoiac always assumes there is some other message lingering a few levels below the verbalized one.

"Nothing."

I could tell it was something, but maybe I just didn't care. "Isn't Susan there?"

"No, she's working and I need to talk to you."

I swallowed and tried to act natural, but how could I when my heart was roller coasting? "Can't you just tell me on the phone?"

"No, I need to see you."

He had me. All it took was a little coaxing and old pushover was his. "Okay, I'll be there as soon as I can." I hung up before I started heavy breathing into the phone.

First I had to find something to wear. Something that would be just perfect. I ran into my bedroom, threw open my closet and started flinging pants and tops and dresses on my bed. At the same time, I was wiggling out of my jeans and hoping to God he meant what I thought he meant.

Within minutes I pulled up in the Rasnick's driveway, having changed to a slinky black top, tight white pants and a pair of high heels I reserved for very special occasions. I'd even sprayed some White Shoulders on and touched up the pores on my face with makeup. It's amazing to what lengths we femme fatales will go. And how soon we'll forget the task at hand whenever love rears its head.

I took one last look in the mirror on my visor before I climbed out and sashayed toward the house, swaying my hips more than usual in case he was watching out the window. A couple of soggy newspapers littered the welcome mat in front of Lou's white stucco one-story home. Letters and junk pieces crammed the mailbox as if no one had been paying much attention lately. Even with Lou's car standing in the drive, I began to wonder if Lou was there.

My heels tapped up the sand-gritted walk, my heart thudding in heady anticipation. I nearly jumped into his arms when he opened the door, but I restrained myself. He had just showered and his hair was flattened down on his head, giving him a little boy look. The kind it's hard to ignore. I followed him inside, wondering if I was going to be able to stand the excitement of the moment without having a heart attack or wetting my pants.

There was a strange smell in the house. Something like stale air and depression. Susan's usual good housekeeping skills had gone by the wayside. Newspapers cluttered the couch and floor and some stale doughnuts and a cup of cold coffee with a slag of gone-bad milk sat on the table. Some dirty clothes lay misshapen and discarded in one corner. I wondered if Sue lay sick in the next room.

But even that thought didn't stop me. Lou wore a red velour top above his tight jeans with the washing direction tag sticking up the back of his neck. When he stopped in front of the couch, I couldn't resist putting the tag back in place. Besides, it gave me an excuse to touch him. The muscles in his upper back were taut and full of tension. Dare I hope it was sexual tension?

"Megan. You don't know how much it means to me to have you here." He turned, took my hands in his and pulled me onto the couch. The newspapers crunched beneath us, but neither of us seemed to mind. My heart trip hammered and I could almost feel the softness of his lips on mine.

His mouth came within inches of my face before I pulled back. "This isn't right. What about Susan?" What a time to have an attack of conscience.

He bolted back on the couch as if lightning had just struck him. His voice was accusing. "What about Susan?"

"But --- but you're married ---"

"Yes, we're married, but that doesn't seem to mean much right now."

Had he fallen out of love with his gorgeous wife and in love with me? How could that have happened without me even knowing about it? Strange things have happened, but even I found that hard to believe. I stared at him. "What do you mean?"

He put a hand on my cheek and pulled my face closer to his. I looked into his eyes, waiting for the inevitable. Just before he kissed me, his handsome face contorted as if he was either going to scream in agony or burst into tears. Was this the effect I was supposed to be having on him? Even I knew it wasn't a look of love. "Lou, what's---what's the matter? Even though I asked, I wasn't sure I wanted to know.

He blurted it out with a sigh of relief. "Susan's having an affair and I don't know what to do about it." His body started shaking and his head dropped in a dismal heap onto his chest. I wanted to put my arms around him and comfort him, but I was afraid to.

Instead, I leaned back and played with the strap of my shoe, hoping my voice didn't come out in joyful squeaks. "Susan? Nah. She loves you." I was trying my best to play fair and I hoped I was scoring points with the someone who keep track of those things.

His head jerked to attention and he waved an arm in the air. "That's what I thought, but there's no doubt about it. Someone saw them together in the linen room on the fourth floor of the hospital."

I tried to hold down my glee and be diplomatic. "It could have been anyone."

He jumped to his feet and started pacing, kicking papers out of his way as he moved. They flew in the air with loud whopping noises, punctuating his words. "You mean nurses and doctors are doing it all over the hospital?"

140

Fear had taken over inside me by then and I was completely unsure of what he might do next. "I didn't mean that exactly ---"

What did I mean?

There were certainly affairs between doctors and nurses, but that wasn't my point. "What I meant was, maybe they mistook someone else for Susan."

He stopped pacing and glared at me. "Susan has a very distinctive look."

"Sure, but in a white uniform in the dim light of a linen room ---"

He scratched at his chin. "No, this person swore it was Susan. Besides she's as good as admitted it."

"She has?"

"She says the romance has gone out of our relationship. She says she never sees me anymore what, with her schedule and mine."

I shook my head. How familiar it all sounded. It had only been a year or so ago when Lou had been lamenting the same thing about us. Things certainly do come around. I had lost all surges of lust by then and was mentally putting on my counselor hat. "Have you talked to Susan about how you feel?"

He gave me an incredulous look. "She knows how I feel." His eyes were almost belligerent.

"Women have to be told these things. So do men."

He plunked down next to me and stared at the peach wall in front of him. "Maybe you're right, but it's too late anyway." With barely a pause, his arms reached for me.

I could feel myself slipping. "Lou. You don't want to do this, Lou," I muttered into the sleeve of his shirt. His arms tightened around me and I felt his energy surging. "Let's talk about this some more." My last words were lost in a very wet kiss.

God, how long it had been since I felt his lips and tasted them. But I hadn't forgotten that slightly metallic taste nor the tightness of the embrace he held me in. I stopped trying to talk then and just kissed him back. His hands were already massaging my back and pulling my body next to his.

After no more than five minutes I used supreme restraint and yanked away. "No, Lou. Not like this. Not when you're on the rebound." His arms fell away. "I've tried that and it doesn't work. If we're going to make love it's going to be when you and Susan have officially called it quits. Not like this. Not when you're hurting so bad."

He looked at me and then I knew for sure he was going to cry. My arms cradled him to my breast. His body shook against mine like a child's. Then I really wanted to make love to him, but it was too late.

He knew it and I knew it.

I got up and poured us each a stiff drink of scotch. We sat staring at the wall and drinking our drinks. Sometime later, I left. Creeping out of his apartment, I felt his sad dog eyes following me. It was one of the hardest things I've ever done.

CHAPTER 26

I went back home and threw the high heels in the closet as if I was trying to hit a bull's eye. The tight pants and slinky top followed. Those I hung on a hanger, but not very neatly.

Pulling on jeans, sneakers and tee-shirt, I headed for the kitchen. Boy was I depressed. Buck was awake, but I put the towel over his cage. That started him talking. "Take the bird," he shouted, then squawked twice.

"I am not taking you this time, Buck."

His John Wayne voice came on. "If you know what's good for you, you'll take the bird."

I pulled back the towel to get a good look at him. "You threatening me?" We stared at each other, neither flinching nor giving ground. Pushover that I am, I broke the silence first. "All right, all right, you can come. After all, you did save my life last time."

He nodded, whistled and rattled the cage door. I threw off the rest of the towel and let him out. He was on my shoulder in a second, muzzling into my neck thankfully. "Sure, now you're going to be nice," I mumbled, walking toward my car.

He didn't say a word on the ride. Three Palms Point is a narrow road that branches out so that most of the homes look out over Boca Ciega Bay. The deeper the water, the higher the price. By my calculations second Palm Point was pretty ritzy and way above my financial grasp. I wondered how Mary and Dennis had spurted up into the high paying district.

The porch light at 4l6 was on. How nice of them to light my way. I turned my Toyota around at the end of the street, doubled back and parked a block down in a lot of a small condominium, using a spot reserved for guests. I figured if I wasn't a guest in the neighborhood, no one was.

I walked the distance to 4l6 on the side opposite the streetlights. I didn't want anyone to see me coming. There were other walkers, snowbirds who loved to stroll the streets at night after their dinners, checking out any FOR SALE signs on houses and dreaming of living in St. Petersburg Beach. In their state of rapture, they hardly noticed a middle-aged woman with a parrot on her shoulder who was singing "Rock Around the Clock" in an off-key.

The moon glinted off the white sparkle paint on 4l6, giving it a nightclub effect. Someone's sprinkler system came on with a hiss and a spurt, making me jump in my tracks. "Steady, Megan," I whispered. Buck's claws dug into my shoulder, reminding me to shut up and pay attention. Very soon I was going to have to look confident and charge in under worse conditions than a little spray of water.

Twin palms wafted above me in the evening breeze and the smell of orange blossom and someone's ham roast came down the street. I walked up the drive to 4I6, my shoes making crunchy noises on the river rocks. I jumped off them as if they'd given me a hot foot. Buck gave me a disgusted glance which I pretended not to notice. Instead, I hurried up the walk being careful not to disturb even one of the stones lining it. Those little buggers made enough noise when stepped on to alert even the deaf.

A light burned in the living room. It was one of those glass affairs with seashells filling the bottom. I had one just like it. Probably every one in St. Petersburg Beach did. I squinted in the window. The polished terrazzo floors gleamed in lamplight. Wicker and rattan couches and chairs with pastel pillows clustered around the large room. It was not the Dwyer's taste. They must have bought the house furnished.

I tried the door. Locked. I took a few steps east and peeked in the kitchen window. Buck moved about nervously on my shoulder. "Something wrong?" I whispered. He nodded as if he had ESP, which I was beginning to think he did. Even so, I wasn't stupid enough to ask him anymore questions. Not right then anyway.

I looked back into the room. The light above the stove was on. This was more like it. Dirty dishes piled high in the sink and buckets of take-out chicken and greasy containers for french fries stood around on the counter.

A barely audible shuffling noise caught my attention. It seemed to be coming from the room next to the refrigerator. Putting my ear to the open window I listened. The sound of tiny feet pushing against metal. "Anybody home?" Moans started, like someone trying desperately to speak through a muzzle. I hesitated. Who was in there? A crazed Itty or Bitty? A mad dog frothing at the mouth? Worse? Buck gave a wolf whistle and snapped me out of my fantasies.

"Anybody in there?" I asked, sounding more frightened than interested. More shuffles and moans. There was someone in that room and if one thing propelled me past fear it was nosiness.

My hands grabbed for the window, pulling at the edges. If they were anything like mine, they would slide right off their holders. Buck grabbed one edge and I grabbed the other. We pulled until the bottom panel released into my hands. I measured the space. Could we fit through it? We'd have to.

My fingers fiddled with the screen until it popped out, slapping me in the face with a whack. Jim Rockford never had these kinds of problems when breaking and entering.

I set the screen down on the sidewalk, grabbed the ledge and walked my sneakered feet up the side of the wall. Buck nipped me on the neck, probably trying to tell me he wasn't going in through any kitchen window. For the second time in two minutes, I ignored him. Inching in on my abdomen, I could only hope Buck's head wouldn't bang against the upper window. One supreme effort and we fell in the sink.

144

Good thing I had on dirty clothes. Buck slipped into a pan of sudsy water and emerged soggy and squawking. "Stop complaining," I whispered. "At least we're in." He flicked his wings, sending a splash of cold, greasy water into my face. Don't expect thank-you from a parrot.

I slid my body out of the sink and down onto the floor. Buck flew to the suspicious room tapping on it with his beak. I followed.

Taking a deep breath and holding it, I opened the door, eyes squeezed tight against what I might see. The moans and shuffles grew louder. I opened one eye and took a look. Even with her white curly wig askew, splotches of gravy on her mint green dress and dirt on her white crocheted gloves, I'd know the parrot lady anywhere. Even if she was lying in a bathtub. "Veronica! What happened?"

Red-faced, with eyes huge with frustration, she shook her body frantically. Buck hovered in front of her, peering into her face. Or maybe he was trying to give me a subtle clue. It finally dawned on me Veronica couldn't answer with a gag in her mouth, so I untied the binding.

After a few gurgling noises, her voice came out through a dry mouth. "Thank God, I thought no one would ever hear me." She looked up at me with a dazed look. "Is that you, Megan?"

"It's me. And Buck." The parrot flew onto her shoulder and started nipping at the ropes holding her down. Together we got her out of some of her bindings and I helped her stand.

Her legs buckled then, but I managed to yank her out before both of us slid to the floor. Buck flew to the counter, not wanting to engage in childish things. Veronica and I sat there looking at each other like two kindergartners in the sand pile. Finally she said, "I've been in the tub all day."

"You have? You must feel awful."

"I ache all over." She thought a moment, then said, "Not that I don't always ache all over, what with my rheumatism and arthritis, but this is the pits." I nodded and started to massage her ankles. She looked up at me with hurt and anger in her violet eyes. "Can you imagine your own flesh and blood treating you that way?"

"Mary?"

"You bet. And that rat of a man she calls husband." She shook her head as if even she couldn't believe it. She glanced down at my hands on her ankles. "Oh, that feels so nice. You have magic hands, my dear, magic hands."

"So I've been told." I rubbed her ankles some more. "Why did they do it?"

"I don't know everything, but they've been holding me hostage for days."

145

I helped her to her feet. When she slumped against me, I propped her up in a chair against the wall, then found a glass and gave her a drink of water. Her hands trembled as she tried to help. "That tastes so good. Having an old sock stuffed in your mouth sure dries you out."

I nodded, refilled the glass and handed it to her. "We thought you were ---"

"Dead? I know. Dennis wanted everyone to think so." She wiped a drop of water off her chin.

"Why would he want us to think that?" I offered her a chocolate chip cookie from the plate on the table, then chewed on one myself as I listened to her.

She rubbed her wrists and sighed. "When Audrey started getting suspicious and sounding off at the funeral home that it wasn't my body in the coffin, they had to cook up another scheme." She handed me back the glass and signaled she'd had enough.

"What did they cook up?"

Veronica looked left and right, then whispered. "I think I'd better tell you when we're safely away. They'll be back anytime and I wouldn't want them to find us."

Her breath smelled of fear and humiliation. I undid the rest of the ropes binding her and helped her out the door. Buck tilted his head as if contemplating a decision, then jumped back on my shoulder. Veronica smiled weakly. "He's become very attached to you, hasn't he, Megan?

"Who? Buck? Nah. Probably only because you weren't around."

She nodded and gave me a curious look as if she didn't believe a word I was saying. I opened the front door and pulled her down the street toward my car, glancing left and right to make sure I didn't see any Ford Festivas. When she was safely settled in the car and I was heading away from Three Palm Point, I asked her about the Dwyer's plan.

"They've been running an insurance scam for years, but each one gets more daring. This time I think they have plans to eliminate me."

Murder was an ugly word and one I didn't like to use. "Eliminate you?"

"Sure. I'm no use to them anymore. I'm just baggage in the way." Her face slackened and she really looked old at that moment. "Children just don't have any respect for their parents anymore."

I nodded and turned at the corner. Her words reverberated in my head and I wondered if she included me in that disrespectful group. A sliver of guilt quivered through me as I remember I had forgotten to send my mother a birthday card the month before.

146

Veronica disrupted my reverie. "Where are we going now? To catch them and make sure they get their comeuppance?"

"You're going to my house and take a little rest."

"Not on your life. I know you're going after them and I'm coming, too."

I looked at the parrot on my shoulder. "Buck, will you please talk some sense into this woman?"

He glared at me, then ruffled his feathers. You can always count on a bird to help you out. I pulled into my driveway. "Let's just stop here and get something to eat. I'm starving. Besides, I need to call Lou. He'll know what to do."

Veronica raised a knowing eyebrow. "The boyfriend," She muttered, climbing out of the car as if she was negotiating Mt. Everest.

"Ex-boyfriend," I said from between clenched lips, putting one arm around her waist and holding her left arm with the other.

"That's what they all say," she said. I swear she winked then, but it could have just been an eye droop from fatigue. The moon hid behind a cloud and a moist, cool wind blew in from the north, making me think that maybe winter was on its way.

Somehow I managed to get my key out of my purse, open the door and guide Veronica inside. I was starting to feel tired by then and began to wonder if I shouldn't let Lou and the police handle the rest of the case.

Inside, we hobbled to my bedroom where I helped her off with her heavy black shoes and propped her up in my bed. "This your room, dear?" she said through a yawn. I nodded and turned on the small lamp beside the bed. "You've made it real nice and comfortable," she said, nodding her head in approval.

"Thanks, I like it." I started to back out of the room. "I'll bring you a snack in a minute." She yawned and waved a tired hand at me. Buck and I went into the kitchen. Even his head was drooping on my shoulder. Once he was back in his cage and covered for a snooze, I took down a can of soup and heated it up. Chicken noodle soup was the one thing that always made me feel better and I hoped it would do the same for poor Veronica.

I glanced toward the Florida room and didn't see my feline friend. The kitty litter smelled like it needed changing, but Samantha was nowhere in sight. Probably out on the town again. That made me thankful that at least I wouldn't have to confront her icy looks. When I tiptoed back into my bedroom with steaming soup bowl in hand, Veronica was cutting some pretty noisy Z's. I set the food within her reach, tiptoed back out and closed the door behind me. She'd sleep for a long time.

I went into the living room and dialed Lou's number. I expected to hear his hurt voice, still wanting me. Boy, was I in for a surprise. Susan, his wife, answered.

147

"Megan? How nice to hear from you," she said as if it wasn't ll o'clock at night and I always made social calls then.

"Susan?"

"Yes, it's me. I guess you're surprised to hear I'm back home."

"Not at ---"

"Sure you are. Lou told me you knew about us."

A rod of anger swelled inside me. That guy couldn't keep the most intimate things private. My mind conjured up an image of Susan and how much I liked and envied her. Envied, hell. I was consumed with purple jealousy. She was the beautiful, tall, thin blonde type. The kind of person who never has to work out or watch what she eats and still looks terrific. Me, I'm always dieting and exercising and still always five or ten pounds heavier than I'd like. There is just no justice in this world. Between the anger at Lou and the envy over Susan, all I could manage was a strangled, "then you're home again?"

"Yes," she gushed. "We worked everything out. I don't know whatever possessed me ---"

I wished it was still possessing her, but then deep down I knew Lou and I just were never to be, so I mentioned the obvious. "Then you're back together again."

I could tell she was taking a drag on her cigarette, probably considering her answer. Maybe lung cancer would claim her in a few days, but then again, I had rotten luck on those kinds of things. "Yes," she said, her voice brightening, "and although we've got a long way to go, I think we can work it all out."

I swallowed my feelings and said, "Good. Great. I wish you the best." Maybe I'll turn out to be a good sport yet.

Her voice turned puzzled. "Is that why you're calling?'

I'd almost forgotten why I was calling, but then Lou (or even the thought of him) always seemed to have that effect on me. "Yes --- I mean, no --- I mean, I need some help on a case I'm working on."

"The double murder?"

Did everyone in the St. Petersburg area know my business? All I could think about then was getting even with Lou for blabbing about me and what I was working on. I clenched my teeth and mumbled, "Yes, the double murder. I need his help. Do you think I could talk to him?"

"You could if he was here. But he's not, so you can't."

I hated her brand of humor or maybe I really was a sore loser. "Where is he?" I can be pretty bold when I want to find out something.

"He's working on some case with his buddy from the station. What's his name -- ah --- you know who I mean."

"Yeah, I know who you mean. Lt. Johnson."

"That's the one. He sure is a slave driver, isn't he? Demanding that Lou help him even when he's not his boss anymore."

Now we were getting somewhere. "What is he demanding Lou help him with?"

"Lou didn't have time to tell me the whole thing. Something about that Rodger's insurance case he's working on and the Single Hearts Club and ---"

"Aha!"

"Aha?"

"Insurance scams."

"Insurance scams?"

Logic was never one of Susan's strengths, but then I probably wasn't being very lucid at the moment. "Never mind, gotta go. I'll catch up with Lou at the Club." I hung up, feeling very much part of the in-crowd.

No sooner had I put down the phone when it rang again. I shoved it against my ear and answered with more than a little irritation. "Yes!"

"Good evening. This is Ruthie."

"Ruthie who?" Did I know a Ruthie?

"Ruthie Wickstein. The one you have a luncheon engagement with tomorrow."

"Oh, yeah, Ruthie." My fingers played with the phone cord. "Shouldn't you be in bed? It's 11 o'clock at night."

"I'm an insomniac."

"That figures."

"What?"

"Nothing. Why are you calling?"

"I want to confirm our luncheon date for tomorrow. The maitre d' gets very annoyed if everyone doesn't show up. He's having the chef make us something special."

"Maitre d'? Were we really having this conversation? I was losing it, but then I'm not accustomed to having eight-year-olds confirm luncheon reservations. I wasn't sure I even believed her.

"You are planning to show up tomorrow, aren't you, Ms. Baldwin?"

"Show up? Yeah, sure. I just have a lot of things on my mind." Why was I making excuses to an eight-year-old? I tried a reverse ploy. "Does your father know you're making late night phone calls?"

"Ira is on a different biological clock."

"A what?"

"He goes to bed early."

"I see. Yes, I plan to show up tomorrow unless something happens."

"What could happen? You're not going after those crooks, are you?"

She had me on the defensive again and my parental voice started to ceep in.

"Ruthie. That is none of your business."

"But I'm curious. I mean, you're the first real live investigator I've met."

"Your father's an investigator."

"Only on dead people. It's very boring. They can't talk or act or do any fun things."

"I guess if you look at it that way, you're ---"

"Can I come with you?"

"No. Definitely not. Absolutely not."

"You're no fun. Just no fun."

"I know. Several people have noticed that recently."

"Maybe you could just tell me where you're going and I could make up what happens."

"What?"

150

"My teacher says I have a very active imagination and so if you tell me what you're up to, I could picture you at the Single Hearts Club capturing the criminals."

"What makes you think I'm going there?"

"You are, aren't you? The murders are tied to the Single Hearts Club. You said so this afternoon."

Smart kid. Maybe too smart. "You never mind where I'm going. I'm hanging up now. I've got work to do."

"Be careful."

"Thanks."

"I wouldn't want you to miss luncheon. Andre would be very angry."

"Thanks a lot and good night." I hung up the phone and prepared to leave.

On cue, Buck woke up and started banging on his cage. His voice was a cross between John Wayne and Clint Eastwood. "Let me out, Pilgrim. This is no job for a woman."

"Not on your life. You're not coming this time. I don't care how much you helped me before."

"Let me out!"

His voice went up a few decibels and I was afraid he might wake Veronica. Then I'd have the two of them yelling at me to take them with me. "Okay. I'll make a deal. Just hold it down in there."

The noise in the cage stopped. I took off his cover and opened the door. He jumped on my finger and up onto my shoulder as if he was the most well-behaved bird in town. What a con artist.

I tiptoed out of the house, making sure to lock all doors so Veronica would be safe. I had no idea what to do to keep me safe so I just climbed in my car and started driving.

Then it hit me. If Veronica was still alive, who was that in the coffin I'd seen at the Whittier Funeral Home?

CHAPTER 27

The neighborhood was pretty quiet by then. The moon had come out from behind the cloud, illuminating my yard and making Mrs. Joiner's palms look like monsters sticking out their tongues and making fun of me. I get very paranoid when I'm scared.

Even Buck was showing the tension, digging into my shoulder with his knife-edged feet. I frowned at him. "Stop that or you'll have to get off me." I get very irritable when I'm scared.

Buck unhinged his feet and gave me a pitiful look. There is nothing more humiliating than being pitied by a parrot. I stepped on the gas pedal, getting us quickly to Gulf Boulevard. Too quickly. One glance in the rear view mirror told me why. The blue Ford Festiva roared out behind us when I took off from the stoplight. "Danger," squawked Buck and I knew he was right.

Had they been following us all along? It didn't matter. What did matter was that Dennis and Mary were on to me. The one thing I had to make sure and do was lead them away from Veronica.

I veered onto the bridge, praying to God not to let the gates go down. They didn't. I squealed off the other side and headed up Pasadena, driving right past the turn to the Single Hearts Club. Then I did something I'd seen Jim Rockford do in one of his shows. Or maybe it was Steve McQueen in *Bullitt*. I swerved down an alley, Buck veering off my shoulder and swearing at me in a Yiddish accent. I made a couple of quick right turns and ended up behind the blue Ford Festiva. Boy, did they look confused. Dennis nearly drove off the road into the Caravan Shoe Store and Mary stuck her head out the window and waved a gun at me. Neither of those things stopped me. I was determined. Crazy, but determined.

They led me on a merry chase through St. Petersburg. Soon we were in north St. Petersburg and things started to look familiar. The smell of the county garbage incinerator made it necessary to close my windows. Even then the toxic fumes made their way inside my car. For a minute I thought Sorita Wyberg might be in on the deal, but we headed past the mobile home park and onto the interstate.

He must have thought he lost me because Dennis pulled off at 22nd Avenue and started to slow down. I thought maybe we were getting close, but he only drove into a gas station and filled up with petrol. I parked across the street and a little down the block. Dennis leaned his heavy body against the side of the car. This time he wore a white velour shirt that looked as if half his plate of spaghetti had taken up residence there.

Mary got out, stretched her massive body and lumbered inside. She wore the same nondescript polyester dress she had to the funeral home. Clothes were definitely not a priority with her. Lurching from side-to-side, she made her way on thick-heeled shoes toward the office. The roll of fat around her waist seemed to have grown since the last time I saw her, but her facial expression was still cold and bitter.

I saw her kick the soda machine and argue with the skinny clerk inside before she appeared a few minutes later with a can of Diet Pepsi in one hand and a candy bar that looked suspiciously like a giant-sized Baby Ruth in the other. So much for nutritious snacks.

They both got back in the car and drove off. I followed at a respectable distance. Dennis turned south on Central Avenue and then picked up speed as he headed west. Boca Ciega Bay flashed by, its dark waters reflecting the lights from the high-rise condos banking it. The Ford Festiva rushed through a light on yellow and I barreled behind, hoping no cops were around to notice. "Prepare to jump ship, mate," screamed Buck in my ear. I brushed him away, seeing what Dennis had in mind. The lights were already flashing for the bridge to go up.

Then I knew he knew I was behind him. He hoped to make it across the bridge before it opened up and leave me on the other side waiting. The gates had already come down, but that didn't stop Dennis, he swerved around a couple of vans and crashed through them. I was a little crazed, but I wasn't a maniac. Buck and I sat behind the traffic, watching the bridge go up and then slowly settle down into its concrete holder. By the time Buck quieted down and returned to my shoulder, he was silent, but looked to be sulking.

I stepped on the gas and zoomed across the highway. The Ford Festiva was long gone. The road ended ahead and I would have to decide which way to go. I chose left.

While we sped down Gulf Boulevard, my mind kept wondering if Dennis might have set up this whole thing in order to lure me away from Veronica. Terrified they might already be at my house murdering the parrot lady, I drove as if my life depended on it. Why had I been stupid enough to leave her alone? And without even Buck to save her. Samantha would be no help whatsoever, even if she was home, which I doubted.

Giving myself mental whiplashes all the way back, I drove dangerously, passing right through two red lights and nearly knocking over the few tourists on foot who dared wander back to their motels across Gulf Boulevard. If anything had happened to Veronica I'd never forgive myself.

I was a nervous wreck by the time I pulled into my driveway. The porch light was still on, just as when I'd left. No sign of the Ford Festiva, but they might have hidden it. Maybe even in my garage. Heart gulping up my throat I rushed to my bedroom window and peered in. No sounds. Well, no danger sounds, only the loud snores of the parrot lady. She reposed peacefully on my bed, one leg dangling over the side and her polyester wig sliding down onto her forehead. She was dead to the world in the best way.

I breathed a sigh of relief and returned to my car. If they weren't after Veronica, what were Dennis and Mary up to?

"Single Hearts Club," Buck crooned into my neck.

"Of course!" I was halfway out of the driveway before I squealed on the brakes and looked at the wise parrot who was hanging onto my shoulder for dear life. "Where did you learn that?" I asked. Buck just clicked his mandibles together and preened his back feathers. Parrots never tell.

I think I drove fast enough to the Single Hearts Club to qualify for the Guinness Book of Records, but since Buck was my only witness, I'll never know. I pulled in the alley two blocks down and coasted a half block closer with my lights and motor off. Above us, the moon glanced off the Single Hearts Club sign, giving it a sickly, shabby look.

The two-story white frame house looked deserted, but one can never tell about those kinds of things. How many times had I seen Jim Rockford stumble into a building only to be knocked out from behind or find a cool revolver jammed into his back? I was smarter than that. I had studied those kinds of things. My VCR tapes attested to the number of times I watched The Rockford Files even when they weren't running on television. I'd studied each and every action, using my pause and slow-motion buttons to take in all the details. I'd even taken notes on what happened.

Feeling prepared for any event, I got out of my car and proceeded on foot. They weren't going to hear me coming. No way. I walked cautiously toward the darkened building, my sneakered feet barely whispering along the cement. Somewhere down the street a baby cried, while inside me, my heart pounded with the strength only real terror can produce.

Someone had left the top off their garbage can and the smells of rotting oranges and other unmentionables blanketed the alley. I breathed through my mouth, closing off the back of my nostrils as I had done as a kid. It was a great little trick that blocked out the stench of the creamery whey heating up in the summer sun in the alley next to my childhood home. Things eventually come in handy if you can wait long enough to use them.

As I hurried along, I wondered where Lou and his police friend were. Maybe I'd beaten them there. Wouldn't that be a coup? I could see the headlines in my mind's eye already:

NURSE INVESTIGATOR CAPTURES MURDERERS

Wouldn't that frost Susan? Who was I kidding? Lou and Susan were back together and they were going to stay that way. Why did I always persist in tormenting myself with what can never be? Must be in the genes.

The closer I got to the Single Hearts Club, the more I realized I had a decision to make and I wasn't sure which way to go with it. Should I just walk in the front door or break in a window in the back? The front door seemed the most law-abiding. It also seemed the most dangerous. They'd see me coming for sure.

Weighing them both, I opted for the back. Maybe because I was thinking so hard, I didn't see the dog. Above me, something sniffed, then punctuated the humid night air with a series of high-pitched barks that no one could overlook. Freezing in my steps, I tilted my head and looked up. On a second-story porch, a German Shepherd stood on guard with ears pricked and scowling face trained on us. Nothing like a welcoming party when you want to make a unnoticed entrance.

I stood there, trying to figure out what to do. Buck decided for me. Using the full volume of his considerable voice, he made even more ferocious barks back up at the Shepherd. The dog squealed, dropped to his haunches and backed up until he was out of sight. For all I knew, the dog backed all the way into the house and was probably cowering under its master's bed by then.

"Good bird, Buck," I whispered.

"Buck's a good bird," the parrot mimicked, then gave a low wolf whistle.

"Shush, now. Somebody will hear us." I looked right and left, but nobody seemed to be around. Still, it didn't hurt to be cautious. I tiptoed around the corner of the Single Hearts Club and there it was. Standing in the moonlight, badly in need of a car wash, was the blue Ford Festiva. I froze again and my stomach did something resembling a flip-flop.

"They're here. My God, they are here," I murmured, clapping my hand over my mouth when I realized they might be able to hear me. I forced myself to calm down and take a deep breath, trying to convince myself I was ready to step forward. I was ready, but my feet weren't. They just would not move. Maybe they knew something I didn't. We stood there for minutes before Buck flew off my shoulder, flapped around to my backside and gave me a nip in the butt.

That'll get you going everytime.

I didn't know whether to kiss him or pull out his tail feathers. I did neither, just inched my way along, hoping the sting in my rear end would go away soon. Meanwhile I looked for an open window.

Unfortunately the only one visible was about five feet off the ground and I don't do high jumps. Some boxes to my right would work just fine as a stepladder, I decided. Buck flew back on my shoulder and dug his feet in. "Not so tight, partner," I whispered, stacking the boxes up under the window, then grabbing for the ledge with my fingers.

I thought I heard voices inside but I wasn't sure. I hoisted my body up and peered in the window. It was so dirty I couldn't see a thing. I used all my strength to push open the window far enough to allow us to get in. I put one foot up and crawled up on the ledge. Darkness blanketed the room so I couldn't see a thing. That was probably why I miscalculated the drop to the floor below, falling with a thud and twisting my ankle slightly on the landing. Buck had already left my shoulder, figuring it would be a rocky ride.

Crouched on the floor, I waited, listening, hoping they hadn't heard me . The voices in the next room quieted. "Now you've done it, partner," said Buck's John Wayne.

"Shush," I mumbled, feeling pretty stupid at that moment. Footsteps clumped across the hall and stopped in front of the ballroom. The door opened, letting moonlight filter through a window in the hallway. It illuminated the dumpy figure of Dennis Dwyer. The gold chain around his neck glittered like a fiendish weapon. I held my breath and hoped he couldn't see, hear or smell us.

"There's no one here," said Dennis' nasal voice. "You must be getting jumpy, Mary. Come here and help me with this." He picked up two metal containers and shook them.

Mary waddled into the hall as if she had all the time in the world. Dennis roared at her, "Where the hell ya been?"

Mary pulled back a strand of hair from her face and sniffed. "Where do you suppose I've been? Getting together all the papers and stuff." Her voice had lost its edge of cheery singsong.

He grunted, then handed her one of the containers. "Pour some of this around. Make sure you splash it all over. Get all those walls and floors." He pointed to some room down the hall then gave her a dirty tooth grin when he said, "We want this to make a nice glow."

What were they going to do? Paint at this hour of the night? As soon as she started to pour the stuff on the floor I knew they had something more devilish in mind. The odor of gasoline stung up my nose. I was torn between trying to stop them and running in the other direction as fast as I could.

Fear won out. "Come on, Buck," I whispered and sneaker-squeaked it back towards the window. At first glance there was nothing to climb up on so I tried to jump up to the ledge. Height and depth perception are not my strong suits, especially in the dark. I jumped, banged my head against the window ledge and crumpled onto the floor dazed.

"What was that?" Dennis had heard and was coming on the run, his heavy feet bounding more quickly across the ballroom floor than I ever would have believed was possible.

The angry glare of a flashlight shined into my face. "Who are you?" he shouted, grabbing me by the scruff of my neck and holding me up in the air. A look of recognition spread across his face. "Why you're the one from the funeral home, ain't ya?"

Buck circled above, then made a few kamikaze attacks at Dennis' backside, but to no avail. Either Dennis had a steel bottom or he was just plain tenacious. He swatted in the air at Buck's head with his fleshy hand until the bird flew for the hallway, squawking and shrieking all the way.

By that time Mary was coming on the run, gasoline can spilling the foul-smelling stuff all over the floor. She glared at me, then at Dennis. "What's she doing here? Isn't she the one from Whittier's?

"Yeah, and I'll bet she's the one that's been following us all over tonight. Aren't ya?"

I stared at him. Sometimes playing stupid works.

In this case, it didn't. Dennis' eyebrows furrowed in thought, then flattened as if a light bulb had just lit in his brain. He nodded to himself. "She must be some private dick or something."

Mary shone the flashlight into my eyes. "Is that who you are, a private detective?"

I decided to take the polite route to answering that question. "No, ma'am. I'm just a private citizen. I came over here to see if I could get a date through the Single Hearts ---"

Dennis grunted. "That's a crock and ya know it. You're the one from the funeral home." He jammed his face so close to mine I could smell his sweat and see the greasy folds of his fatty face.

"I may have been at a funeral home. You see I have a morbid interest in the dead, I ---"

Dennis grabbed my arm and twisted until I thought it might pop out of its socket. "Ow! Do you have to be so rough?"

"Damn right I do. I want to know what ya know."

"Well, I've been to high school and college so I probably know a whole lot more than you do. Where do you want me to ---"

Mary's voice was like chalk across a blackboard. "Cut the crap, sweetie." Mary's eyes squinted out from under their hoods of fat. "I know who you are. You're that friend of my mother's aren't you? The one who drove her to your house from the library."

Dennis peered at me. "You sure, Mary? She looks a little thinner than that one."

"Maybe she went on a diet. No. it's her. I bet she even knows where my mother is, don't you?" She glared at me.

"Sorry, I don't. The last time I saw her was the day I brought her back to your house."

Dennis shook his head and grinned. "Ya know, I just don't believe that. I heard ya left a message with our realtor and I bet ya know about our new house. I even bet ya went over there and fetched Veronica May right away from us, didn't ya?"

Mary jumped at me, but Dennis pulled her away. "Don't get physical, Mary. There are other ways to deal with her." Holding his wife at bay, he snarled into my face. "You been interfering in our business for too long now and you're going to pay." Mary clapped her hands as if she was his personal cheerleader.

"You mean I have to pay you too, just to get a blind date?"

Dennis reached over and pummeled my arm. "Don't be a smart-mouth. In case no one told ya, no one likes a smart-mouth."

"I didn't know this was a popularity contest."

Mary scowled at me. "Go ahead and joke, but you won't be laughing in a few minutes."

I figured I'd try one more ploy. It couldn't hurt and maybe time would buy me a visit from Lou and the police. I looked into Mary's eyes. "I don't know anything. I'm telling you, I'm a single person with a penchant for death who just happened to come here after the place closed."

"Sure and I'm Little Red Riding Hood," taunted Mary, putting her arms on her massive hips and sticking out her tongue.

Dennis gave first me, and then his wife a disgusted look. "Smart ass, ain't she?" He faced me again. "If I was you, I'd make an effort to appreciate these next few minutes."

"Why? Do I get a prize if I do?"

Dennis scowled, then broke into low yelps that I suppose was his attempt at laughter. "Damn right, sweetie and its going to be a corker!"

Mary eyed me up and down. "I know what she's doing here --- she's a spy."

Dennis looked puzzled. "Spy? You're crazy. Who would she be a spy for?"

Mary scratched her chin. "Maybe the insurance company. They're probably on to us."

"We've been too careful for that."

"Maybe you're right. There's no way to tie Cassie's ---"

Dennis glared at Mary, his eyes narrowing into fatted slits. "Shut up! You want her to know everything?"

Mary's lips trembled with anger or hurt. She opened her mouth to speak, then closed it again. She looked away before she smiled and said. "Doesn't matter what she knows, does it? She isn't going to tell anyone about it."

I nodded. "Of course I'm not going to tell anyone."

Mary swiveled to face me. "That's for sure. We're going to fix you so that you -"

"Shut up, Mary," Dennis leaned forward and prodded me with a beefy hand. "Why'd you have to mess in our business? I never did nothin' to hurt you."

"No, but you hurt my friend. Veronica May is a wonderful person and Cassie Saunder's mother is one of my best friends."

Mary clicked her tongue. "Cassie Saunders? That whore?"

"She was straightening up her life."

Mary chortled. "Soon you'll be with her and you can catch up on what you've missed since you've seen her."

The meaning of her words stamped themselves into the front of my mind. My voice rose nearly an octave like a kid who is scared to death and tries to bluff. "I suppose you're going to throw me off the Gandy Bridge, too." I was afraid I'd said too much already, but I couldn't seem to stop myself. "I have friends who'll miss me. Friends who know about this Club."

Mary grabbed for my hair, but I ducked out of her reach. She grunted, pretending she didn't care. "If your friends aren't here yet, sweetie, they're going to be too late."

Dennis shoved his wife out of the way. "Shut up, Mary." He looked at me from behind hooded eyes. "Do you think you're smarter than us, college girl?"

Mary lurched forward again and grabbed for my hair, giving it a yank. "You're not as smart as we are, girlie. We've been to school too, you know."

"Which school? The school of hard knocks?" Mary gave my hair another yank and I wondered if she'd taken a handful of it with her when she let go.

Dennis snorted. I must have hit an educational nerve because his face bathed itself in fury. "You think you're so smart. Are you smart enough to stop us?"

"I don't want to stop you, just find out what you're up to."

Mary made a face like Alice Stremins used to make at me in first grade just before she stuck my pigtails in the paste. "Well, just think again, Miss Smarty Pants.

You're not going to find out one darn thing!" From the smell of her breath, she either had an upset stomach or hadn't brushed her teeth in months. She smiled a tight smile, lifted her open hand and slapped me hard on the face.

Dennis grabbed her arm and pulled her away. "Cut that out, Mary. We don't want to break any bones."

She scowled at him. "Why not? They'll never know."

"Broken bones show up no matter what. Don't you know nothin'?"

I figured it was time for someone to interject some sanity into the conversation. "You could just let me go. I'll never tell." I crossed my heart, hoping they'd be dumb enough to fall for one of my lies.

They weren't. Dennis slammed his hand down on a nearby crate with the velocity of a meteor and noise of a sledgehammer. Then he stared at me, shaking his head. "Sure and snow falls in Florida."

I summoned up all my courage and said, "Actually, snow has on occasion fallen in ---"

"Shut up and let me think!" Dennis gave my head a slap, knocking me half-senseless.

Mary made a few clicking sounds with her tongue, then said, "You better hurry up and finish this, Dennis. She might have brought someone else with her, you know."

He turned toward his wife and gave her a look that made her shrivel an inch or two. "You shut up, too. You broads are what's wrong with this world, if it weren't for you, things would be pretty nice."

Mary grunted, then pulled herself up to her full height, banging her enormous breasts against his flabby chest. "And I suppose you'd be cuddled up with one of your homo buddies right now if it weren't for women."

Dennis swallowed a few times, his look changing from murder to humiliation before he said, "Just you shut up, Mary. I said I was trying to think." He forced me down onto the floor where I cowered at his feet, trying to decide what my next move ought to be. I thought about biting into his thick ankle, but the idea was too repulsive.

Finally Dennis looked at his wife. "Get some of the rope in the office, Mary. We'll just fix this little Miss Interference." A vicious smile crossed Mary's face, then she turned and waddled off.

I consoled myself, thinking being tied up wasn't the worst thing possible. After all, Veronica lived through it. Then I saw the gleam in Dennis' eye. "By the time they find you, you'll be cooked to well-done. Very well-done." To top it off, he laughed a nasty laugh and I knew I wasn't going to get out of this adventure alive unless I thought of something very intelligent very soon.

160

Mary waddled back into the room and handed her husband a piece of rope. "Tie her up over there," said Dennis, shining the flashlight on an old wooden chair in the corner and slapping the rope back into his wife's hands.

She grabbed my arm and twisted, forcing me to my feet. "Over there, sweetie," she shouted, quick-stepping me to the corner. I hate it when people call me sweetie, especially when they're about to murder me. Mary patted the chair. "Sit down!"

I pretended to obey, but instead twisted my body the other way, breaking her hold on me. Then I jumped on her back and went for the bone under her nose with my fingers while I pushed against the back of her knees with mine. I would have wrestled her to the ground if Dennis hadn't dived in, grabbed my leg and yanked me back. I twisted around, arms flailing to reach his hands, but I couldn't.

He stared at me as if I was a museum specimen. "She's a nasty one, ain't she?"

Mary lunged at me. "Let me at her, the bitch!"

Dennis glared at her. "You just calm down and tie her up. We have to get out of here. No more fighting!"

Mary nodded, her lips smiling with cruelty. She hummed as she worked, sitting me down precisely in the middle of the chair, then winding the rope around and around me. She seemed to take great pride and a certain sadistic pleasure in tying the ropes as neatly and tightly as she could. She must have been a Girl Scout because she tied some pretty good knots.

I had one more trick to use, but I took my time and waited until I thought the timing was right. Then I looked up into her face. "I know a lot about you, you know."

She grunted, but kept tying knots.

"I really do know a lot about you. For example, I know your father is a jailbird." The knot she was tying tightened. My trick wasn't working so well. Maybe it needed more polish. I tried again. "I also know your sons take turns sharing jail cells with some of the worse felons in Pinellas County." The ropes tightened around me. "I even know you're in this with Rick Stetson."

Her hands stopped making knots and she shouted over to her husband. "Dennis. She knows about Rick and us."

He smacked his lips. "She don't know enough to do anything."

"How do we know she hasn't told someone else?" Mary breathed some more bad breath into my face. "You haven't told anyone else about this, have you?"

"Who me?"

"You're the one I'm speaking to, sweetie."

161

Dennis stomped over. "Just don't let her get your goat, Mary. She's just talkin', trying to outthink you, and I don't suppose that's too hard to do." Mary took a step back and took a swing at her husband. She missed.

He only laughed and went over and sat down in the other chair across the room. "You women think you're so tough. But when it comes down to it, we men always outsmart ya."

Mary grunted. "Yes, just like you outsmarted Bobby Jim."

"Shut up, just you shut up about Bobby Jim."

Mary opened her mouth, took a look at Dennis, then shut up.

When I was bound in place, Dennis strolled over and made an inspection. "You done pretty good for a woman." He spat the words at his wife, then took a dirty handkerchief out of his pocket. He looked down at me and gave me a nasty smile. "This here's gonna keep you quiet, little girl."

He shoved it in my mouth and tied it behind my head. When he bent over I noticed his deodorant had let him down, but I didn't think it was wise to tell him about it at that moment. I tried to keep the slimy cloth away from my tongue, but I couldn't. There is no pleasure in this world quite so delightful as knowing your mouth is around an object Dennis Dwyer has probably blown his nose into.

When he was through, he stood back and admired their work. "Okay, let's finish and get out of here. No one's going to find her in time. I guarantee it." Dennis turned and lumbered out of the room, following the path of light from his flashlight.

Mary sniffed and flounced out behind Dennis. All I could think about was where was Buck and would he somehow manage to save me? The more I thought about it, the more I realized he probably couldn't. When the going gets tough --- parrots... What do parrots do? I had no idea.

While I tried to solve my own puzzle, I listened to Mary and Dennis arguing in the hall. "You were supposed to bring the matches, stupid," shouted Mary.

"Here's some. Can't ya do nothin' right?"

"I can do plenty things right. More than some crossed-over homo."

I thought I heard the crack of fist against jaw and then Mary yelping with pain. If I was lucky, they'd knock each other out and I'd wriggle out of the ropes.

No such luck. "These are too damp to light, stupid," Mary yelped. "You sweaty pig!" Footsteps echoed down the hall, followed by the banging and crashing of drawers. Dennis shouted first. "Here's a lighter. That'll work."

A minute later I heard the snap and crackle of flames and smelled the deadly odor of smoke. Dennis stuck his head in the door, shining the flashlight under his chin like some Halloween ghoul. "You just rest quietly. We're going to pick up Veronica now." I struggled against the ropes, but they only seemed to tighten. "We figure you got her stashed over at your house. And you know what? I know where you live." Their laughter echoed out the door behind them.

Panic leapt up inside me. Where the hell was Lou? Where was Buck? Where was anyone? The fire was advancing on me and I was powerless to stop it. Somehow I managed to work the gag out of my mouth and shout to no one in particular. "Let me out of here! Somebody! Help!"

CHAPTER 28

Buck! Buck!" I shouted, but he didn't show. That darn bird must have flown out with Mary and Dennis. Just like rats leaving sinking ships, parrots must leave burning buildings.

If I was going to get out of this, it was going to have to be by myself. "Come on, Megan, don't give up," I mumbled, trying to overcome the panic that was already rising in my belly.

I wriggled my body, trying to loosen the ropes. That was something I saw in a Woody Allen movie, but I guess someone hadn't read the script, because they didn't budge.

The fire advanced on me. Smoke and fumes clogged up my throat and teared up my eyes so I had to blink against the burn. Flashes of white and red loomed out in the hall. Beyond the door, paint smoked, bubbled, then surged into grasping fingers of flame. Charred wood and plaster burned merrily. A red flash ran across the floor and up the window curtains on the far wall, creating bursts of bright color and sickening whiffs of melting fabric.

The temperature in the room rose from hot to unbearable and the beads of perspiration on my face flowed into rivulets of salty water. It was only a matter of time now. I had to do something. If the flames didn't get me, the smoke would.

I craned my head around. The open window in the next room looked to be about six miles away. If I could just get closer to it, I might be able to breathe a little easier. Forcing my feet against the floor, I gave a jump and a hop and the chair moved a few inches in the right direction. Success. Bouncing and jumping like a human pogo stick, I made it to the window in the next room.

That was the easy part. Now to get out of the ropes. By rocking the chair back and forth, I eventually tipped it over. I was on the floor, but the ropes were just as tight.

Running out of ideas, I did the only thing I could think of. "Buck! Buck!" I shouted.

When all else fails, scream bloody murder.

I think I must have passed out after that from panic or smoke. Sometime later I heard: "Wake up! Wake up!"

Something jabbed me in the neck. The voice sounded like John Wayne, but the peck was pure parrot beak. "Stop that," I mumbled, coughing and choking on the clouds of smoke enveloping the room. "Get me out of these ropes, Buck."

He gave me a quzzical look, then started gnawing at the cord binding my feet. At the rate he was going, we'd both be up in flames before he got through the first one.

Lou or somebody had to be there by then. Maybe they'd even caught Mary and Dennis. "Get the police. Go outside and get help!"

Buck considered a second, then flew through a cloud of gray smoke out the open window. I felt about ready to pass out again from the fumes or maybe from the thought that I was about to be roasted like a weenie at a barbecue.

Through it all, my head hammered with pain. Mary must have done quite a job on my face and hair. Was I to die a bald woman? I vowed that should I ever catch up with her again, I'd do a little hair pulling myself.

Concentrating all my strength into my legs, I flipped my chair-bound body over onto my knees. Shards of pain shot up my legs, but I managed to crawl to the wall by the window. I had no idea how to maneuver up to the window with a chair on my back, but I was determined.

Grunting, whimpering and slipping, I tried to inch up the wall. It didn't work. Somewhere outside I heard the wail and roar of a fire engine and the siren of a police car or two. It wouldn't be long now, if I could just hold on. Thank God they hadn't put any gasoline in this room.

A male voice shouted through the crackle and bang of burning timbers down the hall. "Megan"? It was Ira's voice.

"In here! I'm in here!" Help was coming at last. Where the hell was Lou? I twisted the chair around to face the door. "Hurry up! I'm in here!"

They came through the door together. Ira Wickstein and Lou Rasnick.

Neither one was smiling. If I hadn't been choking to death, I would have laughed at them. Legs and arms collided. Ira's tall thin body prodded and pushed against Lou's well-muscled torso. Their voices lifted in shouts: "Let me in there, damn it, Megan's my friend!" That was Lou. Always gallant.

"No, you step aside. I'm going in there first." Ira's usual shy smile had turned to steely determination and his thoughtful brown eyes to defiance.

Mustering the last of my voice, I shouted, "One of you step aside before we all die of smoke inhalation!"

That did it. Lou pushed his way in and ran to my side. His hands were already untying my hands when Ira slid in by my legs and started to loosen the ropes around my ankles. "Who the hell is this, Megan? asked Lou, trying to knee Ira out of the way.

I gave Lou my rudest look. "Let him help, will you? This whole place is going to blow up in a few minutes and you two will still be arguing about whose friend I am."

165

That shut them up. Some women like to have men arguing over them. I am not one of those women. Especially when I'm nearly dead.

Buck flew back in and tried to help. His eyes were red from the smoke and he wheezed and coughed like a 100-year-old man with tuberculosis. The best he could do was give Ira and Lou a few nips. "Stop that! Buck, stop that! Let them untie me, will you?"

The men in my life just were not meant to cooperate.

Buck gave me an apologetic look and flew for the window. Wise move. At that moment I wished I had a pair of wings myself. Seconds later, I was loose. "Can you get to your feet?" Ira asked politely, rubbing my wrists. Lou didn't bother to ask, he just pushed Ira aside, picked me up and threw me over his shoulder. He made a dash for the side door. Beneath us smoke billowed and darted. Burning embers popped, crackled and hissed. Lou's sneakered feet pounded along the floor and my aching head reverberated from each thud.

"Get my purse, Ira!" I shouted. A lady just doesn't go anywhere without her purse. Besides, I knew what a hassle it was to replace credit cards and driver's license, having had to encounter that ordeal the previous year after someone stole my wallet in one of the strip malls on 34th Street.

Ira's feet padded behind us, his steps punctuated with grunts and shouts of, "If you hurt her, you'll have to answer to me."

Lou kept running, but managed to shout down my back. "Is that your medical examiner friend?"

"None of your business," I mumbled between bumps against his body. We were in a very intimate physical relationship at that moment, but I wasn't enjoying it at all. I felt like a trussed hog and wondered how Ira would have handled getting out of there. Probably by cradling me in his arms with my face buried in his neck.

Why is it I always fall for the guys who bring me the most indignity? On the jog outside, with my face banging madly against Lou's spine and buttocks, I decided that if I survived this, I was going to forget about a certain private investigator named Lou Rasnick.

Somewhere behind us a wall caved in and crashed to the floor. Lou pivoted, dodged a burning curtain and dove through a doorway that was just about to collapse. Flames licked up Lou's jeans and jumped up onto my hair. My hands pounded desperately at my head and Lou's legs, trying to quell the fire. Between bangs I wonder if Ira had made it.

I swiveled my head around just in time to see him jump through a ring of fire and into a stream of water from one of the firemen. His hands clutched my stone-washed jean purse to his chest. All around us, men in yellow slickers shouted and pointed their hoses at the building. Someone threw a blanket around Lou and wrestled us to the ground, rolling us over and over until the flames went out.

Lying on the ground, looking up at the Single Hearts Club afire, I thought it had never looked lovelier. Windows popped and burst like Roman candles and flames burst up in brilliant patterns. Ira's hand brushed my cheek. "Megan, are you all right?" Before I could answer, he bent down and kissed my forehead.

The moon reeled about me and tears poured down my face. I was alive, but what about Veronica? My voice came out raspy and dry. "I'm fine. Help me up."

"No, you have to rest. The paramedics are coming. They'll take you to the hospital and make sure you're ---"

I sat up and threw the blanket off. "I'm not going to any hospital. Veronica's in danger. Where's my purse?"

"It's right here. I've kept it safe for you."

I yanked it out of his hands. I knew I was being slightly irrational, but I figured I had the right. "Where's my car?" I gazed about trying to remember. I had forgotten where I'd left it. Maybe I was worse off than I thought. My hands patted my hair and body, making sure everything was where it was supposed to be. No broken bones, just like Dennis had said.

Ira's arms came around me. "Hush now, just rest." He smelled like smoky musk cologne and wood chips.

Lou's head burst up from under the blanket. "Who the hell are you to tell her to rest? Who do you think you are anyway?" Lou was on his feet, hands in boxing pose.

"I'm Megan's friend, that's who. Someone who plans to look out after her and love her and ---"

"We'll just see about that." Lou yanked Ira away from me and pulled him to the edge of the crowd.

I grabbed my purse and stumbled to my feet. If they were going to act like children, I would just have to handle this Veronica thing myself. "Don't leave without me, partner," said a John Wayne voice. I whirled. A bedraggled parrot flew in a crooked flight pattern above the crowd and banged onto my shoulder.

"Buck! Am I glad to see you. You don't look too bad."

"You look like hell in a hand basket," he growled.

"Thanks. Are you game for a little more excitement?" For an answer, he tried to preen his charcoal-dusted feathers into place. He'd lost a few tail feathers and soot ringed his face, but otherwise he wasn't any dopier than I was.

Tripping and wobbly-legged, I made my way through the crowd, pushing back the gawking faces and forward-leaning bodies. When I got to the alley, I remembered where I'd left my car. "Megan! Megan!" Unmistakable Lou. "Where the hell do you think you're going?" He was a least a block away so I didn't think he could stop me.

I tried to run, but my legs wouldn't obey my command. Instead, I sort of skip-stumbled to my Toyota, unlocked my door and shoved my aching body in. Down the alley I heard another car rev its engine and take off in my direction I didn't look back, just strapped myself in and drove in the direction of St. Petersburg Beach.

Halfway home I glanced in my rear view mirror. Lou and Ira were in Lou's car, still arguing. Lou was driving like a maniac, swerving in and out of cars, but he just couldn't catch up to me. I lost them at the bridge, finding myself lucky enough to be the last car across before the man in the cement house high above us put the gates down and wouldn't allow anyone else through.

I thought Lou might just be crazy enough to break through the barrier, but he wasn't. Arms swinging and faces red with anger, he and Ira got out of the car and continued their argument. I took one more glance to make sure Lou wasn't shoving Ira into the water, but my red-haired friend was still holding his ground when I roared off the bridge and onto the street.

Car squealing around the corner after the stoplight, I headed toward my house. The movie at the Beach Theater was just letting out and tourists and locals streamed into the street, paying no attention to traffic. I made my way through them, beeping at a few. Didn't they know this was a matter of life and death?

I turned onto 64th Avenue and nearly ran into an elderly lady in a black straw hat and white crocheted gloves. She was moving down the street at quite a good clip. Behind her, lumbering along and shouting obscenities, were Dennis and Mary.

I squealed to a stop, threw open the passenger door and shouted, "Veronica! Jump in, it's me, Megan."

The parrot lady stopped, squinted at me, then fell into the seat. "Megan!" She turned and spied the parrot. "Buck. I'm glad to see you're still around."

"All hands safe," said Buck. I half expected him to give a salute.

Veronica smiled. "You won't believe what's happened." She looked at me. "Mother of God, what's happened to you?" She wet her handkerchief and dabbed at my face while I floored the gas pedal and we sped into the night. Veronica's body lurched backward. She turned to look at the parrot and shouted above the noise of the car. "Poor Bucky. You look like they put you through the wringer."

"Poor Buck, poor, poor Buck," crooned the parrot, eking out every drop of sympathy he could get.

When he had milked the situation for all it was worth, Veronica turned back to me with her handkerchief. I pushed her hand away from my face. "Don't fuss over a little soot. I'm more worried about getting you away from Dennis and Mary. They tried to kill me tonight and you're next on their list."

We spun around the corner and headed toward the Don CeSar Hotel. Veronica grabbed hold of the dashboard and clung to it. "I know. I think Mary is totally crazy."

"And Dennis isn't far behind. They set fire to the Single Hearts Club tonight and left me inside to charcoal broil."

"It's what they do best. They've been setting fires all over the county. They set fire to my house and planned to collect the insurance until they found out I'd written another will leaving it all to my friend, Audrey."

I breathed a sigh of relief that Audrey wasn't mixed up in their murders and schemes, but only for a second. When I glanced in the rear view mirror, I saw the blue Ford Festiva coming on fast behind us. "Hold on, Veronica, we're going to have to really move." The parrot lady fiddled with her seatbelt until she finally got it latched, then she sat back and seemed to enjoy the ride.

Buck dug in his claws and gave a few squawks, but otherwise he was fine. I think he was getting used to high-speed chases. Maybe even learning to like them.

Up ahead, spotlights lit up the Don CeSar like a gigantic pink cake. I turned left at the corner, heading for the bridge back to St. Petersburg. Mary and Dennis weren't far behind. And wasn't that Lou's car a few cars back, horn honking and motor revving?

I grabbed two quarters out of my ashtray and threw them in the slot to enter the bridge. None of us were lucky this time. The bridge was just going up. Dennis must have figured out Lou was after him because he tried to do a U-turn on the entrance to the bridge, but there was no room.

Lou and Ira were on the run toward us, having abandoned their car. I jumped out of mine. "Stop the blue Ford. They set Single Hearts on fire!" Lou gave me a puzzled look then pulled out his gun and ran for Dennis' car. His hand shoved the shiny muzzle inside Dennis' window. Ira ran to the other side of the car and pulled open the passenger door. He offered Mary his arm, but she stood up, purse swinging and mouth yapping. When she hit him in the face with her bag, he grabbed it away from her and held it in the air, a foot above her head. She stepped on his foot, but he pushed her back gently.

Two police cars with sirens and lights blazing screamed onto the bridge. Uniformed-officers jumped out. One of them was Lou's friend, Lt. Johnson. I'd met him when Lou and I were an item. I could tell it was him from the arrogant way he held his head. The other was Jamie Henders, a nice fellow Lou and I had double dated with a couple of times. On Lou's word, they hand-cuffed Mary and Dennis and led them away.

I let my head fall back against the seat. My work was done. Very soon now I could rest.

CHAPTER 29

Lou came to my front door in a new knit candy-striped polo shirt of cobalt and white, stone washed cotton twill trousers of sea blue and dark blue boat shoes. Somehow he'd found time to get a haircut. The sun glanced off the blackness of his curly hair and dazzled me. He'd even shaved which was something he was loathe to do.

He smiled and showed me a dimple in his left cheek. "Megan. you look terrific."

I looked down at my white sundress and ankle straps and hoped it was true. "Thanks. I'm just about ready to go." I grabbed for my purse and stepped outside next to him. Even though I'd sworn to be rid of him, at that moment, standing in the warm breeze next to my arborvitae tree, I wanted him badly. A lock of hair fell across my forehead and I pushed it back. I'd have get a trim soon. Singed ends are not an attractive sight.

"New locks?" he asked, examining the shiny brass on my door.

"Yes. Dennis Dwyer broke in to get at his mother-in-law. Wouldn't you know I have a $200 deductible on my house?'

"Them's the breaks." He smiled at me and took my arm and I didn't feel bad at all about the money I had to spend to get the lock fixed. "Let's take my car," he said, guiding me toward it. He even opened the passenger door for me, something he'd only done once or twice during the entire time I've known him. This was getting spooky.

It was a short drive to Paula's house. Her blacktopped parking lot still smelled of fresh tar but the newly painted white lines had already been smeared by some careless driver. Her beige stucco building showed its age in the bright sunshine. We climbed up to the second floor. Below us some seniors splashed in the pool, taking an early morning exercise class. Paula opened the door and let out the intoxicating smell of freshly baked chocolate cake. "Come on in. I thought we'd have some coffee." Her foghorn voice was still intact.

She looked as if she'd lost a few pounds since Cassie's death, but she looked good. Her eyes were clear and her face nearly unlined about her cotton twill shirt dress of burnished gold. I gave her a long hug, then said, "Looks like you've finally gotten some rest."

She gave me a warm smile. "Yes, Rachel saw to that."

Rachel? Where was the old bat? I hoped she was on a slow boat to China.

Paula led us into the kitchen. The chintz curtains had been freshly-laundered and pressed and the glass jars on the counter were full to the top with pastas, dried beans and cookies. Even the "Bless this House" hotpads looked cleaner. She seated us at the heavy maple table and poured steaming coffee into blue mugs. Before I'd had a sip, a plate with the fudgiest chocolate cake ever appeared at my elbow.

Lou woofed down his cake and had a second helping in front of him before I'd barely tasted mine. Paula passed me the milk and said, "I was surprised you wanted to come over, Megan. I read in the *Times* that you've been through quite a bit lately."

I smiled. I love publicity, even when its a picture of me with my hair half-burned off and soot on my face. "I'm a quick recuperator. Besides, I thought I owed you an explanation for Cassie's death."

I'd forced Lou to come with me and explain. After Mary and Dennis had been hauled away by the police, I remembered I hadn't done a darn thing to find out about Cassie's death and the guilt had been eating away at me since then.

Paula sipped her coffee. "You've found out something?"

I stared at Lou. Finally he put down his fork and looked at Paula. "She was killed because she found out about the insurance scams Mary and Dennis Dwyer were pulling off."

Lines etched themselves into the space between Paula's eyes. "She wasn't involved in them, was she?" She set down her mug and crossed herself. "Oh dear, I had so hoped she was finally straightening up."

I glared at Lou. We didn't think her daughter was involved, but then we'd probably never know. I had already asked him to go easy on Paula, but I wasn't sure he would. I let out a tiny sigh of relief when he said, "Nope. Cassie wasn't involved at all."

Just when I was starting to feel good about the whole thing, the dark figure of Rachel came through the kitchen door. "Ms. Baldwin. How nice to see you." Coming from anyone else, those words would have been believable. Looking at her mud brown eyes, I knew she meant just the opposite.

I introduced her to Lou. She seemed to take a shine to him, smiling and flirting with her hand in front of her face as if she was starring in *Dangerous Liaisons*. She still wore the shapeless black suit and it still hung on her heavy body, but her face looked younger when she smiled, sat down next to him and reached for a slice of cake.

Lou grinned at her the way I'd seen him do with me on occasion and I wondered if his dimples were all for show. He nodded at Rachel. "We were just telling your sister about Cassie."

Rachel leaned toward him in a conspiratorial whisper. "Cassandra was a trial and tribulation to my poor sister and me."

I gulped down my coffee, preparing to defend Cassie, but Paula beat me to it. "Cassie was trying very hard to overcome her past. I give her credit for that."

Rachel grunted and took a big mouthful of cake. Lou nodded. "Cassie was an innocent bystander in the scam going on at the Single Hearts Club."

I sat forward and caught Lou's eye. "Who was involved in it then?"

"Rick Stetson and Gemma Fuller."

I smiled to myself. I'd already figured that part out. What I didn't know was exactly how Mary and Dennis fit in and Lou only came with me to Paula's on the condition he'd reveal the details to her. "How did they suck Cassie in? Through Mary and Dennis?"

"Cassie was Rick's lover and she came back to the Single Hearts Club one night for an unscheduled tryst with him. Only she must have overheard what they were up to and they found out."

I tapped on my mug. "So she had to be eliminated."

Lou nodded. "Exactly."

Rachel shifted her weight toward Lou. "Then Cassie's death was because she knew something about Rick --- ah, Mr. Stetson --- and they were afraid she might tell someone."

I grunted. "Too bad they didn't take the time to figure out Cassie was deathly afraid of heights before they pushed her off the Gandy Bridge."

Lou nodded. "One of their many mistakes." He gulped down the last of his coffee. I watched his Adam's apple go down as he swallowed. He has one of the all-time sexiest ones. I was so mesmerized by it that I almost missed his next words. "You see, Gemma had cooked up this scheme to find well-heeled singles for Rick. His law practice was floundering because of his marathon sexual exploits, so he needed a few easy marks to milk."

"Very interesting," I said, toying with the rest of my cake. "But what does it all have to do with Mary and Dennis Dwyer?"

Lou eyed my cake dish and I pushed it toward him. After taking another fork full of the brown delight and swallowing it, he said, "Rick wasn't satisfied with small-time law clients. He wanted the big bucks. When Mary and Dennis came to him for counsel about a suit against them for collecting illegally on a life insurance policy, he knew he had found his little niche."

Paula shook her head in puzzlement. "I don't understand."

I patted her arm. "I do. You see Rick needed a patsy. Someone to do his dirty work for him and you can't find a dirtier pair than Dennis and Mary."

Rachel honked her nose into a black lace handkerchief. "You mean that lawyer, Mr. Stetson, was paying them to murder people for their life insurance?"

Lou nodded. "Not exactly. They started with small insurance claims at first. Evidently Mary and Dennis can be quite charming when they choose to be." I remembered the night I met them at the funeral home. They hadn't been exactly charming, but Mary was very polite and probably could ingratiate herself with some poor, lonely soul who could find nothing better to do than go the Single Hearts Club for solace.

Lou eyed another slice of cake, thought better of it and said, "In fact, they even got twisted up with a case I've been working on. The Dwyers started to get a little sloppy, and that was when I and the police started suspecting them."

"The Rodgers' case?" I just blurted it out even though I knew I wasn't supposed to reveal the name of any of Lou's clients.

He gave me a disgusted look. "I can't say the name of the party, but yes, it was an insurance case. When my client couldn't get the insurance that was due her, I started to do some digging. It took a lot of work, but I finally learned that Rick Stetson was the person holding up the money."

I was always pumping Lou for information on how a private investigator works and this was no exception. "How did you find that out?"

"Tricks of the trade."

"Seriously," I said, putting on my nicest smile.

"It wasn't easy." I knew he'd tell me. He loves to brag about his prowess. "He was working under a dummy corporation, but I managed to pull a few strings in Tallahassee and find out he was really the owner."

"What else did Mary and Dennis do?"

"They've set fire to quite a few houses, including their own."

"And almost killed Mary's mother in the process."

Rachel shook her head. "Just to get the insurance money?"

Lou nodded. "That's right. They've received 10 checks from their insurance company totaling more than $500,000. They like to buy houses and then torch them. They've also submitted claims that their houses have been burglarized. Some pretty fancy jewelry and a specially-built truck were reported in one."

I took a sip of coffee. "How did you find out about all this?"

"Once we connected them with insurance scams, we started checking claims originating from them. At first they were careful to use different counties, but lately they've gotten fat and lazy and have submitted too many claims in St. Petersburg. Even the insurance company had an investigator looking into it."

Lou pushed my empty cake plate back and nodded a thank you. I nodded back. "You're welcome." I looked into Lou's eyes. "What about Dr. Oakes?"

Lou gave me a puzzled look. "Dr. Who?"

"Stephen Oakes. The guy who wrote Veronica May's prescriptions."

"No connection."

"Don't you think it's funny both Veronica and Cassie were his patients?"

"Probably just coincidence."

I didn't believe it for a minute, the way Dr. Oakes had reacted to my prodding made me pretty sure he was involved in something slimey. Maybe I'd have to show both him and the police a thing or two about that later. Right then I was perfectly happy just to assuage my guilt and pump Lou for all the information I could.

Lou smiled a self-satisfied smile. "And the sloppiest mistake the Dwyers made was to try to collect on Cassie's life insurance policy."

Paula let out a little grunt. "No wonder I kept getting the run-around when I tried to get the insurance money to pay for Cassie's funeral."

Rachel clicked her tongue and patted Lou's hand. "Is there no respect left in this world?"

Lou shook his head and smiled at her, showing a dimple. "I guess not."

I grabbed Lou's hand and yanked him to his feet. I don't mind being bested by a beautiful, young blonde, but when he starts flirting with chubby matrons, I can't stand it. "We've gotta go now. I've got a luncheon appointment." I pulled him toward the door.

Rachel was on her feet and scurrying behind us. "But surely you can stay awhile." She grabbed Lou's hand. I opened the front door and pushed him outside.

Paula winked and waved good-bye, stepping in between Rachel and Lou. Paula knew just how frustrated I had been about Lou and she wasn't going to let her sister add more.

"See you soon," I shouted, pushing Lou toward the car.

He opened the car door slowly. "What do you mean, you have a luncheon engagement?"
"I have a luncheon engagement. How about dropping me at the Ship's Captain."

"I thought we might ---"

I glared at him. "You thought wrong."

"But can't we just be friends?"

"It just won't work for me that way. Not right now."

He frowned and reminded me of Buck when he sulked. "Okay, if that's the way it has to be."

On the ride to the Ship's Captain I almost weakened, but I forced myself to get out of the car when we got to the restaurant. I was stupid, but not that stupid.

CHAPTER 30

Ira stood up and waved to me from their booth by the window. His red hair looked almost strawberry blonde in the sunlight. He wore an expensive blue suit, red tie and an expectant look on his pale face.

I hurried across the gleaming hardwood floor toward him, passing well-spaced tables, each draped in a crisp white tablecloth and decorated with a red carnation in an art deco glass holder. The bar was nearly empty, but the tables were all occupied by pale men in business suits and women in silk dresses or tailored suits. Even at midday the candles were lit and the level of conversation was low and discreet. The place had the aura of new money and big business deals.

The Ship's Captain was one of those seafood restaurants that dandies up all the entrees to look like they're French. Such food usually tasted great to me going down, but the rich sauces always gave me heartburn. It was not the kind of place I frequented, nor did Ira, from the uncomfortable look on his face.

A gamin-faced, red-haired replica of him poked her head out as I trotted toward the booth. Ruthie's voice was too low and sophisticated for a child's. "Ira refused to let me come alone. He said he had a few things to say to you, too."

Ira blushed and indicated a seat next to him. "Ruthie is getting entirely too independent."

I laughed and sat down. "She is a real card, Ira. Sort of reminds me of myself in my younger years." Ruthie beamed and I winked at her. I thought we could just possibly become great friends. "I wanted to thank you, Ruthie."

She fluttered her eyes and looked up at me. "For what?"

"For telling your father I was in trouble."

"Oh, that. Isn't that what good investigators need, a back-up?"

I smiled at her again. "Exactly."

The waiter came by. He was one of those tall, dark types with a somber face who pretends to be French, but isn't. He whipped the huge menus into our hands, then gave Ira the wine list. Without hesitation, Ira announced, "We'll have a bottle of your very best champagne."

The waiter blinked three times, snapped the wine list back into its holder and left.

I leaned over and said to Ira. "That guy makes me nervous."

Ira smelled nice, like pine needles and strawberry soap. He leaned even closer to me and I could see even his eyelashes had a red tint to them. "The waiter makes me nervous, too." That was another thing I liked about Ira, he understood.

He doesn't make me nervous," chimed in Ruthie. "Waiters are supposed to act superior so they get a good tip."

Ira laughed. "One of Ruthie's one million theories on the human condition."

Ruthie blushed and said, "You have to admit Ira, I'm often correct."

He nodded and smiled. "What will you two beautiful women have?"

Before I could even consult the menu, a bony hand tapped on my shoulder. I turned and there she was. The parrot lady. She was dressed about the same as the first time I saw her in the parking lot of the Beach Library---black straw hat with a big red rose dangling off it, white hand-crocheted gloves, black sunglasses, flowered dress, and a tad too much Naples red lipstick. The only difference was the flowered dress had roses on it instead of orchids and the bird on her shoulder was a cockatoo, not a parrot.

Veronica smiled mischievously. "Megan. I've been looking for you."

"You have?"

"Yes." She beamed at Ira and Ruthie. I introduced them.

Ruthie's brown eyes riveted on the bird. "What's his name?"

"Oscar. I named him after my brother."

I cleared my throat. "What about Buck?"

She nodded. "That's what I wanted to talk to you about. I want you to keep Buck ---"

I shook my head. "But I have a cat and they ---"

Veronica shrugged and winked at Ruthie. "I can't take Buck with me."

The little girl reached over to hand the bird a breadstick and asked, "Where are you going?"

"On a cruise. You see, Buck gets seasick and can't go with me." She looked at the cockatoo. "Oscar loves the sea. He reminds me of my brother."

A look of pleasure came over her face and I felt myself beginning to weaken. I stared at my napkin. After all, she was my adopted (sort-of) Grandmother and the least

I could do was keep Buck for her until she got back. I looked back up at her. "When will you be back?"

"In about a year. It's a worldwide cruise. Isn't that great?"

"A whole year?" I didn't know if I could handle him for that long, but Ruthie and Veronica seemed to be in collusion about the matter.

Ruthie turned her big brown eyes on me. "You have a bird, too? I just love birds." Her voice went "little-girl" interested. "Does he talk?"

I nodded. "Can't keep him quiet."

Ira smiled at Veronica. "Why don't you sit down and have lunch with us?" She did sit down and we had a marvelous lunch. On Ruthie's orders, the chef had prepared blackened grouper, endive salad and tiny red potatoes and carrots Andre.

After we had all sipped and tasted and admired, I said, "There are a few things I still don't understand, Veronica."

The parrot lady picked up her linen napkin and wiped a piece of fish from her upper lip before she said, "And what is that, dear?"

"First of all, who was that in your coffin?"

Ruthie's eyes doubled in size and Ira choked on his wine. Veronica reached over and banged Ira on the back before she said, "I have no idea, my dear. That is something for a smart young person like you to find out." Then she winked at Ruthie and started her giggling.

I ignored the laughter and plunged back in. "If you don't know who was in the coffin, maybe you can tell me why Buck attacked Selma."

Veronica's eyebrows shot up. "Buck? That's very unlike him."

"That's what I thought, but the moment he saw Selma, he took off for her hat and took a big bit out of it."

Veronica giggled and swatted a hand at me. "What kind of hat?"

"A black straw. Just like yours. Well, not just like yours. It didn't have the rose, but otherwise ---"

Veronica nodded. "Then that explains it."

I was totally confused at that moment. "I don't see how it explains anything."

Veronica buttered another French roll. "I guess you wouldn't, dear. You had to be there." She popped a morsel in her mouth.

Ruthie pulled at Veronica's sleeve. "What happened? Was it funny?"

Veronica smiled at the little girl, but waited to speak until she took another sip of wine. "It wasn't exactly funny. You see Buck wouldn't get in the cage and I was afraid Mary and Dennis would hear him, so I put my straw hat over him."

Ruthie giggled into her hand. "What did he do?"

"Well, he didn't like it at all. He tried to fly around, but of course the hat was too heavy. So I scooped him up and pushed him into the cage." Ruthie clapped her hands and giggled. Veronica nodded, then turned and looked at me. "That was right before I left him at your house. Dennis had threatened to kill Buck and I had to get him to a safe place."

Ruthie shook her head sadly. "The poor bird." She gave me a devastating look, the kind my mother used to give me to make me feel terribly guilty. "You are going to keep the bird for Mrs. May aren't you?"

I nodded and took a bite of fish. One does not argue successfully when both little girls and grandmothers gang up on you. I sighed into my napkin. It might not be so bad after all. Buck was quite a smart little bird. "There's another thing about Selma I don't understand. You said you lost track of her, but she told me you kept in touch."

Veronica wrinkled her lips. "If you call a card every year or two keeping in touch, then I guess you could say we've kept in touch."

I cleared my throat and asked my final question. "Selma wasn't in on any of the shenanigans with Mary and Dennis, was she?"

Veronica fluttered her eyelashes. "Lands sakes no. She doesn't have a mean bone in her body. Mary and Dennis thought up the whole thing themselves, at least that's what that nice lieutenant told me."

Having no other questions to ask, I concentrated on the wine and the feel of Ira's admiring glance on my face. Veronica was kept busy intriguing Ruthie with stories about her travels and Ira with the way she captivated Ruthie.

Most of the afternoon flew by and it wasn't until I was back home sitting in my living room that I began to wonder how many other women Veronica might have given parrots to. I gazed over at Samantha who was pulling on a string from one of the drapes and getting ready to climb them if it didn't come loose. In the kitchen, Buck was mumbling away to himself in a Scottish brogue.

Were there other women, scattered across this great nation, also sitting in their homes right then trying to figure out what to do with a smart ass bird and a reincarnated ex-mother-in-law cat?

I sighed and took another sip of my peppermint tea. At least I wasn't being bombarded by sun particles and I guess I should count myself lucky for small favors.